Tatiana, all in Moon-Drenched White, Danced Softly Across the Floor.

She turned and reached in the pale air, looking as if she were a spirit of the night itself, a moonbeam that had chosen the form of a woman for an evening. Her long drifting midnight hair, her swirling clothing, her astonishingly eloquent arms and her white swan neck all added to the illusion.

Mesmerized, Roland held out his arms and at once Tatiana was in them. Her cloud of hair fell around him, enveloping him.

Tatiana's eyes snapped open and gazed with wonderment on her own true love, the man she had been searching for as long as she could remember. He bent back her head, his masterful hands entangling themselves in her hair and she was trembling, breathless.

Roland cupped Tatiana's face in his hands and brushed her delicate lips with a kiss. Then he leaped out the door and was gone.

Dear Reader,

We, the editors of Tapestry Romances, are committed to bringing you two outstanding original romantic historical novels each and every month.

From Kentucky in the 1850s to the court of Louis XIII, from the deck of a pirate ship within sight of Gibraltar to a mining camp high in the Sierra Nevadas, our heroines experience life and love, romance and adventure.

Our aim is to give you the kind of historical romances that you want to read. We would enjoy hearing your thoughts about this book and all future Tapestry Romances. Please write to us at the address below.

The Editors
Tapestry Romances
POCKET BOOKS
1230 Avenue of the Americas
Box TAP
New York, N.Y. 10020

Pas de Deux

Louisa Gillette

A TAPESTRY BOOK
PUBLISHED BY POCKET BOOKS NEW YORK

Books by Louisa Gillette

Glorious Treasure
Pas de Deux
River to Rapture

Published by TAPESTRY BOOKS

An *Original* publication of TAPESTRY BOOKS

A Tapestry Book published by
POCKET BOOKS, a division of Simon & Schuster, Inc.
1230 Avenue of the Americas, New York, N.Y. 10020

ISBN: 0-671-61741-9

First Tapestry Books printing July, 1986

10 9 8 7 6 5 4 3 2 1

POCKET and colophon are registered trademarks
of Simon & Schuster, Inc.

TAPESTRY is a registered trademark of Simon & Schuster, Inc.

Printed in the U.S.A.

To: Whitney Lynn and Michael Leo
who danced into our hearts
from the very beginning.

Chapter One

THE LUSTROUS BLACK AND GOLD CURTAIN CAME DOWN TO thunderous applause as Odette, the white swan maiden, helpless under the spell of a wicked sorcerer, glided tremulously away from her beloved Prince Siegfried. The capable, sturdily built ballerina used the heights of her acting ability to create an illusion of supreme pathos. The audience was drawn into the darkly magical forest of the swans, enraptured by the seemingly shimmering lake coming to life in a new dawn.

The enchantment of the tragic *Swan Lake* ballet was temporarily broken by the crystalline lights of intermission.

"Charming," Tsar Nicholas II uttered, beaming a benevolent smile on the nobility privileged to sit in the Maryinsky Theatre's royal loge. "We'll show those

Italians we Russians have something to offer the world of ballet."

"But my dear Nicky," old Princess Lisevetna Ilyovna wheezed.

Her massive, wrinkled form almost required two gilt and velvet chairs to prop up. She tapped a delicate Oriental fan impatiently against the young tsar's knee.

"All of St. Petersburg has already seen *Swan Lake*. And while our sublime prima ballerina . . . what's her name? No, don't tell me. I knew it a minute ago . . ."

"Olga Vorodskya," Tsarina Alexandra murmured.

An anxious glance at her husband belied her usually calm exterior.

"Thank you, Alix, dear," Lisevetna cooed. "You are such a help to us all. Ah yes, Olga Vorodskya. She makes a lovely Odette, but I hardly think she compares to the bravura of Legnani."

She leaned confidentially toward Nicholas.

"When she completed those thirty-two *fouettés* in Act III last season, I thought I would faint!"

The tsar's darkening glare clearly indicated he wished such an event had occurred and that his dear old great-aunt had not recovered. The gentle pressure of his tsarina's hand seemed to calm his smoking temper.

He said with forced patience, "Aunt Lisevetna, I forgive your ignorance. But never assume that your tsar would be content with repeat performances, regardless of their excellence or their foreign tricks."

Once again, Nicholas's eyes sparkled with secret power and scanned the audience below. The air seemed to be charged with an extra degree of anticipation. All was in good order, the auditorium filled to capacity with elegantly dressed ladies in wisps of silk, noble gentlemen in their finest, and the cream of Russian military officers in the familiar dark uniforms with gold-braided epaulets . . . all balletomanes of the most extreme order and all present at the tsar's invitation. Nicholas turned toward his little party in the loge.

"I have a small surprise . . . no, a splendid surprise. . . for all of us tonight. I think you will agree with me after the next act that a fledgling star is in the ascendant."

There was a flurry of excitement toward the rear of the royal box. Half-whispered comments flew back and forth among the assembled courtiers.

"He's found a new one."

"Is she good or just pretty?"

"Isn't Olga dancing the entire ballet?"

The tsar leaned across the old princess to the man on her other side.

"Now you'll really see dancing as the world has never before known."

The imperial smile was fastened on with certain knowledge of the future.

"Even the French will have to sit up and take note of Mother Russia after tonight, eh, Monsieur le Comte?"

The dashingly handsome man in question cocked his blond head to one side in a nod of expectant acknowledgment. There was a shadow of a smile on the comte's face. For a moment, the tsar wasn't sure whether it was offered in bold irony or mutual confidence. But the crystal chandeliers began to dim and the last whispering rustle of silk and jangle of saber steel settled down.

"Her name," the tsar whispered, "is Tatiana Ivanovna Dmitrova."

Nicholas grinned beatifically. He could afford to be

magnanimous at a moment such as this one. Soon they would all know what he had seen in privileged privacy at the Imperial Ballet School.

Eagerly the audience sat forward as the orchestra began the long regal introduction to Act III, including the dramatic theme of Odile, the black swan. Delighted applause broke out as the rich interior of Prince Siegfried's castle was revealed.

As in all fairy tales, the prince had to find a suitable wife and, in *Swan Lake*, Siegfried's mother had arranged a ball for prospective brides. But the prince already had a bride in mind—the beautiful and lyrical white swan maiden, Odette. After a divertissement of native folk dances, the castle darkened mysteriously and cymbals crashed, warning of the supernatural vision to come.

For suddenly on stage was not just a ballerina poised in black tulle with tiny brilliants flashing from her breast, shoulders, earlobes, and tiara, but the stunning image of a princess of midnight. Elegant as a swan, she held her head erect, her shoulders straight. Sharp twists of her head, so precise they were inhuman, made it seem as though her dark eyes moved restlessly about, fire flickering and snapping from their smoky depths.

The prince was convinced Odette had come, not knowing the sorcerer had conjured up this malevolent spirit in imitation of the pure maiden. Siegfried went to Odile as the magic began and trumpets heralded the first steps of their pas de deux.

From the moment this dazzling Odile lifted her eyes, sparkling with cold hard light, to her partner, the spell was complete. She displayed an irresistible power over Siegfried with arrogant pride—first beckoning, then dismissing, next alluring, finally triumphant.

Each gesture and movement was impossibly perfect and precise. Her arms swooped through the air like wings and her feet cut at the floor like knives. Her endless balances, low bends, and devilishly high extensions thrilled the prince. The audience interrupted again and again with roaring bursts of applause.

Confident in her mastery of the prince, Odile paraded across the stage with an accelerating virtuosity that mesmerized all watchers. She completed her glittering assault with a triumphant arabesque endlessly held *en pointe* and an imperious toss of the head.

After Siegfried danced his pledge of love and joy to Odile, she once again demonstrated her tight control over the prince in a lightning display of thirty-two successive *fouettés*, so relentlessly swift and sharp that she seemed to spin like an obsidian top. She dazzled him into a promise of marriage and the audience rocked with shouts of "brava" and loud continuous applause.

The sorcerer then stepped in to reveal the truth behind the malign spirit. She was not the pure Odette, dressed in black, but the sorcerer's creature. Together, the evil ones stood in cruel triumph over the prince and the real swan maiden, who reached toward him pathetically as the curtain closed.

The corps de ballet skittered off stage to prepare for Act IV, accepting towels and glasses of tea, exchanging their court costumes for the white net skirts and tiny wings of the swan forest. In a remote corner back stage, the black swan sagged against a huge crate of props, her heart pounding in her ears. She had done it. Her first performance was over.

And now Tatiana didn't know what to feel. Or rather, she felt so much, it was impossible to distinguish the exhilaration, the free flight of emotion soaring within her as she had soared on stage, from the blistering heavenly pain in her toes. Were her feet actually touching the floor yet? She laughed a low, breathy chuckle as reality . . . for the briefest moment . . . hit home. The beautiful black satin toe shoes were shredding, the compact toe piece smashed and broken down.

Olga Vorodskya sashayed past, waiting for her cue from the orchestra.

"Not a bad attempt for one who hasn't graduated from ballet school yet. A little more practice, dearie, and you'll get your moment in the sun. You can take a little bow with me at the end," she offered in pompous generosity.

She started to step onto the stage, but the veteran danseur who took the role of the prince barred her way. He latched a firm arm about her waist.

"Ah, my valiant Prince Siegfried," the prima began.

"Hush, Olga," he cautioned her. "Don't you understand what's happening?"

He pointed toward the darkened auditorium. The audience sat in complete silence.

"She sparkled, dearie, but what did you expect? A standing ovation for a baby ballerina?" complained Olga.

"You may be aging, dear Olga, but you're not blind," spat the usually convivial danseur. "Open your eyes, if not your heart. Look at the tsar."

Her eyes flew up toward the royal box where Nicholas and his noble party sat transfixed. Then, as the tense quiet shattered, the tsar stood to lead the auditorium in a thunderous ovation. At first it was erratic, like the

6

unsynchronized heartbeats of a thousand different souls. Then a rhythm took hold. The grand old theatre rocked and reverberated with the exultant sound, in unison, of hands clapping their appreciation, admiration, veneration for the brilliant new ballerina.

The skillful danseur had moved to Tatiana's side.

"It's for you, little one," he said to her.

Startled from the depths of her own emotional tide, she stared at him, uncomprehending, the stark lines of her facial makeup exaggerating the size of her eyes. He repeated his words, shouting to be heard over the tumultuous din. While Olga glared in jealous disbelief, he gently prodded his Odile forward, out of the wings and onto the stage to accept her homage.

As the glittering black swan, Tatiana glided to center stage and imperiously surveyed the dark void which was magically producing wave after wave of loving acknowledgment. Shouts of "brava" met her and lifted her onto a gossamer cloud of bliss. She extended an arm gracefully, pointing to each section of the theatre in mute salute. She bent her head low over her breast and placed her other hand to her heart. Raising her head to face her audience, she sank in a reverent curtsy to the floor.

The audience roared its approval, demanding more from its newly baptized favorite. Flowers, tossed by adoring balletomanes, fell in showers of soft scented petals about the triumphant ballerina. Never in her wildest dreams or even in her own naive appraisal of her talent did Tatiana expect such a response to her dancing. Serene on the outside, Tatiana was ablaze within, her soul singing a joyous paean.

She knew in her heart that for her there was no life

without dance. It gave her a freedom, a vision, a passion like nothing else. It made little difference if she danced for herself in her mother's private studio or in school with the other hopeful ballet students or in the rehearsal hall perfecting the age-old patterns and steps. Dance was the breath of life. Dance was happiness. Tatiana inhaled deeply. The perfume of the hot-house blooms gently pelting her exuded their own heady magic on the girl.

No one had prepared her for this kind of reception. Over the years, the voices of demanding class masters and mistresses, her mother's exacting eye for detail, her schoolmates' less than enthusiastic response when assigned to dance with her, all made her aware of her talent. But it all meant nothing compared to her own feelings when she danced. And now, in accepting the audience's acclaim, even those feelings took a backseat.

They approved of her. She had galvanized them to this level of excitement. She had enchanted them just as Odile had conquered her prince. Tonight, she knew what it felt like to be an equal of the gods. Thrilled and trembling, humbled by this pure outpouring of love, she rose and bowed low, her arms arched high over her head like a swan's wings in flight.

And still the audience carried on, determined to end this *Swan Lake* in three acts instead of its usual four. Shouts for encores filled the auditorium. For a moment, the black swan seemed to lose her poise, not knowing what to do.

Her prince valiantly ran out to the teetering girl. As shouts of acknowledgment for him rose up, he bowed deeply from the waist. His mouth, set in a wide grin, belied the awe in his voice.

8

"The tsar has sent word, Tasha. He will honor you now," he whispered.

In an elegant, unstudied move, he shifted Tatiana to face the royal box. Tatiana answered the royal command with grace. In the few moments it took to relight the auditorium, Tatiana flew effortlessly up the special stairway from back stage to the door of the royal box. All eyes were on Tsar Nicholas as he offered his hand to the most dazzling of black swans and brought her forward to the edge of the loge. The crowd broke into yet another deafening roar as Nicholas bestowed a silver box on Tatiana.

"Of course, I should have waited until the end of the ballet, my dear," said the tsar, a twinkle in his dark eyes, "but I thought history ought not record a riot on your first night of triumph, little swan."

Tatiana, eyes cast to the floor, hardly heard Nicholas's wry words. He lifted her chin so that she was forced to look at the imperial face.

"You will come to the Winter Palace tonight," he added warmly, "so that you may dine with us and we may feast our eyes on you."

Somehow she managed to nod her head.

"Good!" The tsar smiled. "Now you must hurry away or we will indeed have a riot of another kind if Olga Vaslova doesn't get her chance to save Siegfried in Act IV."

Suddenly, the real world of the stage performance came hurtling back into Tatiana's consciousness. Murmuring a soft birdlike cry, she tiptoed off, accepting with a distant smile the multitude of compliments she received from the noble entourage.

"Well, Tante Lisevetna," Nicholas began expansively as he settled back in his seat, "you can have Legnani for all she's worth. For my money, I'll take our Russian black swan. And you, Monsieur le Comte," he went on, "what do you think of our ballerinas now?"

Tsar Nicholas turned a deaf ear on his great-aunt as she rattled on effusively about Tatiana Ivanovna and gave all his attention to the Frenchman who blatantly stared at the retreating form of the new prima ballerina.

The comte finally turned to the tsar, ignoring the imperial arched eyebrow—a sure sign of disapproval—and said, "Your Imperial Highness, you must introduce me."

Surprised by the Frenchman's audacity and his zeal, the tsar found himself nodding.

Safely back stage, Tatiana found a moment to herself. As Act IV swept the tragic ballet to its conclusion, with Olga once again in the limelight, Tatiana sat in peace in the women's dressing room, hugging the golden moment to her like the precious warmth of a summer's day. Tentatively she opened her gift from the tsar. On a bed of black velvet lay a gold Russian cross encrusted with tiny rubies, emeralds, and sapphires and outlined in diamond chips. In the center, between the two horizontal bars, stood a large square-cut emerald. She closed the box fast, as if disbelieving her own eyes.

Slowly, she lifted the silver lid until the medallion was completely revealed. Even in the poor light at her makeup table, the magnificent piece was blinding. Her eyes, soft with wonder, caressed the jewels and she let her fingers graze the richly faceted surface before she dared to pick up her prize. It was heavy, as only something so highly given would be, she thought.

Dangling from the cross was a gold double-link

chain. She watched herself in her mirror as she solemnly fastened it around her neck. Like a little girl lost in a daydream, she pretended the tsar was present, first offering her his congratulations on bended knee, then standing proudly to place the symbol of Russian blessing upon her. Obediently she hung her head and—

"Tasha! Tasha!"

The voices of the corps dancers invaded her fantasy.

"Hurry! Olga's taking her bows but they're screaming for you."

They practically pushed her from the jammed room. Spirited along to the wings, she watched Olga bask in success. The stage was strewn with flowers and the ballerina stood with bouquets of white roses in both arms. But when a few people at the far side of the first few rows caught sight of a dark gauzy skirt at the edge of the stage, they picked up their chant for the black swan.

Olga did her best to ignore the audience's growing demand. She offered a long-stem rose to her prince and brought the orchestra conductor on stage for a bow. She even invoked the choreographer, the great Petipa, and his perennial assistant, Lev Ivanov, to stand from their seats for a round of applause. Trying to hide her angry distress, the established prima finally beckoned to Tatiana.

"Your turn, dearie," she said nonchalantly, gritting her teeth all the while.

With great bravado, she walked hand in hand with Tatiana to center stage. Hoarse cries of "brava" ricocheted about the theatre as the two swans—the sturdy white maiden and the flashing black sylph—were given their due.

The outpouring of emotion again overwhelmed Ta-

11

tiana. Tears fell freely down her cheeks, coursing over the stark black mascara and liner. She curtsied in a deep bow of gratitude. More flowers were tossed, and in a moment of impulse, Tatiana reached for one particularly beautiful sheaf of white lilies and offered it to Olga.

The audience raved, stamping their feet against the floor. Her eyes wide with fury, Olga was not to be outdone by this brazen newcomer. A hard smile pasted on her face, she artfully bent down to retrieve a blood-red rose for Tatiana. The audience screamed its approval.

Only the tsar's departure from his box calmed the avid balletomanes. As much as they adored ballet and its stars, they could not be late to the tsar's reception and dinner. The curtain finally rang down and the little bald man who raised and lowered it mopped his brow in spent amazement.

The auditorium grew quiet as the jubilant chatter of the crowd filled the broad avenue outside the Maryinsky and continued unabated to the Winter Palace. The steady backstage buzz slowed to dull silence as stage props and scenery were stored for future performances and dancers in their tutus and tights turned back into mere mortals, hastening to their midnight revelries . . . or a good long soak and a warm bed.

Tatiana deliberately stationed herself beneath a stairwell, her senses keen and alert. Not noticed there in the hustle and bustle, she felt the theatre gradually become an empty husk. When the last soul had gone and the ring of the last footstep echoed into oblivion, she slipped from her secret place.

The black swan wandered onto the darkened stage and absorbed the cool drafts of air streaming in from the auditorium's opened doors. Slowly she circled the stage. A strain of music came into her head and she launched impulsively into a series of tight *chaîné* turns. Through the battered satin shoes, her toes clutched at the floor and cramped.

While she rubbed her feet vigorously, another motif swarmed up and out and she hummed a few measures from the Waltz of the Sugar Plum Fairy. In seconds, she was gliding across the stage, spinning in a triple pirouette, ending in an extended arabesque *en pointe*. Darts of pain shot up the supporting leg but she willed them away. Her ebony eyes were alight with the flame of inspiration and daring.

The tempting mood had caught hold. Tatiana strode to center stage, setting her feet in fifth position. The sequence of thirty-two *fouettés* was Legnani's signature yet Tatiana had duplicated this feat. Could she do it again, she asked herself?

In a low soft voice, she skipped through the melodies of the Black Swan pas de deux, her delicate long fingers dancing the choreography, until she reached the swan's last solo. Now louder, she accentuated the rhythm, building to a crescendo. With a lightning snap onto her toe, she started the long count. She felt a little wobbly. Would her toes take this punishment a second time?

Her outer leg whipped around, picking up speed. She held her spine firmly erect and her arms circled close to her. Her pulse quickened. With each turn, she felt stronger and steadier, as when a fledgling makes the air its own. In her mind, the stage was peopled again. Siegfried's courtiers eyed the black swan in amazement while the prince fell under her spell-binding power. The vision overtook the reality of pain. Twenty-eight, twenty-nine, thirty, thirty-one, thirty-two! Her heart sailing on fairy wings, Tatiana leaped off stage in a series of grand leaps, both feet outstretched and her arms overhead in triumph.

Her heart still aflutter, she made her way to the women's dressing room and to her table, only now acknowledging the screaming pain in her toes. She made up a bowl of soothingly hot salted water for her aching feet before staring long and hard into the mirror.

The black dramatic lines of makeup on her face emphasized the tilted almond shape of her eyes and her naturally arched eyebrows. Looking at the image of the black swan, her jet pupils seemed to flash like meteors against the snowy whites of her eyes. The deep ruby color on her full lips seemed to accentuate the black swan's knowing sensuousness, and the rouge, high on her cheekbones, gave the illusion of elite superiority.

She removed the brilliants from her hair and earlobes, dipped her hand into a jar of cold cream, and covered her face with the cleansing lotion. Towel after cotton towel wiped away the image of the coolly powerful black swan. Her face now purified, Tatiana pulled out the legion of hair pins which had kept her upswept chignon intact. Burnished cascades of blue-black hair fell about her shoulders like a cloak of midnight sky.

She looked back into the mirror. Gone were the suggestions of glittering sexuality, dominating brilliance, magical force. In their place was the face of a young girl with innocent eyes and untried lips. She wondered whether anyone at the Winter Palace would recognize this pale and serious person as the prepossessing black swan.

With a sigh, she put away the bottles and jars strewn about the table. There, underneath the clutter, she found a small note in her mother's hand.

"Tasha," it read, "your performance was worth every ruble I ever invested in you. You have a rich and rewarding future ahead of you, darling. Now, make it pay!" It was signed, "from Mother."

There was a short postscript.

"Don't look for me at the palace. I felt a migraine coming on while you danced."

Tatiana shook her head, half amused, half chagrined. Her mother never had real headaches, only those of convenience. She would never miss an opportunity to attend a reception at the palace. She just couldn't abide being without an escort, even on the night of her daughter's first triumph.

Driving back the bitter taste of her mother's selfishness, she shed the black swan costume, washed quickly, and put on an ivory muslin gown with a soft empire line and full leg-o-mutton sleeves. She wore her hair down, a thin white satin ribbon tied around her head.

She hesitated over the tsar's gift. Should she wear it proudly for all to see or tuck it safely away in her brocaded reticule? Opening the silver box, she stared at the cross of gleaming gems, each facet blinking a seductive message.

"Pick me up . . . put me on," came the hypnotic whisper.

Her hand reached out, closed over the cross, started to bring it close to her.

"I'm beautiful. Wear me and you will be beautiful, too," the cross seemed to urge.

The fantasy had become ridiculous. She laughed, put the cross back in its box, and sharply shut the lid. She grabbed her floor-length fur-lined cloak and flew from the theatre, winging her way to the imperial party.

Chapter Two

ALONG THE EDGE OF THE ICED RIVER NEVA, THE FABLED Winter Palace took up three long city blocks. Inside, it was a symphony in white, with sparkling marble staircases, thick pristine carpets, and baskets of hot-house orchids. Along the corridors through which Tatiana passed, huge framed mirrors hung along both sides of the walls doubling the images of those privileged to walk this path. Guards in ornate uniforms lined the endless corridors like an army of nutcrackers, Tatiana thought.

Finally reaching the grand ballroom, she peered timidly through the great mahogany doors, inlaid with gold, at the multitude of guests. The court officials, military generals, younger officers, and noblemen were sleek in their gold braiding, their chests weighted down with ribboned medals. They were magnificent and more than a little frightening, she admitted to herself.

But it was the ladies at whom the young girl gasped. While she had often seen her mother dressed in her finest gowns with her most expensive jewelry, Tatiana had never imagined the sight multiplied by hundreds upon hundreds. Everywhere about the enormous room, the women sparkled like stars in the sky. They all wore gowns, invariably white and of the lowest décolletage, cut in the latest Parisian styles. While they were elaborately beautiful, it was the fantastic display of jewelry that mesmerized Tatiana. Each woman had huge gems about her head, neck, ears, wrists, fingers, and waist. Only Tatiana had not engaged in the ostentatious display.

She could have stood for hours peeking at the splendor of the guests, but the grand master of ceremonies spied the late arrival and tapped his ebony and gold staff on the floor three times. Tatiana stared at the two-headed eagle atop the staff, caught by the vivid thought of the strong golden bird flying straight for her. On impulse, she might have dashed away except for the chamberlain's firm arm at her back.

"Tatiana Ivanovna Dmitrova!" he announced in funereal tones.

All eyes turned toward the petite girlish figure as she entered and curtsied deeply and reverently before the royal personages. The tsar and tsarina signaled for Tatiana to be brought forward to them. Tatiana hardly dared raise her eyes to Nicholas, stern in his stately military garb, or to Alexandra, resplendent in a silver and white tunic-style court dress with a thick ribbon of mauve running diagonally from one shoulder to the floor.

"Champagne for our new young star," Nicholas ordered.

"But sir," Tatiana stammered in a whisper, "I am too young . . ."

"Nonsense," roared the tsar, who was immensely enjoying his party. "No one is ever too young in St. Petersburg for champagne or vodka. They are our sustenance, Russia's mother's milk—"

"Now, now, my husband," interjected the tsarina. "You're scaring her. She's just a child."

Alix's liquid brown eyes glistened warmly.

"How old are you, little swan?"

"Sev—almost eighteen," came the brave reply.

"You are lucky, my dear. You might pass for twelve on the street, but on stage, no one would dare think of you as other than a mature woman. To have such ageless beauty . . . well, I am envious, my dear." Alexandra smiled.

The tsar stared severely at Tatiana's sweet trusting face before him.

"I must choose someone special for you, my pet. Someone who understands a delicate, as yet unopened bud."

Confused by his words, she blushed at the depth of his stare.

"Alexei! Where is Baron Alexei Ivanovitch Polukhin?" he boomed into the milling crowd.

In answer to the imperial call came a short elderly courtier in tight fawn breeches, polished black boots, and tailed coat. He leaned toward Tatiana, alarmingly close, so that she smelled his liquored breath. His bushy gray mustache tickled her hand as he bent low to kiss her fingers. She looked imploringly at Nicholas and Alexandra for some explanation of this gentleman's forward behavior. The tsar smiled broadly.

"You are a lucky one, Alexei. You shall be the first to dance with our remarkable little starling."

He cocked his head to one side and listened to the orchestra at the far end of the room.

"Are you up to a gigue, Alexei?"

The old gentleman with rheumy eyes and reddened nose saluted his monarch.

"Your pleasure is mine, Majesty."

In a trice, Tatiana was jerked away from the reassuring presence of the royal couple and speeded toward the dance floor. She found the baron surprisingly light on his feet, and his touch, as he led her about, was sure. She could almost imagine him on the stage of the Maryinsky . . . a Bournonville ballet, of course. The gigue had a nautical flavor and she pictured Alexei in middy and bell-bottomed trousers, executing a sailor's hornpipe.

Swept away into her reverie, Tatiana fancied herself the young cabin boy, boisterously echoing the captain's steps. In her mind, the giant columns supporting the cathedral-high ceiling became ship's spars and the massive crystal chandeliers lit up the scene with golden light.

Couples soon stood back for this unprecedented display. As the tune ended, there were explosive bursts of applause. Tatiana was rudely brought back to reality by the ardent, rather physical show of appreciation. Both Baron Polukhin and she were hoisted on the shoulders of a number of overly enthusiastic young officers who were carried away by Tatiana's buoyant dancing, Alexei's valiant efforts, and the inordinate amount of champagne they had already imbibed.

In the merry crush and confusion of the moment, the baron clumsily dismounted from his perch of honor and managed to steer Tatiana's human palanquin toward a quiet corner.

"There, my dear," the old man wheezed. "A place of our own to recover our composure."

Without waiting for a reply, he handed her down and escorted her toward an empty love seat surrounded by potted palms and ferns. Tatiana felt a calm and coolness exuding from the greenery. He took a moment to watch her settle herself on the gently yielding cushions, then turned to a hovering attendant and snapped his fingers.

Before he could lower himself onto the low ottoman before her, two servants had returned with chilled champagne, two fluted goblets, and a tray replete with cold sturgeon, creamed chicken croquettes, toast points, and three kinds of caviar. Alexei waved the servants away and poured the bubbly wine himself.

"Thank you for your attention, Your Excellency," Tatiana began gravely.

All this fuss was beginning to embarrass her. She felt the hot flush of her cheeks fanning her discomfort.

"And please thank His Imperial Highness for presenting me with such an excellent partner."

She searched her mind for the most formal and impersonal of pleasantries.

"Our dance was so enjoyable but I wouldn't dream of keeping you from your other duties."

"Duties?" the baron interrupted.

He drew the footstool closer to the young girl and gazed at her with what Tatiana alarmingly recognized as love-sick eyes. It was the very expression Pavel Sergeivitch, the mime instructor, had taught all third-year ballet students. She tried to edge further back into the settee but to no avail. He grabbed her hand and squeezed it tightly.

"Duties?" he repeated. "Never consider yourself a duty, my beautiful flower. You will be my pleasure, my comfort, my joy, my jewel . . ."

Tatiana jumped up and neatly disengaged his grip. She shook her head, frowning.

"Surely you misunderstand, Baron Polukhin. I'm grateful for your escort, but now, if you will take me back to the tsar . . ."

Alexei stood his ground, chuckling as she spoke. At the mention of the tsar, he let out a whoop of amusement.

"You set your sights high, black swan. Tsar Nicholas loved a ballerina once. But do you think our all-wise, all-seeing tsarina would allow such a thing to happen a second time? Far better to accept one even as unworthy as I."

Tatiana shook her head in chagrin.

"I don't understand what you mean. If you will not take me to my patron, please return me to the company of the other ballerinas. I know Olga Vorodskya and Katincka Antonova are here tonight."

"Ho, ho! So you wish to prance and preen before your rivals. Very well, my dear, I am up to the challenge."

He rose stiffly.

"Let us show the poor unfortunates just how lucky you've been. I wouldn't mind seeing the expression on Vorodskya's face when she sees you with me. You know, little Tatushka"—he leaned forward in confidence—"I was her first, too. Perhaps we shall invite her to dinner one evening for a private tête-à-tête-à-tête."

He broke off in guffaws which quickly lapsed into raspy choking. His face, already a blotchy red from the exertions of the gigue, now took on the appearance of an overheated furnace. Tatiana ignored his physical plight, having begun to realize what rights this awful old man thought the tsar had given him. Was this how it had begun for her mother?

"Never, never," she insisted in a high unfamiliar voice, horrified by his suggestions.

There must be some mistake, she thought. The tsar can't have meant this to be. She broke away and fled toward the safety of the assembled guests. Tatiana leaned against a cool wall and breathed in the exotic scent of lavender hyacinths which bloomed in a lacquered pot beside her. Beyond was a tall Oriental vase filled with delicate lilies. She felt the tension slowly ebb from her body and she banished the chill dark thoughts from her mind.

A wave of hungry guests, led by Nicholas and his tsarina, swept toward her on their way to the dining rooms. The royal couple noticed the slight figure, as pale as the most fragile flower petal, and paused. The tsar's eyebrows flew up in consternation.

"Deserted, little pet? What is Alexei thinking of? You must have someone at your side."

"No, no, please," Tatiana whispered, fearful lest the aging Casanova reappear.

Alexandra murmured into her husband's ear and the fly-away eyebrows resumed their normal place.

"That will stir the old bull up." Nicholas laughed conspiratorially.

He turned to the group of nobles immediately behind him.

"Ah, Monsieur le Comte. There you are! *Venez ici, s'il vous plaît.*"

Tatiana's heart sank. The baron had come back. She cast her eyes to the floor. She would not look or speak to him. She felt a strong firm arm engage hers and she was forced to follow meekly or face the tsar's wrath. A welter of smooth French words bombarded her ears but she refused to react in any way.

"Excuse me, mademoiselle. I must have been mistaken. I was under the impression all ballerinas were conversant in the language of the dance. My apologies."

A chair was pulled out for her at one of the elaborately set dining tables. Tilting her head at an angle, she caught a glimpse of her escort. It was not the horrible old baron!

Instead, before her stood a man of leonine aspect: tawny locks shot through with gold, insolent eyes flecked with nutmeg brown and sunlight, chiseled bones, full and brooding lips, a tanned complexion completely out of place in a Russian winter, and a well-built lean body. He was not quite right for a dancer but she had a flashing impression of an animal on the prowl, watching, judging, biding his time till the moment to strike came.

She still couldn't speak as the intensity of his gaze fell over her. She had to look away, gasp for air. He must think her stupid, she thought. Of course she knew French. She was fluent in it. French was spoken everywhere in St. Petersburg: in the palace, at school, in her own home.

By the time she raised her eyes, a tiny speech on her lips, he was gone and sitting down next to her was

Baron Alexei Ivanovitch Polukhin. From behind his back, he produced a single dawn-tinged rosebud and placed it in Tatiana's wine goblet.

"Lambkin," he began with a hint of concession in his voice, "you see I do understand."

She searched his face for signs of more playacting. She could detect none.

"I accept your apology," she said gravely. "But you must understand . . ."

She raised her eyes to his and stared deeply with all the passionate fire she could muster.

". . . there will be no repeat of our earlier scene."

The baron started to laugh off this trifling young maiden's concern for her virginity. But the sound died on his lips. For, worldly as he was, he could not disavow the force of meaning in those ink-lit pools, charming him, compelling him to accept her demand.

"Of course, my shy peach, my hot-house plum, it will be as you say."

He patted her hand and brought his chair closer to hers. Lifting her napkin from the table, he shook out the folds and laid it tenderly in her lap, artfully grazing his liver-spotted hands across her thighs. Tatiana blushed furiously and repositioned the heavy linen herself.

"I'm not a child, sir. I don't need you to cut my meat for me."

A puzzled frown added more wrinkles to his furrowed brow.

"But without me, you'll have no meat to cut, Tatushka."

He leaned even closer, breathing in the scent of her hair and the pearly skin of her neck.

"The tsar always gives me his tenderest flowers. Trust me, my little swanling, and I will teach you the game of love."

Tatiana looked wildly about the table for some means of escape. Her partner to the left was already engaged in conversation, as were Tsar Nicholas at the head of the table and the imposing grande dame seated next to him. Was there no one to save her from the baron's bald advances? She would rather die than be locked in the prison of patronage.

"Surely you can think of some small service I may perform for you."

Alexei, undaunted by her lack of enthusiasm, was kneading her fingers. Then she felt an insistent rubbing against her gown. His hard boot was bruising her leg. She squirmed unhappily.

"Tatiana Ivanovna, my queen, can't you find it in your heart to need me just a little?" the old courtier implored in his most chivalric tone.

She pulled her hands away and half rose from the massive chair in order to push it as far from Polukhin as was politely possible. She dared not look at him. She was afraid any gesture, the slightest glance, might encourage the incorrigible old goat.

"You must not say those things," she whispered, her voice cracking.

She reached for her water glass and the fine edge of the glass seemed to bite into her sensitive flesh. She sipped and choked. With an anticipation faster than her reflex, Alexei dabbed the drips on her chin dry with his own napkin. Instinctively she flung it from his grasp to the floor. Her cheeks were stained red-hot with mortification.

"Please," she begged earnestly, "you're embarrassing me."

In despair, her eyes sought refuge with one understanding soul, but the ladies at her table all seemed to be engaged in the business of flirting. They glanced out of the corners of their eyes at their male dinner partners. They laughed and feigned modesty at the gentlemen's jokes. They lifted their forks to their mouths with overt sensual relish. Tatiana couldn't bear the thought of eating, much less playing the same games with Alexei Ivanovitch.

The gentlemen, too, seemed perfectly happy and well occupied between the ripostes of their glittering ladies and the subtle bite of the tsar's finest vintage vodka. That is, all the gentlemen but one . . . and he was studying her with savage relentlessness. It was the man of mystery who had escorted her to dinner. If only he were to leap across the table, without upsetting the dinner, of course, and pummel the old baron until he agreed to leave Tatiana alone . . . If only he were to beg the tsar to reassign him as her patron, if indeed she had to have one . . . If only . . .

But time and reality dragged on. The handsome stranger with his penetrating stare stayed seated at the table with grim-set shoulders and a frown spreading over his brow. Defeated, Tatiana sank back in her chair, picking at the tsar's delicacies, forced to listen to Baron Polukhin blatantly bribing her with promises of furs, jewels, her own apartment, vacations in Europe, parties every night.

". . . and if there should be a child, of course, I will provide . . ."

All color drained from the young girl's face. Abruptly she stood up and almost jumped away from the table as if it had bitten her. Barely touching the ground, she flew to the tsar's side, one hand clutching at her head, the other at her heart.

"Serene Highness, please forgive me. I . . . must go . . . my head . . : feel sick . . ."

Her inarticulateness must have touched the imperial ruler.

"Of course, little pet. Even victory can be difficult to digest. Alexei . . ." he began to call out.

But the frightened girl closed her hand over Nicholas's signaling fingers.

"Please, no. Too much . . ."

The tsar was willing to overlook the child's impertinent grasp in light of her obvious gratitude.

"As you will. Run along, then, Tatiana Ivanovna, with my blessing. But next time . . ."

She had kissed his ring and flown from the room before she could hear what he might have in store for her next time. Two men rose from their seats, their eyes following the willowy figure out of sight. Alexei Polukhin shrugged his shoulders, puzzled. But the French comte, Roland de Valois, had the look of a man determined to get what he wanted.

Chapter Three

TATIANA HUDDLED DEEP IN HER FURS AS THE SLEIGH driver urged his horses down icy lanes toward her mother's apartment. The headlong pace, the soft hiss of the sleigh's runners breaking through the crusted snow, the frozen wind that snatched at her hair, all comforted Tatiana. Behind her, the tsar's looming Winter Palace dwindled to nothingness. She had escaped.

She was rushing through an enchanted landscape. The spires and cupolas of St. Petersburg glistened in a flood of moonlight, hanging above her in the iced velvet air. They looked as insubstantial as a frost fairy's fingerpainting on a windowpane. The buildings seemed to have lost their sturdy brick facades and turned crystalline with icicles and starlight.

Adrift in each golden pool of lamplight, the snow-flakes flickered and swayed to the wind's chilled breathing. The Neva River slumbered like a furred sinuous beast beneath its white coverlet. Overhead the northern lights, saffron, salmon, and flame-blue, twisted and danced up the night curtain.

She closed her eyes. The drifting snowflakes became Father Winter's kisses, falling on her cheeks, her lips, her eyelids. Calm thyself, little one, they seemed to whisper. Their sweet wet touches gave her tiny shivers of delight.

Tatiana's thudding heart slowed. She was lulled by the beauty about her. Her mind floated on ahead, to her doorstep. She would soundlessly unlock the front door, negotiate the long shadowy hall, and fall with grateful limpness onto her goose-feather quilt. Its lushness would engulf her tired limbs and she would slowly sink into a welcoming, perfumed, bosomy cloud. The world would drift far away, far far—

"Here we are, miss."

Tatiana sat up with a start. The horses' breath plumed out into the night. Above her, the driver's bearded face smiled as he offered her a helping hand. Then, jingling her kopeks in one fist, he slapped the reins smartly and the sleigh moved off.

Tatiana sighed gratefully. Only a moment remained before she could give herself to sweet darkness. Her hand shook with cold as she tried to insert her key into the lock. Before she could, the door was flung open and a wedge of harsh yellow lamplight invaded the snow-hushed night. Her mother beckoned to her imperiously with an impatient toss of the head.

At thirty-seven, fading prima ballerina Lydia Petrovna Dmitrova held her thin body arrogantly upright, pointed chin atilt at a haughty angle. Her face was a yellow-tinged, pale oval without its usual layers of artful makeup. The heavy, coarse black hair, usually piled in an elaborate jeweled coiffure, hung down her back to her hips. One large graceful hand held the expensive mauve silk dressing gown closed at her throat while the other pulled Tatiana into the foyer and propelled the unwilling girl into the front parlor.

"Tell me everything that happened," Lydia demanded in her rushed husky contralto. "What did Tsar Nicholas give you? Who did he choose for you? Did you sit at the great table?"

To Tatiana, her mother's tawny eyes gleamed like twin agate daggers, seeking to pin her to the horsehair sofa. Tonight the girl was too weary to struggle. She took the cross out of her purse and wordlessly handed it to her mother.

Lydia seized the prize, turning it over and over in her hands, visibly weighing it on one wide palm. She ran a long crimson-lacquered fingernail appreciatively along one exquisitely sculpted edge. Then she breathed on the large central emerald and rubbed it carefully with the ostrich-feathered hem of her dressing gown. Holding the jewel up to the lamplight, she tilted the cross back and forth to examine the facets and check for flaws.

Why doesn't she just bite into the gold, like any suspicious onion-selling peasant? Tatiana thought irritably.

"If you're finished, Mother, I'd like—"

"You've done very well, little Tasha," Lydia said. "When I danced the first time for Tsar Alexander, the reward he gave me had only two small rubies, and one of them was flawed."

She stroked Tatiana's cross as if it were a kitten nestled against her breast.

"But this, this is a triumph! I believe you could get a thousand rubles for it, perhaps even twelve hundred."

She shot her frowning daughter a look of professional admiration.

"If your price starts so high, you will command the best from this moment on."

Tatiana interrupted her mother's excitement in a low unbelieving voice.

"That's all this evening means to you—my worth on the open market? You haven't said a single word about my performance."

"Bah, I am a dancer. I know your toes are aching. Maybe they even bleed. But what does it matter? Isn't it worth a few bruises, this jewel from the hand of His Imperial Highness? And it's only the first. Someday you will have a chestful, a barrelful of riches."

Tatiana's sigh was steeped in melancholy. No one, least of all her mother, seemed to care for the one dream that shone at the center of the girl's soul. It was all dachas and summerhouses, furs and diamonds.

"Let me go to bed, Maman," she said wearily, holding out her hand for the cross.

But Lydia Petrovna clutched the jewel to her.

"No, you will not go to bed. Not until you tell me who the tsar chose for you."

Tatiana sank back against the hard sofa, mumbling the name of the aging nobleman she had hoped to forget. Her mother stamped her foot.

"Who?" she insisted.

With another sigh, Tatiana repeated, "Baron Alexei Ivanovitch Polukhin."

She shuddered at the memory of his rheumy eyes measuring her body.

Lydia Petrovna threw herself on the couch, placed the cross on an antique table, and grabbed her daughter's shoulders. The older woman's avaricious smile dominated her excited face.

"But that is completely wonderful! He's worth at least ten million rubles. What did he offer you, the villa at Antibes? It's well known that Marya Vassilovna got an estate on the Black Sea. People say it could almost be a palace. Quite a parting gift, no? And that bitch, Anna Feyodovna, still parades his brooch with the egg-sized pearl everywhere she goes."

Tatiana threw herself to her feet.

"Why don't you take the wrinkled old goat if you find him so magnificent? He couldn't be any worse than your current lover, General Boris Comansky."

Her mother drew herself up haughtily. A savage frown appeared on her face.

"You dare to judge your mother after the struggles and sacrifices I've made for you. What was I to do? Tell me the answer."

Lydia Petrovna's dramatic, waving hands and her thinly plucked, swooping eyebrows punctuated her performance brilliantly while her ocher-hued eyes remained watchful.

"It was winter, we had enormous bills to pay, and Prince Andreyev had just deserted me. How can you be so ungrateful, so spiteful, so cruel?"

Tatiana was unmoved.

"I don't want to live like this, Maman."

Her sweeping hand indicated the clutter of expensive gilt and mahogany furniture, the sparkling collection of Fabergé eggs, the priceless rugs, the double cabinet crammed with heavy crystal—all the accumulation of a kept and pampered ballet star.

"And how would you want to live, then?" Lydia Petrovna sneered, the thin line permanently etched between her brows deepening. "Like that poor wretch Svetlana, maybe, widowed at twenty, pawning her wedding ring for bread, wearing the cast-off toe shoes of others? She no longer dances, they say," added Lydia Petrovna with an unmistakable twist of satisfaction on her thin lips. "She crippled herself in worn-out shoes."

The older woman's eyes swept over Tatiana with disgust.

"I'm sure you've never lowered your lofty mind to consider sordid details such as the cost of custom-made pointe shoes, but the time has come. How do you plan to survive on the sliver of a salary the Imperial Ballet pays?"

"There must be a way to dance and still have dignity," came the quiet answer.

Her mother's eyes narrowed to slits.

"At least four evenings a month, I sweep into the palace wearing my sables, crowned with the tiara that was placed on my head by the tsar himself, my arms so heavy with diamond bracelets I can hardly raise them high enough for my hand to be kissed. Are you stupid enough to believe that anyone, anyone would find me undignified? You are a fool, Tatiana Ivanovna, and I find it hard to believe you are my daughter."

As her mother raged on, Tatiana thought to herself,

and every one of those nobles watching you parade by can name which lover bought which bracelet. Your jewels are your scars, Maman, your medals of a war without honor.

Tatiana's earliest memory was of her mother's terrified weeping as a door slammed shut. The tall mustachioed man with the spurs never returned and there were days with only soup on the table. Then a new "friend" appeared, a cold-eyed, bald-headed tub of a man who insisted the three-year-old call him "Excellency." It was a hard word to say, and probably why Tatiana remembered him at all. He had lasted only a few months. And Lydia had gone back to weeping.

Over the years, Tatiana watched the cycle. First there would be gaiety, parties where Lydia wore her new jewels and her new patron watched her possessively as she charmed his friends. A feverish excitement would take hold of her mother. The front doorbell would ring constantly as tradesmen brought in new purchases and Lydia would direct them to place that étagère there, this vase here. Months would go by. Sometimes years.

Then the fights would start, always over money. The patron would accuse Lydia of extravagance while she would protest he didn't love her. Tearful reconciliations, armed truces, heavy pouting storms—her mother was expert at them all. But in the end, she was always left alone, with piles of unpaid bills.

The cycle would plunge downward. Her latest purchases would be repossessed as Lydia alternated between panic and an utterly calculated search for a new patron. She would entertain old lovers, hoping for introductions to their friends. She attended every salon, every party, every opera or ballet performance, always dressed dazzlingly, always watching for the admiring male eye. At home, she dropped her sophisticated airs and gave way to her fears with hysterical weeping.

Finally a new man would agree to support the famous ballerina. And the cycle would begin anew.

"But I forgive you, little Tasha," said her mother with a wide, thin-lipped smile. "What experience have you had, after all? You've never known hunger, never lacked for anything."

Nothing except love, thought Tatiana bitterly. Nothing except security. Her throat felt tight with unshed tears. She concentrated on keeping them from spilling out, knowing she could expect nothing but an impatient grimace from her mother for any display of sadness. She tried to shut out the woman's infuriating lecture.

"How could you know you can't refuse Count Alexei Ivanovitch's offer? He's the wealthy, generous, dependable patron little girls like you should dream of as they clasp their toe shoes to their new breasts."

Tatiana winced. Had Maman ever clasped anything but jewels to her bosom? She must have been born old, sucked cynicism with mother's milk. It seemed almost sacrilegious to hear the older woman talk of the dreams of youth, dirty them with her grasping hands.

Lydia Petrovna leaned closer to Tatiana to confide, "He won't want much from you in bed. After all, he's an old man."

She leaned back again.

"Of course you will take him," she said with a toss of the head, "and when you're riding in your own carriage with new furs around your shoulders and sapphires at your ears, why then we'll laugh at this night together."

Tatiana had endured as much as she could.

"Am I the only one, besides my father, who believes in true love?"

Lydia cringed, her hard glare giving way to an uncharacteristic falter. She looked down at her hands, white-knuckled in her lap.

"Is everyone for sale to the highest bidder? No, Mother, I will wait for love, if it takes forever."

Tatiana threw herself out of the crowded parlor, away from her mother and everything she represented, away to the night and its silver moon, who alone understood her heart.

The man with golden hair leaned forward and rapped on the sleigh driver's high seat back.

"Faster, driver, faster!" came his impatient, French-accented Russian.

Thank God for Princess Tchernushnya, Roland de Valois thought fervently. That old flirt with her twenty chins would give away the color of the tsar's underclothing, if only one agreed to attend her precious salon. Inveigling Tatiana Dmitrova's address out of the simpering octogenarian had been child's play. The only problem had been extricating himself from her barrage of stories in time to chase down the amazing young dancer.

St. Petersburg rushed by in a blur of brick and ice, crisscrossed by icy, arching bridges, watched by a solemn, broad-faced moon. Spirals of snowflakes floated down the sky, churning endlessly in the bright light. They were like Tatiana, Roland thought, beautiful and fragile, and unaware of the ground toward which they fell.

In that ambitious, self-assured crowd of sophisticates around the tsar's table, she had stood out like a dewy child. Those huge black tilted eyes had viewed the assemblage with serious study. She had listened to the polished entreaties of the baron at her side with awkward, endearing earnestness, her slender hands folded like a schoolgirl's in her white-clad lap. She seemed surprised at the attention, as if she had no sense of her own innocent, enthralling beauty. When a compliment seemed too much for her, Roland had been charmed by the spontaneous blush that rosied her face.

And then, when she all but ran from the party, her vulnerability had touched him deeply. She had fled like a small, hunted thing, with little defense against the bejeweled, aristocratic predators that stalked her. How young she had looked, poised in her simple ivory gown against the tsar's forbidding military tunic, as she clasped her hands and begged his permission to retire in a shy voice.

There had been nothing of that girl in her dancing earlier in the evening. On stage, Tatiana Dmitrova had been all ice and white fire, a poem of sharp, exquisitely etched lines that burned in the mind long after she had moved on. Her black swan embodied the cruelty of beauty—its uncaring, impersonal power that could cut a worshiping lover to ribbons. More than technically perfect, her dancing was eloquent, utterly convincing. She gave herself to the role, held nothing back. Ballerinas with twice her experience would have been proud of such a performance.

The contrast between the coldly sensuous knowing woman on stage and the gentle innocent at table astonished Roland, fascinated him. He had never seen anyone who could so passionately lose herself in a dance. Roland knew he had to have this ballerina, to make her his alone. It seemed he had come to Russia for nothing else.

Roland rapped again on the sleigh, and the driver's rough voice answered, "Almost we are there, good sir."

Even as he spoke, the horses turned down a narrow street, slowed, and came to a halt. Immediately Roland leaped out and slapped some money into the man's gloved hand.

"*Spaciba*," he muttered as the sleigh slid away.

He climbed the stairs to the elaborately carved front door, his shadow dancing velvet on the snow behind him. There Roland paused. It was well after one o'clock in the morning, he realized belatedly. Why was he so intent on overtaking her now, when tomorrow would certainly do as well? He was no boy, to be swept away by a momentary passion. But his need to be with her pounded in him. Had her near-flight simply released his instinct for the chase?

Roland whirled around, certain he had heard someone call his name. A shiver shot down his spine. There was no one there. And who would speak in such a clear, sweet, inhuman voice? Roland's eyes swept the street, the front of the apartment. All he found in the mysterious Russian night was a glimmering path painted on the snow by the moon.

"I must be mad," Roland said to himself, as his feet leaped down the stairs and followed the beckoning silver stream of light.

He was on the trail of an urgent impulse he couldn't resist, did not want to resist. It drove him to the back of the shadowy building, across a sleeping winter garden to where the moonlight played on a set of studio doors. With no awareness of his action, Roland pulled them apart and stopped short at the sight of a vision.

A slender figure, all in moon-drenched white, danced softly across the floor. He had heard the phrase "light as air" used many times. It was a cliché critics and ballet goers alike used for a dancer who gave the illusion of weightlessness. Usually it was a gross over-statement. Once or twice, Roland had actually seen a ballerina sustain the illusion for a moment or two.

But the girl turning and reaching in the pale air looked as if she were a spirit of the night itself, a moonbeam that had chosen the form of a woman for an evening. Her long drifting midnight hair, her swirling draperies, her astonishingly eloquent arms and white swan neck all added to the illusion. Roland could swear that the tips of her toes only touched the ground to accentuate the rhythm of her dance. She wasn't bound to the earth at all, only gracing it with her presence.

Tatiana was dancing to Love. The endlessly held attitudes, soft exquisite arabesques, the slow drifting leaps, all reached toward the one perfect partner who was her destiny. Her arms cried out in longing. Her silvered fingertips yearned for that other soul, the other half of herself, with whom she would attain a final merging somewhere high above the earth.

The utter beauty of her idealism, her dream, was a sweet pain shooting through Roland. Here it is, a voice kept repeating within him, here it is. Unknowing, he was about to take a step toward her when, miraculous-ly, she began drifting in his direction. He held his breath as she began a lingering set of pirouettes, whirling in and out of pools of light, disappearing,

appearing, in time to his thudding heart. The turns became faster, wilder, ever closer to where he stood.

Mesmerized, Roland held out his arms and Tatiana was in them, his insubstantial moon spirit made flesh. She was warm, firm, pulsing with life. The odors of her skin, her breath, were intoxicating, reminding him of a summer meadow at twilight. Her cloud of hair fell around him, enveloping him in her private incense. He was lost in her, happily drowning.

Tatiana's eyes snapped open and gazed with wonderment on her own true love, the man she had been searching for as long as she could remember.

He was everything she had dreamed he'd be—golden, strong, tall, sure. His body fit hers exactly, its broad chest an ideal resting place for her head, the wide shoulders meant for her hands, his muscular arms supporting her slenderness with perfect ease. She had danced a spell of enchantment, Tatiana thought with astonishment, as he lifted her exuberantly into the air.

As he brought her gently back to earth, his golden eyes drank in hers exultantly. She had woven a net of dreams and caught this gorgeous, leonine man who pressed her so tightly to him, against his strong sinewy thighs, his flat abdomen, his hard maleness. His touch communicated volumes to her—hunger, worship, tenderness. He bent back her head, his masterful hands entangling themselves in her hair and she was trembling, breathless.

"Tatiana! Tatiana Ivanovna! I will have no more sulking from you. Where have you hidden yourself?"

Wrenched from their private dream, the pair froze at the grating sound of Lydia Petrovna's voice growing louder and louder.

"I will not have you exhausted for the audition tomorrow!" came the intrusive words.

The key of the inner studio door clicked. Roland cupped Tatiana's face in his hands and brushed her delicate lips with a kiss. Then he leaped out the back door and was gone.

She touched her burning mouth wonderingly, unable to catch her breath. She would never be alone again.

Chapter Four

THE POLISHED WOODEN PLANKS OF THE IMPERIAL BALLET School's stage echoed with the hollow little thumps of hurrying toe shoes. Boris Gregorivitch Tumkovsky, the school's ballet master for thirty-two years, stood front and center, legs planted wide and arms folded on his chest as his fledgling dancers scurried about him. He was a huge, husky bear of a man dressed in black trousers, a billowing ivory shirt, and a tight crimson sash.

Under his white bushy brows that crawled like shaggy animate hedges toward his shining pate, Boris Gregorivitch's round blue eyes twinkled as he called encouraging comments to the three girls in their sparkling costumes. He consulted a pocketwatch and his eyebrows soared.

43

"My little chicks," came his booming voice, "you must assemble immediately."

He clapped his broad hands sharply.

"The great French impresario, Roland de Valois, will be here in five minutes. No, no, no, Elena," he directed, striding toward a strong-looking blond girl. "You will enter stage left. Wait here," he said, giving her square shoulders a final push toward the wings.

He looked across the stage to the right wing where peach-cheeked Irina and pale little Tatiana stood.

"Good," he said, giving them a satisfied nod. His eyes lingered approvingly on the shorter girl and a proud smile touched his lips for a moment.

"So, my little ones, remember that one of you could become the next toast of Paris. It has happened to more than one of de Valois's ballerinas. He is a genius, as we all know. So dance with all your hearts this morning and perhaps he will take one of you away with him."

Boris Gregorivitch's eyes rested mournfully on Tatiana, as if he were bidding her a private farewell. Then he straightened briskly and barked out last-minute reminders to the nervous dancers.

"Your arabesques must be precise, Elena," he said with a frown. "I have spoken of this many times in class. Think line, line! De Valois knows almost as much about the ballet as I do. He will be watching."

He chucked the tall strong girl under her chin. The big man passed to Irina.

"Now, you, Irinichka. We all know your line is excellent, but do not neglect the feeling. Remember why you are moving, yes?"

Over Irina's bowed bronze head, Boris Gregorivitch looked at Tatiana, standing quietly with an expression in her huge ebony eyes that seemed a million miles away.

"As for you, my Tatushka . . ."

He paused, at an uncharacteristic loss for words. Boris Gregorivitch sighed a long lugubriously Russian sigh.

"Dance. Just dance."

Too much vodka, Roland de Valois told himself as he strode through the crunching snow toward the renowned Imperial Ballet School. Either that, or I was drunk on the tsar's brandied cherries.

Roland had awakened under four luxurious quilts in his fancifully carved oak bed at the Empress Hotel still haunted by the image of a young girl made of moonlight dancing through a deserted studio. He also remembered—and the memory made him wince—that he had believed she was his destined soulmate.

Roland shook his head ruefully. It must be the heavy atmosphere of mysticism that clung to everything Russian. It had penetrated what he liked to think of as his practical French aestheticism. When dancers turn to mist fairies and invite you to fly away with them, he told himself, it's time to return home.

No one is really weightless. Yes, Mademoiselle Dmitrova had danced a brilliant black swan, but the rest? She was real enough in your arms, wasn't she? he asked himself caustically, so intent on that memory that he missed the admiring glances of two befurred and bejeweled ladies who were passing him. It was not like Roland to ignore inviting looks from pretty women. But he was momentarily lost in the shapes and textures and scent of Tatiana's willing body, indelibly etched, it seemed, in his memory.

An inviting child-woman, he admitted to himself. But the rest must have been a trick of chance lighting and his own overheated imagination. It's time you stopped looking for some sort of romantic ballet ideal, Roland insisted to himself. Every dancer has flaws and certainly every dancer has weight. Tatiana Dmitrova obviously will have both. All he would have to do is watch.

Now here was a place to cool one's heels, Roland thought as he entered the cloistered atmosphere of the school. In the gray fortresslike building, furniture was sparse and simple. The director, a ramrod-straight man who looked as if he'd never eaten a full meal, offered Roland a restrained welcome before directing him to the student theatre. Pupils glimpsed along the way were dressed in unrelieved gray and acted overly quiet, being either incurious or very busy. The tsar's personal nunnery, Roland thought, amused, as he entered the dusty, little used theatre.

"Ah, my most esteemed Monsieur de Valois," boomed a hearty voice. "We have been waiting."

Walking down the aisle of the auditorium, Roland eyed the massive ballet master who was standing on stage, hands on hips, framed by shabby olive curtains.

"I was told that Russians never looked at clocks," Roland said easily, his deep expressive voice conveying friendly apology.

"It's true what you say," Boris Gregorivitch agreed, giving Roland's outstretched hand a hearty shake, "but I didn't expect a Frenchman to conform to our ways. Come, we will talk."

He waved his guest to a faded seat in the first row of the audience and lowered his own bulk into the neighboring one.

46

"So, you must tell me what you are looking for," Boris Gregorivitch said. He added chummily, "His Kingship, the director, only told me, 'He wishes to find a dancer from among our ranks.'"

The ballet master's imitation of his superior's officious expression was perfect. Roland grinned.

"All I'm looking for is technical perfection, brilliant acting, complete versatility—you know, my friend, the woman I'll never find."

Boris Gregorivitch did not share Roland's rueful smile.

"Did you see the black swan last night?" he asked.

Roland's eyes narrowed.

"Quite a phenomenon," he agreed casually. "But can she do anything else?"

The older man smiled, rose from his seat, and climbed up onto the stage.

"Let us begin," he announced. "The three young women you will see this morning are the cream of my graduating class. Each is assured a place in the corps of the Imperial Ballet, unless, of course, monsieur, you steal one from us."

Boris Gregorivitch signaled the first dancer to be ready to take her place on stage.

"May I introduce Irina Vassilovna Nimzova from Kiev. She is nineteen years old and will dance the doll sequence from Act II of *Coppelia*."

The tiny, withered woman at the piano began playing as a small, graceful beauty ran out onto the stage and took up the mock-mechanical pose of Swanhilda, the vivacious village maid, pretending to be the life-sized doll Coppelia. Roland watched her carefully, noting the precise positions, the exact line, the perfect timing. She had been well trained indeed. He was impressed.

47

But Roland shook his head sadly at the waste. She would never rise further than the corps of any ballet company.

Irina Nimzova lacked humanity in her dancing. She had sacrificed feeling for technique. How clever of Boris Gregorivitch to pick a mechanical-doll dance for his mechanical dancer. But Roland was not fooled. Even at their coldest, Coppelia's movements should suggest the teasing sly intelligence of Swanhilda, who was only pretending to be made of wood. Nimzova's girl could have been carved out of marble, for all the feeling she displayed.

When the dance was finished, Roland applauded politely, his light claps swallowed up by the empty auditorium.

The second dancer, Elena Alexandrovna Tcherenska, was a pleasure to watch. She was tall for a dancer, and very strong. She made the spirited movements of Kitri, the youthful Spanish heroine of *Don Quixote*, splendidly fiery and dominant. But her very strength was also her downfall. Tcherenska's athleticism was too enthusiastic and at times overwhelmed the confines of the role she was dancing.

Kitri had another side to her, one that the dancer seemed incapable of displaying. As well as being wild and powerful, Kitri was also in love. Elena brought no softness, no romance to the dance. Roland knew she would be a crowd pleaser in short set pieces but a disappointment in a full-length role where complexity of character was called for. Roland's applause was stronger for this second dancer as she bowed with innocent pride in her physical achievements.

Roland tapped his strong fingers restlessly on the wooden armrest of his seat. He could find this caliber of dancer in any capital of Europe. Boris Gregorivitch was playing the game very skillfully. After Nimzova and Tcherenska, Tatiana Dmitrova would shine incandescently.

As the husky ballet master returned to the stage to introduce the dancer he clearly preferred, Roland tightened his resolve. He had been in the business of judging dancers for fifteen years. No cagey teacher, no trick of moonlight was going to subvert his exacting standards. He would see her for what she was: human, flawed, possibly talented enough to join his company, more probably not. His arms folded on his chest like a barrier to illusion, Roland listened to the opening bars of the second act of *Giselle*.

The first act flashed through his mind. Giselle, a fragile, naive, emotional village maiden, had unwittingly fallen in love with a disguised nobleman. When she discovered he was betrothed to another, she lost her mind and killed herself. Act Two opened at her grave. Roland leaned forward in unconscious anticipation as the curtain parted to reveal an empty stage.

Tatiana huddled in the wings, imagining the darkness there to be that of the grave. Her mind added damp and silence, heavy air and pressing soil. She was nothing, at peace in the moldering earth.

As the piano sang out its plaintive wail, she felt a magical tugging at her breastbone, an irresistible call. A slicing beam of ivory light penetrated the murk of her grave and somehow she pulled herself from her heavy slumbering body and stepped out into the world again, onto the stage.

Her steps were hesitating, trembling, as if she were not sure her limbs could move. She was cold, so very cold. Her arms hung in front of her awkwardly, as if they had forgotten how to embrace a loved one. She was a spirit newly called from the grave.

Tatiana's intense imagination peopled the empty stage. She envisioned the mysterious, ever-present mists of the night forest, the two lines of Willis, vengeful ghosts of girls who had died of unrequited love. In her mind's eye, she saw Myrtha, the imperious, ice-hearted queen of the Willis, who had just called up Giselle's soul from the grave and now commanded her to follow the rest of the malign spirits.

At first, Tatiana's movements were exact and lifeless, moving only at the queen's command, following the queen's steps. Myrtha turned and ordered the girl to dance alone. Tatiana danced, at one with the curls of mist and the ghostly company. She was free of the earth and she danced a simple paean to her liberation, her discovery of her own weightlessness. She leaped and turned, threading through trees, trailing the midnight mists behind her.

Her sister Willis watched her sadly, for they too had had this moment of freedom before cruel Myrtha had bound them to her forever. Tatiana imagined the sorrow in their faces and her dance took on a tragic cast, as if poor Giselle knew how short her moment of transport was going to be. With a final astounding leap, edged with the pathos of a trapped creature making a final doomed bid for freedom, Tatiana disappeared from the stage.

There was a long pregnant pause. The piano player, the curtain hand, and the ballet master burst into spontaneous applause. Boris Gregorivitch looked out at the silent French impresario and smiled.

Roland de Valois looked like a boy brought face-to-face with a vision. His sophistication, his air of com-

mand, his hard-cast business acumen were all gone. In
their place stood an innocent youth, idealism shining in
his eyes, worship in his clasped hands. Then Roland
caught Boris Gregorivitch's knowing glance, and the
boy was gone as though he had never been. By the time
the old ballet master had made his way to Roland's
side, the impresario was his usual faintly smiling,
imperturbable self.

"So. Now you tell me, Monsieur de Valois. Can
Dmitrova do anything but the black swan?"

"She's extraordinary, as you're well aware, you old
fox," retorted Roland, an unwilling grin on his face.
"I've never seen anyone to remotely match her."

He eyed Boris Gregorivitch curiously.

"I don't understand why you're so eager to give her
up. If she turned up in a school of mine, I'd move
heaven and earth to keep her."

The husky ballet master shrugged.

"Monsieur, a dancer like Tatiana Ivanovna turns up
once in a generation, once in a lifetime. Shall I keep her
locked away here in Mother Russia where only the
tsar's court will see her?"

He ran his bulky fingers through his remaining hair.

"Bah! It would be to my shame. She belongs to the
world, and you, I am sure, will take her there."

"You are a generous man, Boris Gregorivitch,"
Roland said. "In your place, I might be considerably
more selfish."

"You would be more possessive, my friend," the
ballet master corrected, "perfectly reasonable considering the difference in our ages. If I were thirty years
younger . . ."

"I'm interested in Tatiana Ivanovna as a dancer, not
as a woman," Roland stated dryly.

Boris Gregorivitch gave the impresario a doubtful look.

"Well, it is with the woman you will have to negotiate. Shall I bring her back on stage?"

"Please."

The older man disappeared behind the curtain to speak with his trio of waiting ballerinas.

"Our visitor was very impressed. I am sending all but Tatiana back to their classes."

He patted her pale cheek.

"De Valois would like to speak with you, little one."

The other would-be candidates scattered disappointedly, favoring Tatiana with envious glances. She scarcely noticed. Nothing except the performance itself had pulled Tatiana out of her dream of the magical meeting of souls she had experienced the night before. His golden leonine hair, his eager tawny eyes, his starlit smile flickered and glowed through her mind, calling to her even now. Who was he? When would she see him again?

"You are so far away, my Tatushka," said Boris Gregorivitch with a bemused smile. "Aren't you interested in meeting this famous man who wants you to dance for him?"

"I . . . I . . . yes, of course I am. Forgive my inattention, maître."

"I am used to it, you know. But this is your future we're talking about."

He gave her a serious, fatherly look, bristled eyebrows meeting above his searching eyes.

"Have you thought at all about Paris? He will make you a great star, you know. But are you prepared to leave your home and live among strangers?"

"I'm not sure. It would all depend . . ."

Her voice trailed off.

"Depend?"

His frown grew deeper.

On whether my love was with me, Tatiana's mind finished silently.

Boris Gregorivitch waited in vain for her reply.

Finally, with an impatient snort, he said, "So, come and meet the famous man. Maybe he can convince you."

Putting an arm about her slender shoulders, he shepherded her out onto the stage.

Tatiana stopped short, her eyes enormous. It was he, the man of her moonlight dance. He was de Valois. A legendary name in the world of dance. And he looked at her with an impatient businessman's frown, as if assessing her worth. For an instant she stood rooted to the worn planks of the stage as if struck by lightning. Then, overwhelmed by her discovery, she rushed away, leaving the two men staring after her, nonplussed.

Why did I flee from him, Tatiana wondered as she sat cross-legged in the center of her luxurious four-poster hugging a pillow to her breasts. She had run all the way home from the Imperial Ballet School stage, fiercely slammed her bedroom door, and flung herself into the waiting, unquestioning arms of her own bed. Now she shivered at the exciting thought that she would be dancing with him, for him, in fabled Paris. For he was a lion of the dance and he was her love.

Tatiana threw herself from the bed and danced ecstatically around her small room.

"Oh, Marie, he is so beautiful," she caroled to the set of Taglioni prints of the famous ballerina that graced one wall.

53

The legendary dancer smiled delicately back from a cloud on which she was floating, the tip of a rose where she balanced *en pointe,* and a brook over which she leaped, tightly clustered curls flying.

Tatiana spun by the row of porcelain figurines she had won in dance competitions at school. She blew each posed little ballerina a kiss, one from each fingertip.

"He's going to take me away with him," she cried.

As she passed the full-length, gilt-edged mirror that had seen so many struggles, she whispered to her image, "You are a lucky, lucky girl, Tati. Remember that!

"Oh, Papa," she murmured in heartfelt tones to the framed portrait of a dark, handsome man with night-black eyes that stood in a place of honor at her dressing table. "Your little Tati is going to be so happy."

Tenderly she pressed her rosebud mouth to the picture, gave it a searching glance, and replaced it carefully amid the pressed flowers and fading dance programs that crowded out two bottles of scent and a hairbrush.

Roland looked so different from her father, Tatiana mused, yet she knew their spirits were alike. She took hold of a bedpost with one hand and swung around slowly. So golden he was, she thought. Strong, sure, and yet young too . . . She was seized with an impulse to draw him, to bring him to life before her eyes. Taking up a sketch pad and a stick of Conti crayon, Tatiana leaned back among the plump pillows of her bed and began working. Time passed unnoticed.

Without so much as a tap at the door, Lydia Petrovna burst into the room to find Tatiana doodling away, surrounded by crumpled pieces of paper. The girl looked up, started, and shoved her pad under a pillow.

"You minx, you sly little minx," cried her mother, waving a hand-delivered letter before her. "Why didn't you say anything?"

"About what, Maman?"

"You've got the great de Valois panting for you, and you don't even tell me?"

She snapped the note impatiently.

"He'll be here in a few minutes with a contract, a contract!"

Lydia Petrovna's saffron eyes glittered gleefully.

"Three hours after he's seen you dance, and he's ready to put his money on the table."

Tatiana's hand stole under the pillow to touch her picture of Roland. So soon she would see him again.

"I'd better dress," she said in quiet joy.

"We've got him just where we want him," Lydia Petrovna continued, oblivious to her daughter. "You'll have enough money to bathe in."

The doorbell rang downstairs. Lydia Petrovna's face tightened with avid anticipation.

"I'll entertain him," she assured her shining-eyed daughter. "Take all the time you need. And you must wear the necklace the tsar gave you."

With that final directive, the aging ballerina was gone, leaving Tatiana to quiver in a rain of excited feeling before she rushed to her closet.

Very nice, Roland thought as a servant led him into an up-to-date, richly furnished parlor. Tatiana's mother has done quite well for herself. And here was the lady, hurrying toward him, slim and graceful as all good dancers must be, but hard-edged and burnished as an old depreciating coin. Her diamonds were no harder than her eyes, he thought, moving aside a bracelet to kiss her proffered hand.

"Comte de Valois, I am deeply honored to make your illustrious acquaintance."

Her voice was husky, seductive.

Men must have fought over her twenty years ago, Roland thought as he replied with practiced gallantry, "Ah no, madame. The honor is mine. I have long dreamed of meeting the famed Lydia Petrovna Dmitrova."

Although he had never heard of her before coming to Russia, Roland knew what flattery was required.

She smiled complacently as she demurred. "Perhaps your father could make such a claim, but I have not starred on the stage for years now."

"Your legend will always grace the ballet, madame," he offered, not missing a beat. "We will not see your like again."

Paying homage to faded stars was as much a part of his business as judging talent or inveigling funds out of jaded aristocrats.

"You are far too kind, Comte de Valois," Lydia Petrovna purred, "but I thank you."

She waved him to a couch and sat down at his side in a flurry of expensive silk and perfume.

"Have you enjoyed your visit to Russia?" she asked, her eyes moving over him calculatingly.

She is sizing me up as carefully as a cocky banker with a rich client, he thought amusedly, as he replied obediently, "Very much, thank you."

"May I offer you a little refreshment?"

She rang a tiny bronze bell and the maid reappeared with an elaborately scrolled and incised silver platter. On it rested three bowls of caviar, black, red orange, and amber. Perfectly browned triangles of toast filled a basket and there were two crystal shotglasses brimming with ice-cold vodka.

"Nowhere but in Russia can one enjoy such caviar," he said after a taste of the delicacy.

He took another bite.

"Only the tsar serves as fine a treat."

"Your palate is quite discriminating, monsieur. That caviar was a gift from the palace."

Lydia Petrovna preened herself visibly.

"I spend a good deal of time there."

Roland wearied of the polite, empty exchange. She was clearly waiting for him to make the first move. If she felt that put her at an advantage, so be it. She would learn differently soon enough.

"Forgive me, Madame Dmitrova, but I have a limited amount of time," he said in a clipped voice.

He drew a contract out of his inner coat pocket and placed it carefully on his lap.

"I wish to hire your daughter Tatiana Ivanovna Dmitrova for a period of three years with an option to renew if both parties are satisfied."

As Lydia Petrovna stretched out her red-taloned hands for the contract, Roland raised one hand to stop her.

"Before you read, madame, let me say that I seldom make this kind of offer to a beginner, but in your daughter's case . . ."

Lydia Petrovna did an excellent imitation of an indignant mother.

"Monsieur, I am shocked. My Tatiana is no beginner at all, but a brilliant star. Surely you're aware of her unique talent."

Her words seemed to glance off him like arrows against a granite wall.

"One always takes a chance with a young dancer, as you are well aware, madame. How will she hold up under the pressures of the professional stage? Will the freedom go to her head? Will she fulfill her promise? All in all, I feel this is a very generous offer. Read, madame."

Lydia Petrovna gave the impresario a glance of grudging admiration as she accepted the closely written document. Many minutes passed as she read and reread the legal clauses.

"Pah!" she cried, flipping the contract back onto his lap. "Tatiana is lucky she has an experienced mother. There is nothing here about the dance itself. Is she to deliver herself over to you body and soul?"

"I don't believe I mentioned either one," Roland interjected with one raised eyebrow.

The histrionics were quite familiar to him, and he was not impressed.

"Perhaps if you could be more specific?" he prompted.

He was soon sorry he had asked as Lydia Petrovna's sharp words came like a rush of bullets, hammering home her points.

"Her first season, yes, you will choose her partners. But after, she will pick who she dances with. Also, she does not begin as a soloist but becomes a principal dancer immediately. She is to dance three full-length ballets a year, and six solos. She is free to dance as a

guest for other companies after these performances are
finished. After two seasons, she has the right to decline
any new productions that might offer a risk to her
career. Costume, scenery, music—she has a veto in all
at this point. If a soloist displeases her, the girl will be
dismissed."

Roland allowed a long silence to develop after she
had finished her shopping list of outrageous demands.

Then he said lightly, "Had I been looking for someone to take over my position and that of my choreographer's, madame, don't you think I would have said as
much when we began?"

Back and forth they fenced, two seasoned duelists, as
Lydia Petrovna secured for her daughter considerable
say in her own career and Roland successfully resisted
giving away any of his real power. What they finally
agreed upon was very close to the concessions Roland
de Valois made to any star performer. Tatiana would
simply have them in writing.

"Then we are agreed, madame?"

"You have heard most of my objections, Comte de
Valois. These last I'm sure we can settle quickly," she
said graciously.

Immediately Roland became wary, recognizing the
ploy. The most absurd demands were about to begin.
Would this aging, grasping woman demand something
he could not give? Then what would he do? Tatiana
Ivanovna had to be his. Roland let nothing of this show
on his face, presenting the same calm, ironical facade
he had maintained throughout their contest of wills.

"Indeed, madame? Pray mention these few and
paltry details."

"The salary, as you are undoubtedly aware, is barely

adequate. The daughter of Dmitrova is, *bien sûr*, accustomed to a life of luxury. One does not expect you to supply her with Fabergé enamels."

The former star gestured at her own collection.

"But neither should she fall to the level of a starving charwoman, mending and remending her one pair of gloves. I am sure you agree."

She paused calculatedly.

"*Mais oui.* We are completely agreed, madame, that Tatiana Ivanovna will not be reduced to one pair of gloves."

She gave him a disappointed look, as if sadly questioning his sincerity.

"It is little enough to ask. You will supply her with the furnishings of her apartment, with a cord of firewood each year, with a new fur for winter, and with a dozen lengths of fabric in spring and fall."

She ended with a satisfied little nod.

Roland's merry laughter jarred his antagonist.

"Madame Dmitrova, you are badly confusing two worlds. I am not offering to be your daughter's lover but her employer."

Lydia Petrovna raised one slender eyebrow as if to say, "Indeed?" She reached behind her and rang the bell for a servant.

"Ask my daughter to join us," she ordered the maid when she appeared.

In a moment, the black-and-white-uniformed servant returned with Tatiana trailing considerably behind her.

The young dancer was biting her lips. It wasn't the right dress, she thought in despair, shaking out the pale yellow gathers that belled out from her rust-sashed waist. But none of the six gowns she had tried on had looked beautiful enough to wear for Roland. This one was too pale and too girlish, though the lace on the bodice fell in a pretty cascade. The next moment, all thoughts of clothing fled her mind.

Seated next to her mother on the parlor sofa was the man himself, so magnetic he took her breath away. He was a lion on the prowl, his broad shoulders hunched forward eagerly, his sinewy thighs tensed, though his long artistic hands rested with deceptive nonchalance on a sheaf of papers in his lap. There was fire in his eyes, the flame of inspiration and breadth of vision.

She had seen him, by royal candlelight, by secret moonlight, in the theatre's shadows. Now, in bright daylight, she saw him whole for the first time. The handsome and sophisticated nobleman, the vulnerable romantic, and the hardheaded businessman all came together in a combination so potent she couldn't move. She could only stare, her heart speaking in her huge, tilted, night-black eyes.

Roland caught a glimpse of Tatiana and deliberately turned back to her mother, to stress the indifference he felt toward the girl.

"Come closer, Tasha, closer," grated Lydia Petrovna with a beckoning scoop of her crimson-nailed hand.

As Tatiana approached the sofa, her subtle personal fragrance of a twilight meadow, warm and sweet, assailed him. Despite all his attempts at self-control, Roland rose to his feet and looked into her eyes. He was lost. Lydia Petrovna smiled with satisfaction.

"Now tell me, monsieur. How can it be that Tatiana Ivanovna Dmitrova isn't worth an apartment, a bit of wood and fur, some dresses?"

Slowly the dancer and the impresario looked at the

61

woman as if she were a stranger bursting into their private room. Tatiana's eyes narrowed and she shot her mother a long speaking look.

Turning back to Roland, the girl said in a voice of quiet conviction, "I will agree to any terms you offer, Comte de Valois, for I trust you."

"Don't be a fool," cried her mother, leaping up.

She grabbed Tatiana's upper arm and shook it.

"You can't let him have you without—"

Roland removed Tatiana from her mother's grasp.

"Be quiet, woman," he growled. "You've had your life, and a glittering one it must have been. Now it is her turn."

Lydia Petrovna sat down suddenly, mastered by the great impresario.

"Read the contract, Tatiana Ivanovna," Roland said, turning back to the bewitching young ballerina. "You must protect yourself."

"It's not necessary," she told him in a low voice. "My destiny lies with you."

Something in Roland was stirred profoundly at her words. She had crystallized his feelings of the moonlit studio. They belonged together. It was true. But the rational side of him surged forward, threatened by this strange romantic chaos she seemed to touch in him. He scarcely knew her. She was a silly, dream-ridden child who was also a brilliant dancer.

"Still," he pointed out in his best avuncular style, "once you sign this contract, my dear, it will be too late to turn back. For your own good, Mademoiselle Dmitrova, read it carefully first."

Tatiana smiled mischievously, grabbed the pen and sheaf of legal documents from his hands, and signed her name with a flourish.

"Now there is no turning back, monsieur," she murmured.

A shriek of pure pain interrupted them. Lydia Petrovna wrenched the contract from her daughter's hand and pored over it, hunched like an aging, molting hawk.

"It is done, madame," Roland said.

He had gotten what he'd come for. A small mocking voice inside him added that he'd gotten, perhaps, more than he'd come for. Pulling his sophisticated air of gallantry about him like a protective cloak, he smiled in a fatherly fashion at the glistening young star he'd just acquired.

"You will love Paris, mademoiselle. She is a city full of wonder and light, kind to artists."

Tatiana listened to him with shining eyes.

"Is it very different from St. Petersburg?"

He smiled kindly.

"It is wider, more open, full of possibility. In comparison, St. Petersburg is like a lovely crystal, polished, glittering, complete. Paris is more a beautiful woman who may be gay one moment, tragic the next, but who is always endlessly fascinating."

"I can't wait to meet her," Tatiana breathed. "When will we leave?"

"I have reservations on the four o'clock train tomorrow afternoon," he said, rescuing the much-creased contract from the numb hands of Lydia Petrovna. "If you will meet me there at three o'clock?"

Dazed by the startling turn of events, the older woman said mechanically, "Of course, Comte de Valois. We will be there."

"Then I will bid you both adieu," said Roland, bowing. "It has been a pleasure negotiating with you,

Madame Dmitrova. And I look forward to a long and prosperous working relationship with you, mademoiselle. Au revoir."

He bowed himself out of the room, leaving the vanquished mother and the victorious daughter together on the couch.

Chapter Five

"ANYONE WOULD THINK YOU'D NEVER BEEN TO THE TRAIN station before," Lydia Petrovna fussed at her daughter.

The woman deliberately emerged slowly from the sleigh, scooping her myriad furs about her as a shield against the penetrating cold . . . and the lower classes. Lips pursed tightly, she watched Tatiana skip over to the conveyance directly behind their sled and pull at the suitcases and trunks before the driver could reach for them.

"Child," she called out, "remember your place. Let the cur do it."

Tatiana spun around.

"Maman!" came her embarrassed plea.

Her mother had used a word denoting the lowest form of peasant.

"There is no need for insults," she whispered.

"I'm sorry, Tasha. It's just that I'm losing my baby. You've no idea what that means to me."

Her long fingers flapped helplessly about like autumn leaves caught in a wind. Lydia hunched her shoulders forward as if to steel herself against the force of her pain. She clawed through her purse and, finally, from the depths of her sable muff, extracted a gauzy handkerchief and dabbed at her nose.

"Hurry up, my good man," she cautioned the sled driver. "I don't have all day."

She sidled up to him and flashed her most winning smile. She offered him a whole ruble, as if the extravagant amount easily made up for her ugly words and poor manners. He looked at the painted not-so-young woman, bit the coin, pocketed it, and spat into the gutter. Lydia paled. She hastily linked arms with her daughter and retreated into the station.

"Tasha, sweet," her mother begged, "look in my purse for some headache powders. My head throbs from the cold."

The girl felt as eager as a racehorse champing at the bit, but she found the patience to rifle through Lydia's petitpoint bag, finally bringing forth a small opaque bottle.

"And now some water . . ." Lydia said, and smiled coquettishly, enjoying the attention her daughter was giving her. "Or perhaps you could find me a little wine?"

Dutifully, the girl walked off, determined to keep her ebullient mood. She wandered past the ticket cages and the vendors hawking last-minute necessities—a sewing kit, thick leather luggage straps, hot piroshki, and tea.

Then she caught sight of the trains with their sleek coal-black cars and powerful steam engines. Clouds of white-gray vapor puffed vigorously from between the silvered wheels. She was drawn to the trains, absorbing their compressed energy into her own already seething excitement.

People scurried back and forth along the platforms as if reaching their destinations were a matter of life or death. Some scowled; some beamed with expectation. One lone masculine figure stood out, bathed in a ray of sunlight streaming in through the ceiling-high windows. Apollo himself could not have shone with more radiance, Tatiana thought. The man turned and she gasped. She ought to have expected it to be her Roland. Somehow, even from this distance, she felt scalded by the heat of his presence.

She waved wildly.

"Coming, my love, I'm coming," she whispered, her voice drowned out by piercing train whistles.

"Tatiana Ivanovna Dmitrova! What is the meaning of this?"

Her mother's nearby voice sounded harsh and sulky.

"I've been waiting and waiting. Where is my wine? My water? And where are you going now?"

Even Lydia's pettiness couldn't dampen Tatiana's enthusiasm.

"To Paris, Maman," she cried, her dark eyes aglow with youthful fire. "There is Roland."

"Ah, the great Comte de Valois." Lydia snickered. "Of course I know you're going to France, silly child, but play the grand lady. Pretend you don't see him. Make him come to you."

Her words were wasted on the chill moist air.

Helpless to stop the girl, she watched her daughter run shamelessly toward the man, flying to her future like a homing pigeon drawn to its nest. An envious frown wrinkled her forehead, and with reluctant steps, Lydia trotted after the girl to the Paris-bound train.

Roland glanced irritably at the large clock hanging from the center of the station. He pulled out his watch, consulted it, and tucked it back into a pocket. He glanced up at the clock again. A quarter to four, damn it. The train would pull out at four. Had he told her the right time? She must be coming, he thought. He looked down at the litter of bags nearest his sleeper car. The tags had the name Dmitrova printed on them. How many Dmitrovas could be traveling to Paris?

A small figure in dove gray breezed toward him. Her squirrel-fur hat flew off in her hurry, revealing a stream of silky black hair. His heart seemed to skip a beat. Yes, it was Tatiana. How could he mistake those eyes soft as mink, those vaulted brows, and the rosebud mouth . . . and her skin. How he wanted to touch the warm pearl marble of her neck, her breasts. She exuded vitality and hope and he wanted to feel her youth, be a part of it with her.

He took a few hesitant steps, then broke into a run, making a dash for her. She was grinning broadly and her arms were open to him. He stopped abruptly. What are you doing, man? he asked himself harshly. This is business. You're not a schoolboy on the way to his first affair. He shook his head as if to knock some sense into it and only succeeded in tangling his golden hair into a storm of waves. Adopting a serious expression, he waited for her to reach him. Gravely he shook her hand in welcome, fighting an urge to take her into his arms.

"So, you have come," he said, trying to insert a degree of coldness in his voice.

"Did you have any doubts, monsieur?" Tatiana replied.

She searched his face and was rewarded with the hint of a smile. Her heart leaped within her, knowing he was happy to see her. She faced her mother.

"I'll write to you, Maman," she said calmly.

"Just send me your press clippings, darling," returned Lydia Petrovna, true to form.

On impulse, she pulled her daughter to her, embraced her tightly, and pressed a scarlet kiss on her cheek.

"I think I shall miss you, Tatushka," she murmured, her voice cracking.

Pushing the girl away, the older woman attempted to recompose her face. Roland stepped forward, his hand already claiming Tatiana's.

"Have no doubts, madame. I will take the finest care, the greatest interest in your daughter . . ."

He frowned. His speech hadn't quite given the right impression.

"Professionally, that is," he added.

There was a knowing little smile on Lydia's face as if she saw through to his intentions. But there was no time for protestations or explanations. Tatiana's luggage was being stored on board and the conductor called out for the last time. With the gentlest pressure, Roland escorted his charge up the steps and down the aisle of the sleeper car to her compartment.

Opening her window, Tatiana waved at her mother, watching Lydia grow smaller and smaller as the train gathered up speed and distance. Then it was good-bye to St. Petersburg as the huge palaces of red and gold, blue and white, lit by the last rays of the sun, beamed and winked through thin-crusted sheets of ice.

"Adieu," she whispered to the frozen city. "Farewell to my childhood fairyland."

The massive public buildings with their ornate moldings and columns made her think of elaborate doll houses. The smaller brightly painted residences seemed like fanciful wedding cakes. She found herself laughing and crying all in the same minute.

Roland had stood back, giving her this private moment. Now he was sure it had gone on long enough.

"Away from the window, little waif," he commanded.

She turned to him with glittering eyes.

"Or Jack Frost will turn those tears to icicles."

He had meant to be jocular but she seemed to be taking him seriously.

"I'd much rather you wipe them away, Roland," she murmured.

So she knew the game after all. She was smart and fast . . . and a consummate actress. He'd have to be careful.

"It's Comte de Valois to you, mademoiselle. Remember, I'm your employer and twice your age, you know."

"Yes, Your Lordship," she simpered and sank into a curtsy, looking at him from the corners of her eyes.

"Behave now, or I'll return you to the tsar," he cautioned lightly.

She knew he was teasing but the reality behind the threat was too fresh to disregard. With effort, she closed her mind against Baron Polukhin and all he stood for. She had escaped that kind of life forever.

"Yes, Monsieur le Comte, I'll be good."

She sat down on a padded bench and folded her hands in her lap. He studied her silently. She was still a child, he concluded, the mixture of mercurial sprite and serious student unsettled in her blood. He had a sudden vision of the womanly beauty to come during her moment of quiet. Then, with an effervescent bound, she was out of her seat, lifting her arms overhead and twirling around the roomy compartment.

"I'm sorry. I can't sit still. It's all too wonderful."

She breezed about, peeking in, on, and under every conceivable surface. She loved the satin pillowcases, the smooth porcelain washstand, the nubby carpeting, the brocade of the curtains, the intricate moldings around the door. This compartment was the hub of her new world and no other mattered to her.

She was like a giddy puppy, he mused, free at last from the confines of its leash. He laughed along with her, feeling like he was eighteen again. Impulsively the girl turned to him and kissed his hand.

"Thank you, Roland, for wanting me."

She stared at the play of dark and light flecks in his eyes, her emotions naked to him. He stepped back from her gaze, troubled and frowning.

"You must not say things like that, mademoiselle . . . and you must not kiss my hand. In France we don't expect such subservience from our employees."

Artlessly she held her ground with the man of her dreaming heart.

"Or your women?" she asked without shame.

"Especially our women!" he retorted. "Just wait till you meet Micheline Arnot, our current prima, and Zazou, proprietress of my favorite café. You'll see what I mean."

She would need schooling to survive in Paris, he reminded himself. There was no pretense about her, just a bundle of raw youth, naive energy. For a moment he let himself stare at her youthful slim figure silhouetted against lighted draperies.

Diana the Huntress, he mumbled under his breath, goddess of the moon and protector of the young . . . Could Martinon fashion a ballet for her around those motifs? The thought rekindled his own energy and excitement. Yes, he thought, his eyes traveling over the slender form with its hint of virginal womanhood, I must have her . . . for the company.

"Roland, Comte de Valois," Tatiana cried. "Are you all right? You look so strange."

His vision cleared and, to the girl, he seemed to stand taller. His voice crackled with electric authority.

"I've never been better or hungrier."

He consulted his watch.

"Can you be ready for dinner in half an hour?"

"In five minutes, if you wanted it," she said quietly.

He was closing the door when he heard her call his name.

"Yes?"

"I've never been happier, Roland." She smiled.

A rosy flush suffused her cheeks, lighting her face, confirming the purity of her feelings. Roland stared hungrily at the girl and then turned quickly away to his compartment.

Precisely thirty minutes later, he was back in full evening dress, knocking at her door. It slid open at his touch. The room was neat as a pin and Tatiana sat demurely staring out the window. At the sound of his footstep, she looked up at him. He was stunned by the womanliness he now saw in those ebony depths. Gone were the little-girl clothes, the childlike attitude.

Calm and assured, she swept up her shawl and offered it to Roland. She stood before him in a gently flowing sea of aquamarine taffeta, billowing at the shoulders into leg-o-mutton sleeves and gathered tightly at the waist and neck with broad bands of ivory moiré. The tsar's cross hung at her neck.

"Lift up your hair," Roland directed.

Tatiana obeyed wordlessly and secured her heavy tresses with several mother-of-pearl pins. De Valois stepped close to the girl, near enough for her to be aware of his scent of sandalwood and lemon. She shut her eyes, blotting out everything but Roland, and swayed slightly. He removed the heavy jeweled piece from her neck. Without it, she felt heady and light, as if nothing now kept her feet on the ground.

"But why . . ." she began.

"Because I know what's best for you," came the gruff reply.

She felt something delicate rest on her collar. Opening her eyes, she looked at Roland. She could tell he was pleased by the decided arch of his eyebrow and the deliberate nod of his head. She went to her looking glass and gasped. A row of delicate deep blue sapphires winked up at her from a chain of white gold.

"It's beautiful," she breathed. "But why . . . when?"

He covered her with her shawl, his hands lingering on her shoulders, stroking the length of her back.

"After the audition at the school. I knew then I must get you to Paris at any cost."

"For the Companie Valois," Tatiana concluded.

73

Their eyes locked in the mirror, hers pure dark pools and his lit with leonine fire.

"Now that I'm here," she mused aloud, "signed, sealed, and delivered, so to speak, exactly what do you have planned for me?"

"Ah," said the comte, as he wrapped her arm about his and led her to the door, "I'm glad you asked that question, mademoiselle."

He began to tell her about the Companie Valois as they passed through the elegant saloon car with its painted ceilings and silk draperies, its Oriental carpeting and ornately carved upright piano. They were still deep in conversation when they walked down the long smoker, complete with comfortable sofas, fresh flowers to mask the smell of tobacco, and a safe for valuables. Both cars were crowded with flushed excited passengers, but Roland and Tatiana were oblivious to all but their own intimate world.

In the dining car, Roland and Tatiana were seated at a table for two. Formal settings of china and silver were arranged on spotless crisp linen. Clusters of chrysanthemums graced the table in a crystal vase.

"But your vision is extraordinary," Tatiana cried in amazement. "I never heard of anyone with dreams like that for ballet."

"It's no dream, Tatiana," Roland enjoined. "It can be done. I've done it."

He warmed to his subject, waving away the intrusive waiter who tried to take their order.

"Last season the Companie Valois presented five new works, uniting the efforts of Paris's finest. Louis Lavois and Pierre Doreau composed suites specifically for Caillege's adaptations of Fontaine and for Jules

Breton's original story. Morais and Carteret designed and painted the sets and the master, Léon Martinon, created all the choreography."

He sat back expansively, replete in the memory of his success.

"We got incredible reviews."

Tatiana sat like a little girl wrapped up in the magic of a fairy tale.

"How did you ever accomplish it all? Breton, Doreau, Morais, Carteret . . . their names have reached St. Petersburg as well as the reputation of their tempers. What's your secret?" she asked.

Roland sipped at his champagne and grinned like a cat with a secret.

"Have you heard of Montmartre, Tiane?"

He shortened her name, gallicizing it. Tatiana smiled to herself. That was her third gift from him, counting the contract and the sapphires. Her hand flew up to the cool stones.

"Mont . . . mar . . . tre," she repeated slowly as if tasting the tang of each syllable.

"It's the melting pot, the meeting ground for all the arts in Paris. Along the boulevards, in the galleries and halls, it's war. Artists and sculptors fight each other for patrons; musicians and dancers scrap for the sous thrown their way."

"This is Paris?" Tatiana asked in alarm.

"We aren't under the whimsical protection of a tsar," Roland wryly noted. "But there are the cafés of Montmartre and there the truces are established. We eat and drink together; we sympathize with one another, share our hopes, and damn our enemies; and there, Tiane, is where I carry on my business."

She looked puzzled.

"I don't understand. What do you have to promise them?"

He chuckled.

"I promise them the moon, of course. Whatever working conditions, billing, pay they want, I promise it to them. Don't look so horrified, *ma petite.*"

He leaned across the table jovially.

"The secret is they all want the same things: a chance to work, to produce their best, a full belly, and fame. And it's worked! Their names are known as far as St. Petersburg, aren't they?"

Tatiana had to laugh. Roland's infectious charm and description of his work enchanted and astounded her. But one question remained.

"Why me, Roland? You have a brilliant company already, producing one success after another. What do you need another ballerina for?"

"Not just another ballerina," he said, impassioned, "but the world's greatest ballerina. You will be my star, my treasure. You will be the catalyst igniting my artists to their greatest inspiration. With you as my prima assoluta, my company will be unsurpassed. We will be immortalized, Tiane . . . you for your incandescent dancing, me for my humble efforts to create the ideal creative arena."

Tatiana sat silent, her eyes looking into the future Roland had made real.

"I believe you," she said earnestly. "I believe you can do it."

"With you at my side, I know I will."

On impulse, his hand shot out to hers which rested on the table. Cradling her hand as though it were the highest prize, he heated her cool fingers with the warmth of his passion. He stared at her with a mixture of triumph and hunger. She felt his strength cresting through her and she returned his steady glance with her own message of hopes and dreams. Slowly, he withdrew his hand, but his dominant smile remained.

"Enough about me . . . I'm starved."

She laughed merrily. All his moods were contagious, she realized in surprise as she felt a very real hunger pang begin to gnaw at her.

"I'm ravenous!" she chimed in.

As he whisked his napkin from the table, he glanced at her shrewdly.

"And then, perhaps, you'll tell me all about yourself?"

They feasted on tomato mousse with quail's eggs, lentil soup, broiled breast of duck, chicken in mushrooms, succulent lobster dipped in blanc beurre sauce, and vegetables in puffed pastries. Roland downed the exquisite meal with champagne, Tatiana with Vichy water. Apple beignets, liberally sprinkled with powdered sugar, were served for dessert and the Frenchman introduced the Russian girl to her first cup of coffee. She sat back, happily stuffed.

"No argument, now," ordered Roland as he fed her the last bite of the fluffy beignet.

"You've got it the wrong way around," Tatiana said, wiping a speck of sugar from her chin. "It was Eve who gave the apple to Adam, not the other way."

Roland laughed but his mind sped ahead, fed by her suggestion. He could see a ballet with Tatiana as an enticing Eve, luring Adam past the brink of temptation, the wily snake never far from her side. Roland vowed to make a note of the idea along with the Diana concept. Next season would shape up well, he thought.

"And ballet, Tiane?"

He called her that as if she had no other name.

"Who first tempted you to dance?"

She breathed deeply and, in her mind's eye, looked back into the past.

"No one needed to tempt me," she explained. "My mother says I danced before I could walk. I remember a certain music box Maman had in her boudoir. The tune was a Chopin waltz and Maman tells me I learned to count by my second birthday because of the tempo. A fat-cheeked cherub with pointed toes was painted on top. I thought the cherub was a picture of me. So I'd point my toes, sway back and forth lisping 'one-two-three,' and waddle about while my mother put on her makeup."

"I'm sure it was no waddle," Roland added quietly. "You were born graceful."

"Perhaps so"—she nodded—"but I had my share of mischief. When I was a little older, I was fascinated by some porcelain figures given to my mother by one of her lov—friends. I was forbidden to touch them. Maman said they were of great value. But when she was busy, I would pretend the figures came to life and I would invent little plays and dances about them.

"I had two favorites. One was a solemn-faced Buddha, wise but mute. I believed if I went to a certain land—usually the one behind the velvet settee—I could find a bell with a human voice. If I danced well enough, I could return to my Buddha and give him the bell. Then he could ring the bell and it would speak for him."

Roland was touched by the innocent yearnings of the child Tatiana had been.

"And your other favorite?" he gently prodded.

"Oh, she was a tease," said Tatiana with a smile. "She was a shepherdess with a crook and laughing eyes. She always got me into trouble. Once I pretended she'd found a magic stream of perfume. If you washed your hair in the stream, it would turn any color you wished for.

"One day, I gathered up all of Maman's perfume bottles and emptied them into her bidet. I danced a wish dance around it and dunked the shepherdess and my fat curls into the mixture. Maman was furious. My hair stank for a week and all the paint came off the shepherdess. But I still loved her . . . the shepherdess, I mean."

Uncontrollable thoughts of her father charged ahead, trampling the harmless childhood memories. Tears formed in Tatiana's eyes and welled forth, unchecked.

"My father . . ."

The words had tumbled from her lips before she could stop them. The girl coughed, trying to clear her throat. She felt an urgency take over within her and a voice seemed to whisper, You can confide in him. Tell him. She had told Roland so much already. Of all people, she knew she could tell him anything, everything. Taking a deep breath, she tried again.

"It was about that time that my father . . ."

Her voice dried up. She started to choke and a wild look of panic seemed to jump from her eyes. Her hand flew to her throat.

"Tiane, my darling . . ."

Roland rushed to her side, picked her out of her seat, and clasped her in his arms. Amidst the curious stares from the other dining passengers, Roland grabbed her shawl and practically carried her from the dining car.

Hurrying to a rear exit, he rammed open the door, letting fresh night air pour over the pale girl.

Moonlight swathed them in a silver shimmer. She was nestled safely in his arms and the haunting vision of the moonlit maid dancing her heart out struck him again. When she'd fallen into his embrace—was it only two nights ago?—she had seemed the ultimate woman, brought to life by the breath of the moon. She was ethereal, shimmering, almost intangible.

Now she was real, her vulnerability exposed to him. She hurt and needed someone . . . him. He held her more firmly against his chest, hoping the steady beat of his heart would calm her. The world of St. Petersburg, of Paris, even the lumbering train, melted away. He only knew the two of them were clasped together by moonglow.

Tatiana had never known such peace. Only a moment ago, she felt such turmoil and loneliness as memories of her father flooded her soul. Nothing had ever taken away the pain of his loss . . . until now. Suddenly there was a safe harbor for the unruly tide of her emotions.

Roland had come to her as in a dream, unexpected but just what she needed. And she would hold on to him now and forever. Her convulsive sobs stopped. She breathed slowly. Her pulse matched Roland's.

"Better now, sweetheart?" he asked.

His lips caressed the top of her head.

"Yes, thank you. I can tell you now."

"You don't have to say anything, Tiane."

She leaned into him, relaxed and ready.

"I want to tell you, Roland. I want you to know everything, things I've never told any other living soul."

She left his arms and leaned forward against an iron railing at the edge of the car. She stared at the echo of the moon, lighting the train tracks.

"My father was also a dancer. My mother and he met while still at the Imperial Ballet School. They fell in love and my mother became pregnant. My father begged her to marry him but she refused. She had her sights set higher. But when the dance master found out, he forced her to marry. It was that or be tossed out of the school. So they were wed but my mother wouldn't live with her husband.

"Soon after I was born, my mother resumed her career and attracted her first patron. She allowed my father to visit me once a week then. When she lost her lover, she didn't know what to do. My father took over and cared for me while Maman had her tantrums. Then she found another patron and my father was expelled. The pattern repeated itself many times until finally, on my fourth birthday, he came to see me, bringing me a beautiful doll. He kissed my face as one would kiss a cross. When he left, he went to his studio and shot himself to death."

Fresh tears ran down the girl's face but Roland knew they were tears of release. The pent-up agony was over. He clasped her tenderly to him as if she were the most precious thing on earth. To tell the truth, she was, and it didn't seem important whether he meant for the company or to himself.

She sagged against him.

"It's been a long day, Tatiana Ivanovna Dmitrova, and all good little ballerinas should be in bed."

"All right, Roland." The exhausted girl yawned. "Whatever you say."

She straightened for a moment and caught his eye.

"You've been very good to me and I'm truly grateful."

Her dewy gaze touched him deeply.

"You can always trust me, Tiane," he whispered, his breath teasing her ear. "But you've had enough for one night," he observed, taking her back down the corridors to her compartment.

"Good night, my . . ."

She searched her mind, dismissing "prince," "boss," "savior," settling on "love." But he had already opened her door and propelled her into the room.

"Sweet dreams, my swan," he called out, and was gone.

Chapter Six

ROLAND SLOWLY WALKED THE FEW STEPS TO HIS COMpartment, deep in thought. Tatiana had bared her soul to him, not unusual for a young impressionable girl to do. But she was no ordinary young impressionable girl. Part minx, part woman, part child, part sylph, she was unlike any female he'd ever known.

His mind flitted past the numerous dancers and artists' models of his current acquaintance. He lingered on Georgette, his last mistress, but shook his head, recalling her overly ripe body and demanding exotic tastes. He went further back into his youth. He never thought about his family anymore. They were gone from his life forever. But the face of his softly pretty mother and the bright eager eyes of his little sister suddenly loomed before him.

Damn! He slammed his compartment door shut and

the spectral images vanished. Tiane was too powerful for her own good, he thought, disturbed by his reawakened memories. She made him vulnerable to himself and the past he was done with. He rubbed his jaw and felt bristling stubble. He was a grown man, a successful entrepreneur with a challenging business and a wide circle of friends and admirers. He was rich; he lived and traveled well; he got whatever he wanted.

Roland jerked off his evening coat, collar, and cuffs and stared into the bureau mirror. Why, then, did he feel like a lad, wet behind the ears? He knew in his heart as much as with his cold business sense that what had attracted him to her to begin with was her capacity to feel and to draw on those feelings when she danced. Now he was beginning to realize that was how she lived, how she was.

The cold fear of panic closed in on Roland. What would it be like to feel everything as deeply as Tiane did, to acknowledge his emotions as freely as she did? It was one thing when the Paris critics tore a production of his to shreds. But to expose himself, to make himself completely vulnerable to another person . . . No! Those days were over and done with.

He grabbed for a washcloth and plunged it into a basin of hot water. Tearing off his shirt, he laved a thin layer of sweat from his face, neck, and shoulders. Tiny rivulets sluiced through the brown and golden curly hairs of his chest. He dried himself quickly.

In the mirror, his eyes hardened and, once again, Roland stared back at the impresario in control of his company and his life. Mademoiselle Dmitrova was like a seething caldron of emotions, unpredictable and unmanageable. She created dangerous visions of impossible fancy. He would keep his distance from her.

Their relationship would be one of business only, he decided. Nodding crisply, he strode to bed.

Tatiana woke with a start in the rumbling darkness of the train. She sat bolt upright, shivering and hugging her blanket to her breast. She was out of breath as if she'd been in a race. She got out of bed and lit a lamp. Her eyes fell on the tumble of her gown lying on the floor where it had dropped from her weary fingers. The white sash and collar seemed to leap out at her. She took a deep breath. Now she remembered. She'd been dreaming. . . .

She had found herself in a perfect porcelain garden of white flowers. She also was wearing a flowing dress of white gossamer. But for all the beauty in the garden, there was no life, no breeze. The flowers were hard and unbending. Worse, they had no scent. She was unhappy and incomplete in the lifeless perfect garden.

Then she had felt a change in the air and a strikingly handsome faun entered the garden. He seemed to be oblivious of her, so intent was his gaze on the rigid flowers. He trotted over to each one of the flowers, touching them lightly with a staff of white-gold light. One by one, they sprang into colorful life. She was glad he'd come to save the flowers and animate them. She danced joyously in his shadow.

Finally, when the last bloom had turned its rightful hue, the golden-brown faun turned his startling eyes on Tatiana. With a knowing grin, he began to stalk her, his staff outstretched to touch her white gossamer. Suddenly frightened, she fled from the riotous garden, just beyond his grasp . . . and woke up.

Tatiana smiled. It was a wonderful dream and now she wasn't frightened at all. Now she wanted to absorb its beauty. She climbed back in bed and lifted the curtains. Staring at the moon as it traced its path from night to morn, she reenvisioned the beguiling figure of brown, gold, and tan. It must have been Pan, she mused to herself, with the strength and purpose of a stag or a lion.

She lay back and wondered why she'd run from Pan. In the old myths, he ruled the woods, bringing sunshine and life to them. Wasn't that exactly what Roland had brought to her in St. Petersburg? Her mind's eye pored over the figures of the faun and the tawny Frenchman. As she grew sleepier, the figures merged. At dawn she finally fell asleep and dreamed again. This time she ran back into the waiting arms of Pan.

Roland was in the throes of a nightmare. A huge black swan was chasing him, flapping her great wings, forcing him toward a seething caldron. Roland scrambled up its sides only to find himself at the edge of a violently churning volcano. The great bird pushed him to the very brink where he teetered precariously. She brushed him with the tips of her wings and immediately he felt an urgent stirring of sensual hunger waken and seethe within him. Weakened by his need, he could do nothing to fight off the swan. A wild demonic smile on her face, she touched the lip of the volcano.

Certain the volcano would erupt, Roland was ill prepared for the implosive force which sucked him into the cone's blinding heat. He fell headfirst. Lava licked at his heels, closing in on him, consuming him. He shut his eyes against the furious avalanche, ready for death. He fell slowly, inexorably down to the core of the mountain.

But he didn't die. He opened his eyes to see the black swan soaring beneath him, beckoning with her wings. Flames danced about them but didn't burn. They were ice cold, purifyingly cold. Together Roland and the swan reached the bottom.

From a long low couch, the black swan, now a woman with a black feathered mask, offered him a golden goblet brimming with melted emeralds. The aroma was pungent and teasing and he knew he must quench his thirst. Joining her on the couch, he gulped down the tangy green fire.

She seemed different to him then. He saw they were both naked and he was driven to couple with her. He was on fire with the tingle of their bodies intertwining. Never had he felt so aware of his own body's reaction as well as that of the woman he was having. At their climax, together they burst into flames.

Roland woke, drenched in hot sweat. All he could remember was the fearful heat of the volcano, its unexpected implosion, and the feeling of falling into the chaotic avalanche of red flame and black rock. The vivid memory kept him awake the rest of the night.

It was late in the morning and the ravages of the night had taken their toll. Roland, grim-faced, made his way to the dining car, hoping breakfast, or at least coffee, might still be served. Automatically, he stopped before Tatiana's compartment. He raised his hand to rap at the door and hesitated. For some inexplicable reason, the image of a black swan rose before him, spreading its wings and dancing before his eyes. He shut them, dismissing the mocking dreamlike apparition, and knocked a little too loudly on the door.

"Is it you, Roland?" came the familiar low voice.

"Who else?" he muttered irritably, then louder, "Yes."

She opened the door. He remained in the corridor and glanced quickly at her. Her color was pale, her eyes vague, and her hair drifted about her shoulders, reminding him of drooping petals. She hadn't slept well either, he concluded, and averted his gaze.

Tatiana stood rooted at the threshold, still caught in the spell of her dream. The train lurched suddenly and she fell forward into the Frenchman's arms. Content in his grasp, she lifted her face to laugh along with him at this convenient twist of fate. She was dismayed to read embarrassment in his eyes. He stiffly pushed her away.

"Damned peasants can't lay the track straight," he swore under his breath.

Tatiana stared in surprise. Where was the Roland of yesterday, her willing playmate, her chosen confidant? Where had this gruff stranger come from?

"I think we both could use some breakfast," he said impersonally.

He waved his hand and pointed the way to the dining car.

"After you?" he offered.

Clearly, she was not to take his arm. Clearly, she thought, something had driven a wedge between them. Miserable, she led the way to the empty diner. As soon as they sat down, the train lurched again, upsetting a tiny vase of violets at their table. Water streamed toward the comte before the waiter could mop up the damage. Tatiana was instantly at Roland's side, sponging off his damp leg with her napkin.

"Stop that," he ordered harshly.

He wouldn't be so easily seduced again into her

unreal world of soggy emotions. Even her simple touch was a test for him.

Her hand froze where it lay and she looked at him with imploring eyes.

"I just wanted to help," she said quietly.

Mustering up his impresario's charm, Roland put his hand on top of hers and raised it to his lips.

"Of course, my dear," he said in suave practiced tones, "but you are my employee, not my servant."

He couldn't let her know how much her touch had stirred him. A vague memory, uncomfortable and ill fitting, seemed to nag at him. He shook his head to clear the cobwebs of the night from his mind. He was a professional, and it was about time he acted like one with his latest acquisition.

Courteously, he reseated her and made several clever remarks in Russian about the waiter as the little man scurried back and forth to fetch a new napkin, another sprig of violets, and their breakfasts. Roland had only ordered coffee and Tatiana was satisfied with tea and rye toast. At the next lurch, it was her turn to try to avoid the overturned teacup. Roland reached for her instinctively and their hands lingered on each other.

"The train scheduler should do something about his timing. Better to sleep through the Polish forests than be caught eating on this obstacle course!" Roland quipped.

Tatiana laughed, happy to feel at ease with her love. With the safety of the table between them, Roland felt in control again. He took command of the conversation.

"Tell me, Mademoiselle Dmitrova, what roles do you know?"

"Well, Monsieur le Comte," she responded in kind,

"I've been taught the great classics as well as a range of contemporary ones. I know the lead, secondary, and corps roles in *Coppelia, La Sylphide, Paquita, Giselle, La Fille Mal Gardée, La Bayadère, Don Quixote,* and the three Tchaikovsky ballets."

Roland was amazed. It was customary for a dancer to learn the corps role first. Then, if she were lucky enough to rise, she would learn the steps of the secondary lead, then the soloist, and finally the prima's role.

"How could you . . ." he began, but she had guessed at his question.

"Do you think with a mother like mine, I would be taught anything less?" she said laughingly.

She warmed to her subject, wanting to tell him every detail of her training and career.

"It might interest you to know my very first appearance on stage really took place when I was just a baby. My mother appeared in Petipa's *Dance of the Caryatids* in which the corps dance with baskets on their heads. At the end of the ballet, the baskets are to be opened and from each a tiny child pops out. You can guess who was in Lydia Petrovna Dmitrova's basket!"

Roland could not hide his amusement and they both laughed wholeheartedly.

Tatiana added, "Of course, you've seen me as the black swan."

Tatiana as the black swan . . . on stage at the Maryinsky—his first galvanizing sight of her—and, he now recalled with numbing disquiet, in his dream. Now he knew it was her, invading his sleep as well as every waking moment. Both memories jarred him and he was silenced.

"Roland . . . Roland, I'm speaking to you," Tatiana

repeated. "Where are you this morning?" she demanded.

With effort, the comte steeled himself, dismissing the dream once and for all as silly and inconsequential.

"Thinking ahead, Tatiana, to Paris," he said smoothly, "to where you'll live."

She clapped her hands with childlike delight.

"Oh, tell me, please."

"Most of my dancers share ateliers along the Left Bank. But I don't think that will suit you. I have in mind a rather pretty suite in a residential building directly off the Opera Quarter. You'll have a splendid view of a little park. You'll see children playing, lovers at their rendezvous, the latest fashions—"

"Is it the busiest place in Paris?" interrupted Tatiana.

"You'll have your privacy," he replied coolly.

In a dreamy voice, she mused, "I wish I might have a garden."

Roland stared at the girl, struck again by her innocence and vulnerability.

"You should have flowers about you . . . all species of white blooms to complement your skin and set off your eyes and hair."

She stared at him, her dark eyes brimming with questions.

"I had the oddest, no, most fantastic dream last night," she began abruptly, "with a faun, something like the old Arcadian god Pan."

She glanced past him with a dream-dazzled expression.

"Have you ever seen Pan?"

There she went with the unexpected again, setting him off stride. But a distant, long-buried image slowly began to materialize in Roland's mind.

"When I was a lad, just out of short pants, my father took me to Greece. Occasionally, he'd let me go off on my own. I seem to remember stumbling on an old ruined garden. It might've had some order to it once, but now the old flowers ran riot in all colors of the rainbow.

"I remember the sound of the wind, whispering in the trees. I almost thought it was calling my name. Then I tripped over some marble stones of a decayed shrine. The place must've been a sacred glade at one time. And I could swear I saw the trace of cloven footprints in the earth."

Tatiana started out of her seat, the nape of her neck tingling and taut. In her mind, she saw the garden of her dream and it was identical to Roland's. She consciously brought the faun into the picture, staring at its tawny hair, upswept brows, the penetrating eyes sunlit with the mystery of the forest, the flaring nostrils, the full bold lips etched in a wise knowing grin. Now she knew it was Roland, smiling at her, wanting to touch her with his life-giving staff. She gasped and her hand flew to her mouth.

"What's the matter?" Roland asked, uncomprehending. "Did you see something?"

She sat back down. A warm luminescent smile spread across her lips and her inviting eyes said everything to him. Roland felt a numbness overtake him. The Russian girl's expression was the same as the black swan at the precipice of the volcano. As if the dream had come real, he felt again the hot lava rise within the volcano, within himself. He couldn't let it happen. No! He leaped up, pressing his knuckles against the table.

"Finish your tea. We're done here," he said harshly.

"I don't understand," Tatiana said, confused.

She looked at him with eyes of immeasurable sadness.

"What've I done to make you so angry? Is it something I said last night? Did I bore you too much with my stories, my confessions?"

Her eager bloom was gone, and he suddenly thought of her as a hurt little child whose best friend refuses to play anymore. He was hurting her, and he knew it wasn't her fault. She couldn't help baring her soul so openly and generously.

Why did he keep forgetting she was only an inexperienced child? Why did her very presence, her slightest expression, the sound of her voice, tear into him so? He clenched his jaw and released the table from his viselike grip.

"I'm not angry," he gritted, seeking control over his roiling emotions.

He stared through her, past her, not at her at all.

"I didn't sleep well last night . . . I never sleep well on trains."

"Oh," she said in a tiny voice, and he knew he hadn't explained anything to the girl.

Tatiana rose, feeling helpless and miserable. She didn't want to be apart from Roland but he obviously didn't want her. Roland, too, stood in uncomfortable silence. He needed peace and solitude to regain his resolve and his purpose. But what good was it without this sweet temptation of a ballerina to fulfill his dreams?

The train lurched violently. Tatiana was thrown forward and Roland reached out for her, pulling her to him. She clung to him, feeling the rightness of their embrace. Never mind St. Petersburg or Paris. Here, here in his arms was home for Tatiana, her slim pliant body stretched against his firm muscles. Again she felt a flood of fulfillment surge through her, just as it had at the studio when he had appeared from nowhere and caught her in a lover's embrace. She had danced in despair and yearning and he had answered her call. It was the same for her now and she raised her face to receive his kiss.

Roland was spellbound, caught off guard by the compelling perfume of her hair and skin, the magnetic allure of her body pressed to his, the sweet trusting face turned up to him. She was everything he ever dreamed of.

He felt the fire of his need rise and seethe. He closed his eyes, lowering his mouth to meet her lips. His head swam with the heat of her nearness and the throb of his hunger. Pictures flashed through his mind—Tatiana on a silvered night, the black swan dancing, the red-black caldron, falling . . . falling . . .

His whole body stiffened. Quick as a cat, he unpeeled her arms from his neck and thrust her away. She went limp as a rag doll and clutched at the table for support.

"Why?" she cried, wild with hurt. "Why are you tearing us apart? We're meant to be together. You know it as well as I. Why do you fight me?"

Her words rent him, exposing the truth. It was the truth of illusion, of youthful dreams, he insisted to himself. It had nothing to do with life's hard realities. He cloaked himself in the blind convenience of superficial fact. He made his eyes bore into her with calculated cruelty.

"It's romantic nonsense, a child's whim. We've been together . . . what, three or four times in the last seventy-two hours? You've danced for me; I've interviewed you; we've taken meals together."

He smiled at her as if she were a harmless lunatic.

"But in my world, *ma petite*, that is how I hire a dancer, not fall in love with a woman."

Crushed and in tears, Tatiana could barely look at Roland.

"Don't you know," she breathed in an agonized whisper, "I love you?"

She broke from the table and ran out of the car.

Roland was struck dumb, his feet rooted to the expensive carpet. He was burned by the image of huge teardrops rolling down Tatiana's pale shocked face. In his mind, they washed away the malevolent memory of the voracious black swan in his nightmare. He sat down with a jolt and jammed the heel of his palm against his forehead.

He was a fool and he knew it. Here was the most exciting complex creature he had ever met, offering herself to him, wanting nothing but the comfort of his love. And what had he done? Sent her packing! He slammed his fist against the table. It was time to admit the truth and the force of his feelings. To hell with the ballet company! Roland wanted Tatiana for himself. I want her and I . . . I love her. The words tumbled silently from his mind, dusty from long disuse.

Blood coursed through him, from his loins to his head, filling him with the vigor of youth and hope. He covered the distance between the diner and her sleeper in great strides. Pulling open the door, he swept her in his arms and planted row upon row of adoring kisses on her eyes, cheeks, neck, and mouth.

He snatched moments between his rain of kisses to

whisper, "Tiane, Tiane, I love you . . . love you . . . you."

Tatiana's unhappy tears turned joyful and she melted into him.

"Is this real?" she cried.

"My eyes are open," he breathed, lost in the clean scent of her thick silky hair.

She sighed in sweet surrender.

"I am yours, Roland," she murmured. "Make me yours."

He stared into the deep darkly glimmering pools of her eyes, drowned in the tide of passion he saw within. Slowly, keeping her gaze on Roland, Tatiana removed her clothing until she stood before him, devoid of any trappings. Love for him and womanly power radiated from her, warming them both. He'd never seen such luminosity. It wasn't merely in her glance. Her hair, her skin seemed to glow with the pearly essence of a moon goddess. He stepped forward, then back, feeling surprisingly inept.

"You've done this before, yes, Roland?" she asked, half in wonder, half teasing.

All suavity and polished experience fled from him. She made him feel as if it were for the very first time.

"Perhaps not quite like this," he rasped.

She held out a hand to him and he came to her. She was feather-light in his arms yet cool and real. He laid her on the bed. She stretched languorously, devastatingly sensual. Yes, she was all woman, he thought, but even more innately a dancer.

Her slightest movement betrayed her—the delicate arch of her neck, the forward set of her torso, the long extended poise from her arms to her fingertips, her legs to her slender feet. He stared at her dainty toes and wondered, in awe, at their strength. How fragile she seemed. Yet he knew from his own dancers of their enormous capacity for endurance.

"Come to me, Roland," she murmured.

It was half question, half demand. She made him forget everything but his need for her. He tore his clothes off, giving Tatiana her first full glimpse of him.

She had appraised him correctly at the Winter Palace. He was limber and muscular, but not like a dancer. No, his virility gave him the appearance of an Olympic athlete from ancient times. She recalled the faun of her dreams and smiled. Roland would touch her and make her glow with the color of life.

He lay next to her, adjusting his length to her petite form. Their mouths came together in a soft and gentle embrace. Roland meant to take his time, guiding her in the mysteries of lovemaking, giving her time to respond. But his own need to brand Tatiana his coursed through him and dominated.

His demanding lips claimed her and she was engulfed in his overwhelming urgency. She began to tremble and clung to him as if the ground beneath her were moving. Afraid of bruising her, he became teasing, nibbling at her mouth, thrusting the velvety tip of his tongue into her sensitive corners. He licked at her moist, slightly parted lips, which opened at his unspoken command. He ran his tongue across the top row of her teeth before plunging into her welcoming warmth.

Tatiana's senses were aswirl at Roland's bold onslaught. The exotic heat of his tongue intoxicated her. She molded herself closer to the contours of his body.

"Tiane," he groaned, running his scorching hand down the pulsing column of her slim neck. "There is only you."

Roland lowered his head to the shallow cleft between her firm breasts and pressed a kiss there. He breathed in her musk and blew enticingly on each blushing nipple. She quivered and moaned in wonder as her flesh constricted and hardened into tiny peaks. He leaned back and gazed at her small perfect mounds.

"Like alabaster," he rumbled in a voice thick with desire.

He began to trace the underside of one breast with small kisses, then trailed his tongue lazily over the other, bringing fevered gasps from Tatiana. Her nipples strained against his fingers as he stroked the excited peaks. A tidal wave began to build deep in her body, flooding her senses with surging passion.

He lay over her, pressing her hard against him. The tawny hairs of his chest tickled and enflamed her breasts. Her hands ran over his back from neck to buttocks, feeling the solid muscle and animal tension of him. She felt him push against her thigh and she parted her legs in answer, opening like a flower to him.

"Soon, my love?" she moaned in innocent fervor.

"Not quite yet, *ma fleur.*"

He leaned back on his knees, lifted each of her legs, and bent them to kiss her toes.

"I must pay homage to the source of my good fortune," he teased. "Without this one . . . and this one"—he paused to kiss each digit—"and this one and all these others, there might be no Maryinsky, no Companie Valois—"

"—no miraculous train ride," Tatiana proclaimed jubilantly. "But there might still . . . somehow . . . be us."

She extracted her toes from his grasp and rested

them beguilingly on his chest, pausing to tug and tease at the curly pelt.

"Ooh! Devil!" he howled, and thrust her long legs over his shoulders.

She surprised him with her strength. With only the pressure of her calves and thighs, she inexorably pulled his head down in submission onto her breasts.

"Hah!" she cried in triumph.

In a moment, her voice changed to breathy tones of wonder as the mane of tawny gold descended lower down her belly. His fingers caressed and unfolded the secrets of her core and she felt the budding flower contract and release within her. From her depths, a languid shudder built up and exploded. She dug her hands into Roland's waves while her body arched. She felt like a hot-house under the life-giving rays of the sun.

"Now, Roland," she entreated.

"Now, my Tiane," he echoed.

He held her hips up and guided himself into her fiery core with tender relentlessness. In a moment he penetrated her final barrier.

"Now it will be pleasurable, my love," he spoke softly above her.

He began to build a rhythm, kindling and quickening their passion. Equal to his fire, she responded by undulating her hips, pulsating within. She was soon dewy with the fevered glow of their bodies.

United, they were soaring to the heights, where the sun and moon are one. They trembled on the brink of all-consuming possession and erupted in silver and gold incandescence, fused in the tides of passion. Together, they clung to the inner flame, making their love a communion of dream and reality, miracle and fact.

They lay in each other's arms. Her long tresses rained over his chest. His hand easily sheltered her breast while his heavy breathing slowed and quieted. The ebb of passion gave way to the serenity of fulfillment.

"It's a dance," Tatiana stated blissfully.

"How so, my love?" Roland asked, fondling a curl about his finger.

"Well," she began shyly, "everything we feel in our hearts, our bodies say for us."

Roland listened intently to the young woman locked in his arms, touched by her simple description. She gazed up at him, her eyes like moonbeams casting light to a lonely voyager.

"Isn't that the same as loving, Roland? Don't we find the greatest reality of life through love? Isn't that how we find happiness?"

With heartfelt reverence, the comte cupped the face of his beloved and breathed kiss after kiss on her eyes and lips. She nestled against him, warm and secure.

"I am a lucky man, my precious Tiane, a lucky man."

Chapter Seven

THE VIVID GLOW OF THE WINTRY SUNSET FILTERED through the curtains of Tatiana's compartment, flickering on the closed eyelids of the lovers entwined in each other's arms. The play of light and shadow gradually entered the consciousness of the sleeping girl. She blinked and her eyes opened fully.

Tatiana was overly warm. Deftly, she kicked the sheets from her body without disturbing Roland. The air felt deliciously cool on her skin and she nestled in the heat of her beloved's body, inhaling the familiar scent of sandalwood and lemon now mingled with heady musk. He was all she would ever need.

She had already memorized the line and curve of his body. But to touch him, to feel every muscle ripple and grow taut against the slightest pressure of her fingertips made Tatiana feel alive in a new and evocative way. One hand traveled over him, barely grazing the tawny down of his arms, the heavier fur on his chest, the coarse thatch below his belly and the curly hairs of his thighs.

Roland stirred beneath Tatiana's provocative stroking. The muscles of his arms bunched and relaxed. His breathing grew heavy, making his chest roll like the ocean's tide. The girl smiled to herself. I wonder what would happen if I . . . Her hand snaked up to the hollow of his neck, past the firm jaw, to the soft skin of an earlobe and across his brow. She poised herself over him, breathing warmly in his ear, feeling his hair tickle her eyelashes.

Her tongue inched forward and gently lashed at the whorls of his lobe. The upper part was bony but the pliant lower skin gave easily to the flicking of her tongue. A lazy groan of pleasure escaped his lips.

Fascinated by the effects she was causing, Tatiana was caught unaware as Roland, with the lightning reflexes of a cheetah, tossed her onto her back and positioned himself over her, ready to pounce on his sensual little kitten. Although his hazel eyes sparkled, the lids lay heavy, masking the green and brown flecks behind a veil of sensuous satisfaction. He resembled nothing less than a lion, king of the pride, smugly satiated from the fruits of a hunt, thought the object of his desire.

"Hungry for more?" he asked teasingly.

"I think I could develop an appetite . . ." she began.

He caught one of her perky nipples between his teeth and casually flicked his tongue over it. Her eyes glazed over as a thrilling heat ignited within her.

"Oh, Roland," she sighed, and urged his head toward her waiting lips.

He kissed her with a resounding smack.

"Yes, I'm starving, too," he said matter-of-factly, looming over her.

She smiled and her eyes spoke her hunger for him.

"But, my sugarplum, I want some real food. Now, now," he cautioned at her disappointed pout, "you know how much I want you, Tiane."

He smoothed a tangle of black curls from her cheek and planted a row of kisses in their place. His eyes lingered on hers and she knew he spoke his true feelings.

"But my energy is spent."

Tatiana blushed at the double-edged joke.

"After all, neither one of us had much sleep last night. We ate practically no breakfast. Then we discovered our rather voracious appetite for each other, resulting in, at least, my utter exhaustion . . ."

"All right, all right," cried Tatiana. "I yield."

She blushed again. Was everything, from now on, going to sound as if it had two meanings? Would Roland think she had only one thing in mind?

Still poised above her, he lowered himself onto her nude form, but then reluctantly, sensuously, rolled off to one side.

"There'll be plenty of time, sweet Tiane," he rumbled, "for the bed. As for eating . . . you don't know how stimulating a meal can be," he suggested with all the lure he could muster.

Tatiana was intrigued.

"Very well, Roland," she said, lowering her gaze. "If you'll teach me . . ."

He promptly sat up, a broad grin on his face. Cupping her chin in one hand, he gave her a quick buss, then returned for a more complete sample. She twined her arms around his neck, yielding to the simple pleasure of his mouth pressed against hers.

"You are a fast learner," he murmured before pulling away.

Hauling on trousers, a shirt, and shoes, he blew a kiss to her as he left her compartment.

"I won't be long," he called out. Then, ducking his head back in between the sliding doors, he added in a hiss, "Don't get dressed."

Tatiana fell back against the plump wall of pillows and luxuriated in this bed of satin sheets and feather quilts. She drew the bedclothes up to her chin and thought of her childhood cot in St. Petersburg. How many nights for how many years had she clung to her blankets with tears in her eyes, dreaming of dances, yearning for love to light her life?

She pictured her life in St. Petersburg, had she remained there. Cold and closed off, she might only have had the dance as a voice for her fiery feelings. She saw herself as a small stunted figure, unloved and unloving, eroded by the paralyzing ice of the city, her mother, a string of would-be patrons.

But Roland had come and, like the blazing sun, melted her grim prospects into harmless imaginings. Under his aegis, she would bloom, becoming the best ballerina, the happiest woman she could be. She would dance, live, and love without the tragic endings of the theatrical tales she was used to. For Roland and herself, life would be a continual party, celebrating the arts and the senses . . . just the two of them, together . . . like the sun and moon on their eternal dance about the heavens . . . like this train hurtling past foreign landscapes on a route of their own making . . . like . . .

There was a loud thudding at the compartment door.

"My hands are full," came the terse message.

She swathed herself in a satin bedsheet and flung aside the door. In marched Roland with a huge salver piled high with all sorts of delicacies. Over one arm lay a large linen cloth; clutched under the other was a magnum of champagne. With wolfish glee, he deposited the tray, then himself on the bed, and beckoned to Tatiana to rejoin him. Bemused, she stepped forward and up onto the bed, settling the sheet about her like a cloud of petals.

"Some caviar, mademoiselle?" Roland offered.

"*Mais oui,* monsieur," she simpered.

He began to uncover a silver-domed cup and then stopped as if he suddenly remembered something important.

"One moment, *s'il vous plaît,*" he said with a gleam in his eyes.

In a trice, he discarded his clothes and leaned casually across the bed. Tatiana giggled, wondering where this incongruous tea party might end.

"Roland, how do you expect us to eat? There are no plates, no silver . . ."

"Like this, my dove."

He extended a manicured finger into the chilled crystal bowl and withdrew a scoopful of the dainty roe. Confused, Tatiana stared at the man across from her. She caught the ardor in his eyes and she smiled imperceptibly. The nature of the game had become clear.

She opened her mouth. Slowly she extended her tongue, letting it explore the contrasting textures. Her eyes bored into Roland's like jet magnets, as she sucked his finger clean.

Roland was amazed at how quickly Tiane caught on. She had taken up the game like an expert, though he knew, perhaps better than anyone, what an innocent she really was. She just seemed to possess this confounding ability to give herself up to the demand of emotion, whatever the lesson to be learned, be it dance or life or love. When he was with her, there was no beginning, no middle, no end. There was only Tiane.

He found himself totally absorbed by the pull of her luring eyes, the pearlescent sheen of her skin, the deft passion of her tongue.

"You are an apt pupil," he rasped. "Perhaps too apt. Come here now and feed me some grapes."

He lay back with his feet at the pillows. She had to come to him and drape herself over him to offer a cluster of succulent flame-red orbs. Now it was his turn to stare deep into her being, willing her to him, demanding that she offer herself. One by one, he plucked at the woody vine, seizing each piece of fruit with his teeth. With slow exaggeration, he sucked the juice, then ate the flesh. At the end, he thrust his head upward and neatly caught onto her breast. With a gasp she fell onto him and his hands roamed freely over her.

"But the next course, Roland," she breathed, panting for air. "What do we do with the soup?"

Laughter overtook both of them at the ludicrous notion. They lay side by side till tears streamed down their faces.

"Tiane Dmitrova," he announced hoarsely, "you are incomparable!"

"Comte de Valois," she echoed earnestly, "let's eat. Now I'm ravenous."

They tore into cold squab, artichokes, French baguettes, and sliced hot-house strawberries, devouring each dish with gusto. Only the dessert remained—a frothy Black Forest cake of chocolate, whipped cream, and glazed cherries. Tatiana stared at the rich confection, knowing that with one bite, she would burst. Roland eyed the cake, then Tatiana.

"You know," he said in masterful tones, "those cherries would taste much better on you than on the cake."

Shivering with anticipation, Tatiana leaned back into the pillows while Roland extracted the nine rosy globes from their chocolate posts. He removed the tray from the bed. With the deliberation of an artist, he positioned the fruit in a line extending from the circle of her navel, up the slim abdomen, within the cleft between her breasts, and into the hollow of her throat. Tatiana barely breathed, allowing him, wanting him to shape her to his will.

Returning to the lowest point, he began to nibble up each cherry, tickling and arousing Tatiana at the same time. He rode over her, coming nearer her face. When he leaned into her throat to take the final cherry, she closed her eyes and buried her face in his tawny mane.

Roland took the last cherry between his teeth. Instead of crushing it, he raised himself over her, close enough to kiss her, and, with the kiss, he offered her the final fruit of their feast. Tatiana's eyes shot open in wonder. Seeing the love in his glance, she received the cherry into her mouth and chewed at it slowly.

"Rubies against pearls," he whispered.

As if unleashed from a spell, Tatiana began to

107

respond with all the passion she felt for this man. Twisting out from under him, she knelt over Roland. She kissed his face and breathed the hot air of desire into his ear. Her erect nipples pressed against his chest and she dragged them languorously down the length of his torso. Finding his male nipples, she teased them with her tongue. She curled her legs about his knees to sit upright. Slowly she traced a path from his inner thighs up the engorged shaft of his manhood. Her fingers circled the velvety tip, making him quiver and move beneath her.

Throughout her relentless examination, Roland watched his questing conqueror with a bemused eye while his senses were being devastated. For an innocent, he thought, her touch was certain and its effect expert. It was almost as though she were born with a second sight, knowing just how and where to arouse him. He found his detachment harder and harder to prolong as she continued her shameless assault.

"Enough, merciless explorer," Roland rumbled, "or the master will have nothing left to instruct with."

He reached for her hips, lifting her up and over the root of his pleasure. With sure aim, he entered her moist recesses and experienced the sweet spasms of her taut inner muscles. She rode him like a wild horse, twisting to the stormy rhythm of his bucking and gyrating to match it.

Faster and faster they sped on their journey to its peak, holding furiously onto the moment, then plummeted to the drifting clouds of completeness. When it was over, Roland lay within the soft confines of Tatiana's arms, his shaggy head nestled between her breasts. They seemed to float lazily in a dream of endless summer, far from the harsh reality of winter outside the train's window. No words were needed. Their bodies had expressed every emotion they wanted to communicate.

Later, in the distance of the early evening, a lone shrill whistle pierced through the peaceful quiet. Tatiana shivered and closed her arms tighter around her beloved. Roland, too, was shaken by the screeching wail. From the forgotten shadows of his mind, a vivid memory came flooding forth.

"That whistle . . ." he said in a voice far away, "like a death cry and the first wail of mourning combined in one."

Tatiana felt a chill of surprise. It was just a whistle, unexpectedly invading their own sheltered world. She looked up at him and was shocked to see his eyes intense with pain. He reminded her of the sun suddenly thrust behind clouds, revealing lurking shadows.

"What is it, Roland? You can tell me, my love," she begged.

He stared at her, into her. Since the journey had begun, they had eyes for only each other. The train might as well have been occupied by them alone. But their idyll would come to an end as soon as they reached Paris. And then what? he asked himself. Would his life resume the old way? Would he seek out life but be afraid to feel it fully? His eyes seemed to plunder the depths of Tiane's soul. She wasn't afraid to feel deeply, even if it meant exorcising ghosts from the past. If it worked for her, maybe . . . He looked away and spoke.

"How long ago is it now? Fifteen, twenty years? I was a cocky young lad then, bent on my own path of dissolute amusement, not too different from the other male adolescent nobles of my circle. The de Valois holdings were tucked away in the Midi, the south of France, and from the age of fifteen, I took any opportunity to escape to Paris to sample its exotic temptations.

"My family, at least my parents, were greatly opposed to my jaunts. They wanted me to settle down immediately. Forget the hot blood of youth. Just learn to administer the de Valois properties. Find a charming young girl of good breeding and carry on the family line.

"Needless to say, I was their only son, and needless to add, I was dead set against their stodgy plans. I had dreams of my own . . . which I shared with my younger sister. Dear little Mady."

Roland heaved a deep sigh and paused to collect himself. Madeleine's death had been the worst of the shock, he recalled painfully.

"She was always eager to hear my schemes. And now I think she egged me on a little, knowing her life would be so different from mine. In any event, I proposed living in Paris, following a career in the arts—painting, sculpting, even architecture. My parents opposed all my suggestions, especially the singing and dancing lessons. No de Valois would ever be associated with the stage or the canvas except as an anonymous benefactor or a collector.

"Of course I rebelled. I went to live among my new acquaintances, the artists, dancers, musicians of Paris. My parents cut me off from the family purse strings, but I didn't care. I was doing what I wanted. Unfortunately, I wasn't very successful. All the wish and the will in

110

the world didn't make up for lack of talent. I found, after exhaustive effort, I had two left feet, no sense of perspective, a tone-deaf ear, and a range of less than one octave. In short, I was an artistic disaster!"

"But, Roland, you are a man of considerable talents," Tatiana insisted. "Look at the success, the very existence, of the Companie Valois."

He lifted her hand and gently kissed her fingertips.

"Thank you, *chérie,* and it's true. I do have talents. It just took a few years longer for me to understand and develop them. I seemed to be at my best when my friends were gathered about me. I had an endless supply of grandiose plans for exploiting, in the best sense of the word, my friends' talents. Occasionally, I'd be able to arrange special one-man shows or one-time performances at restaurants, hotels, small halls. I began to develop a reputation as an impresario. And I began to dream of forming a unique alliance among the arts."

He ran impatient fingers through his wavy hair and half sat up, supporting himself on one arm. His face was a palette of conflicting emotions.

"I went home to ask my parents for their support. They refused both their finances and their approval. They also refused to let me see Madeleine. There seemed to be some question about my disreputable influence. For some reason, I stayed the night. Shortly before midnight, my mother visited my rooms, begging me to understand ánd comply with my father's wishes. Stubborn in my youth and my zeal, it was my turn to refuse. She kissed me and left in tears. At dawn, Mady sneaked in to give me a hug and her piggy bank. She flashed me a smile and was gone."

Roland was forced to pause. The muscles of his jaw clenched and his eyes looked muddied. Tatiana grabbed his hand in mute sympathy. His grip was tight.

"That was the last time I saw any of them alive. A month later they took a holiday in Switzerland and were caught in an avalanche. All three of them—my father, mother, and Mady—were killed outright. I went on to found the Companie Valois with the good wishes and support of my friends, for in the end, my father had the last word. I claimed the family title, but the lands and money were entailed to a nephew. As my father disinherited me, so I chose to divorce all memory of my family from my life. They were, are, dead and gone from me . . . except when a lonely whistle pierces the night. It brings back the cry of the train I rode when I brought back their bodies for burial."

The pain was visible on his face.

"I think your family would be proud of you today," whispered Tatiana, "and celebrate in your success."

"Maybe yes, maybe no," Roland mused. "But I know one thing."

He looked squarely at her, naked and vulnerable to her alone.

"I knew if I let you into my life, you'd make me feel the heights and depths again. I made my life an endless sunny day. Now I know it was empty . . . without you, Tiane. But with you, the sun has begun to burn with real brightness."

She kissed him tenderly. Like a child, he leaned into the comforting warmth of her breasts and was soon asleep. She lay beneath him, watching silver strands of moonlight thread through the silken draperies at her window and crawl across the floor. She caressed the tousled tawny locks of her beloved and her fingers strayed along the smooth skin of his neck. A tear fell from her eye onto his cheek. This lion of a man, for all his demanding dominance, was a sad, hurt boy at heart.

They were alike, she and Roland, both afraid love would never come to free them, her from her aching dreams and him from the nightmares of his past. Together, they seemed to heal one another. Roland had given her joy, a reason to dance beyond her own need, a place in his world. And now she knew what she could give him. Through her youth and the full bloom of her emotions, he could be young again, experiencing all of life—its bliss and its sorrows—accepting all that he was meant to feel.

Tomorrow, she thought, all the tomorrows are ours. She slipped her hand within Roland's warm grip and closed her eyes. All she could hear was the deep even breathing of the man at her breast. Soon her body adjusted to his rhythm and she was asleep. Moonlight danced through the darkened compartment, celebrating love's mysteries, casting an aura of hope on the lovers' serene faces, keeping at bay the inexorable glare of reality.

It was a clouded gray morning, weeks later, as the train slowed and made its way toward Paris's grand station. The lovers had wakened early, refreshed and excited to be at their journey's end. Roland burst forth with a never-ending travelogue of the city sights, stabbing his finger at the glass to point out the still-distant locations of his favorite places. All Tatiana could make out were tall elegant trees, and through their bare branches, the occasional top of a church spire, clumps of smoke-spouting chimneys, and the iron-dark peak of something Roland called the Eiffel Tower.

When the station grew near, Roland grabbed the slight girl and pulled her from her compartment to the doorway of the sleeper car.

"Such a frenzy, Roland," she remarked, giggling at his boyish enthusiasm. "And all for a city!"

"Not just any city," he cautioned her in a voice brimming with joy, "but Paris, the city of life and love. You'll see. Just wait till you meet my friends, Tiane. You'll see how the world lights up."

He leaned as far forward as the railing would permit. A tiny blob of color met his eye and he thrust Tatiana in front of him so she could see too.

"Look there," he cried. "I knew they'd come."

Tatiana strained to distinguish Roland's blob from among the shadows and shapes so far ahead. The closer the train pulled ahead, the stronger an undeniable feeling of alarm reverberated inside the girl. The station seemed normal enough. Freightmen and baggage haulers bustled about the tracks. Many wore black thick jackets and flat red caps. People waiting for passengers strolled along the walkways, their faces uplifted and eagerly searching each set of windows.

But there was one circuslike group, so loud Tatiana could hear them all the way to the moving car. Apprehensively, she whipped her head around to Roland. He was waving wildly, a beaming smile plastered on his face, and shouting to that very gaggle of human geese.

"*Mes amis*," he was calling, "I have returned victorious with a prize unimaginable."

Tatiana wanted to shrink back and run for the safe private confines of the train compartment. But Roland had such a firm grip on her waist that her efforts to escape were futile.

"Ah, Tiane, just wait and see. You shall be my

partner in everything," he proclaimed, gesturing broadly. "Like a wild bird newly tamed, Paris will be eating out of our hands . . ."

What had come over him? Tatiana wondered. Had the zest for life she meant to give him taken root so fast? He didn't even sound like himself, more like an overblown court poet praising his monarch than her masterful hero who had seen and done all life can offer. She searched his face for the man she knew.

"You're overwhelming me, Roland. Couldn't I get used to your home first before we conquer the city?"

Roland laughed heartily.

"But you're joking, of course. The gang will have brought my new motorcar and they will be expecting a small parade, at the very least, from the station to Montmartre."

Tatiana felt completely lost, as a child in a darkened forest. Her face crumpled into a helpless frown. In a moment, she was swamped by a sea of waggling hands, waving jerkily and reaching for Roland. The train came to a halt. The rush of passengers behind Roland and Tatiana stampeded forward, sweeping the two out of the car and depositing them in front of the oddest mix of people Tatiana had ever seen.

"Look who's here," Roland shouted gaily. "Any excuse for a party here in Paris, right, my friends? Even greeting a weary traveler back from the hinterlands of the Russian bear."

"Quick, Jules," cried a tall gaunt woman, made up to look like a tiger, "write that down. Roland has turned poetic in his old age."

Everyone chuckled and white clouds of vapor escaped from their mouths. As Tatiana looked from face to face, she could only think of smoke-breathing dragons. And these were Roland's friends. There were almost a dozen people crowding around Roland and pushing Tatiana further away from him. She shifted from foot to foot, uncertain whom to stand near.

First, there was a woman of rotund proportions whose mottled, red-veined skin was echoed in the riot of red hues atop her head. She was swathed in a black cloak so old it looked green. When she laughed, she unashamedly revealed several gold teeth.

Then there was a curious duo of a man and a woman dressed as if they were on their way to a masquerade. Each wore bright red-and-yellow-checked trousers over which hung two shirts of red violet and blue violet, a bottle-green jacket easily two sizes too big, several scarves of different lengths and fabrics carelessly tossed about their necks and shoulders, and matching peaked English hunting hats.

"Aha," Roland remarked, "so the seduction is complete, eh, Carteret?"

"But the question remains," interjected the woman of the pair, "who really seduced who?"

"Marguerite, you are a scream," yelled the gross older woman.

"With a voice such as yours, Zazou," Roland added, "you are the only scream around town."

The group erupted in laughter and Tatiana was pushed again to the outer fringes of the circle. Feeling desperately alone but afraid to cut a path back through these grotesque Parisians, she was left to cling to the edge of the group. She found herself next to two men still dressed in evening wear. Their black tails and top hats looked singularly out of place, both for the time of day and considering the rest of the crowd. She overheard one say to the other he didn't know who these people were but they certainly knew how to have a good time.

The other one replied, "You can say that again. I've been following them around since eight o'clock last night and they haven't stopped drinking yet."

The two men exchanged glances, tipped their hats, and continued listening to the noisy group. Taken aback, Tatiana stepped away from the questionable gentlemen and knocked into another group of men bending over in heated discussion.

"I'm terribly sorry," she said.

One of the men lurched around and belched loudly. It took him a moment to focus and less time than that for Tatiana to realize the entire group was drunk and passing a bottle among them.

"You wanna swig, honey?" he managed to ask.

"Oh!" Tatiana cried out in a voice strangled by shock.

She jumped as though she'd been shot at and, in her hurry, clumsily knocked against a beautiful young woman in an elegant wool coat.

"I'm sorry," repeated Tatiana.

Was that all she would ever say in Paris? Her cheeks were crimson. Why wasn't Roland taking care of her?

"Is this the little wonder you've been telling us about?" asked the beauty in mocking tones.

Roland twisted around.

"There you are, Tiane. Been exploring on your own? Didn't I tell you you'd love Paris?"

His exuberance was irksome but the pressure of his arm about her shoulders was reassuring.

"Roland?"

She felt suddenly shy in front of his friends . . . as though she hardly knew him.

"Could we go?" she whispered.

"But I haven't introduced you properly yet," he boomed.

He planted her squarely before him in the center of the tight circle.

"Everybody, may I present Tatiana Ivanovna Dmitrova, the next empress of the ballet world."

They all clapped and shouted bravo.

The men affected low bows and the women eyed her knowingly. Tatiana's embarrassment grew with each intimate glance thrown at her.

"Tiane," Roland commanded, "meet La Maigre the bewitching cat, Jules Breton our distinguished owl of a poet, Zazou Picard café proprietress, the soon-to-be famous painter Camille Carteret, and his good friend and model Marguerite, my lovely ballerina Micheline Arnot, and I don't know who those other people are but they are welcome to join us."

Again there was riotous laughter. The raucous noise and press of the group engulfed Tatiana. Even Roland was laughing. Whether at her or something else, she was no longer sure. She teetered precariously. Was Paris so hot in the winter, she wondered in a daze? She opened her fur coat and fanned for some fresh cool air.

"My motor?" inquired Roland. "Where's my motorcar?"

Carteret indicated with exaggerated gesture the direction of the nearby boulevard.

"Let's go then."

He whirled Tatiana about.

"Ready, my love? Your city awaits you."

"Please, Roland," she implored. "Can't the city wait until tonight?"

He stood still and stared down into her face. Her

dark eyes held no mystery for him this time. She wanted him, needed him. Galvanized by the energy of Paris vibrating about him, he felt magnanimous, larger than life.

"For you, anything, Tiane."

The sun broke through the clouds behind Roland's head and Tatiana was blinded by the glare. Bright golden rays seemed to emanate from her lover's tawny head. Tears of relief washed over her eyes. She let him escort her to the curb of the wide boulevard where a rumbling metallic contraption on rubber wheels threatened the passing horse-drawn carriages. She had heard of the newfangled invention but hadn't seen any in St. Petersburg.

"We must postpone our parade," he announced to his friends, nodding at the petite woman at his side. "My goddess has given me different instructions and her word must be obeyed."

He leaped into the motorcar after placing his passenger and the luggage in their proper places.

"But Roland," yelled Zazou, "what shall I tell Yvette? She still wants to audition for you."

He revved up the motor.

"For heaven's sake, Zazou, she's a coarse little can-can dancer," he said impatiently. "Ballet is another world . . . for finer feet than hers."

He waved good-bye to the group, grinned forcefully at Tatiana, and drove off in a cloud of black smoke.

Chapter Eight

"JACQUES, THIS IS MADEMOISELLE DMITROVA," ROLAND said the next day to the uniformed doorman who guarded the main entrance of de Valois's Théâtre de Paris. "She's to be given access at any time of the day or night."

"*Bien sûr*, Monsieur le Comte," agreed the barrel-chested, white-gloved attendant as he bowed deeply before the pair.

He made a notation on his log before opening the door and ushered them through the dimly lit foyer and into the theatre. It was a noble hall, from its chandelier-studded ceiling three floors above them to its plush carpeting in wide swaths of ivory and teal blue. The tiers of balconies gleamed with beautifully carved scrollwork, answering the rich cedarwood of the luxuri-

121

ous ground-floor seats. Velvet draperies caressed the walls in muted shades of sapphire and amethyst.

The same rich fabric framed the lighted stage, from which a furious voice was heard shouting, "Imbecile! Donkey! Your legs are heavy as cannon. You've no more feeling than a plank of wood. We'll do it again, and again, and again, until you get it right. And one and two, three . . ."

The speaker was a wiry little man with blazing round black eyes and a veritable mane of silver-white hair. He wielded his stick as if it were a rapier, whipping it through the air to stab the floor.

Tatiana recognized the recipient of his imprecations. It was Micheline Arnot, the beautiful prima ballerina who had been among the group at the train station. Now she didn't look beautiful at all but harried and on the verge of tears. Her body was bathed in sweat as she strove to satisfy the irascible man's demands.

She was really quite good, Tatiana observed. Arnot was very strong and centered, which gave her movements a classically clear line. She had long lyrical arms and knew how to use them to suggest the ebb and flow of a movement. Better even than Olga Vorodskya, Tatiana decided, though she noticed Arnot's somewhat short torso was held too stiffly.

The man slammed the floor with his stick.

"No, no, no!" he cried.

The exhausted ballerina stopped and brushed a dripping chestnut curl off her forehead, her shoulders sagging.

"You move without a crumb of feeling. Where are your hands? Dangling at the ends of your wrists like two dead fish!" Arnot burst into tears as he yelled,

"You are impossible, impossible! You can do nothing right."

He raised his stick and Arnot cringed.

"Go. Get out of my sight."

He brought the stick down against her derrière and the demoralized girl, with a shriek, ran off the stage.

Tatiana looked at Roland with alarm and found him grinning from ear to ear.

"Up to your old tricks again, I see," he boomed with a jovial laugh.

The old man looked out at his audience of two.

Unfazed, he demanded, "When are you going to bring me someone who can dance?"

Roland guided Tatiana down the aisle toward the stage.

"As a matter of fact," he retorted smugly, "I've done just that. Léon, this is Tatiana Ivanovna Dmitrova. Tiane, meet Léon Martinon, the famous and, as you may have noticed, difficult choreographer."

The formidable older man took a closer look at her.

"This pretty child?" he asked skeptically.

"Why don't you try her out?" Roland suggested on a challenging note.

He looked down at his woman with his eyes sparkling and gave her a loving nudge.

"Show him, Tiane," he growled softly.

Léon Martinon raised one bushy eyebrow very high.

"You have your shoes?"

Tatiana exchanged a merry, conspiratorial look with Roland and put on her ballet slippers without a word. She handed him her coat.

"Come," said the choreographer after eyeing her in the revealing practice clothing.

He led the way to the stage.

Over his shoulder, he threw the words, "She looks like a stiff breeze would blow her over."

"Like a sylph, perhaps?" the impresario called back. "Or Giselle?"

"Hmph," was all the response he got.

Martinon stalked off to the far left of the stage and planted himself there with finality.

Fixing Tatiana with a look, he barked, "Eight *chaînés tours, brisé, brisé,* four *sissones devant, pas de bourrée,* four more *sissones, pas de bourrée, attitude,* eight *fouettés, attitude.* It must be allegro."

Tatiana nodded once.

"But I must warm up first, monsieur," she added politely.

He scowled at the delay, his stick punishing the floor with an angry staccato as she stretched her slender limbs and supple torso repeatedly, unhurriedly. She ignored his growing impatience until she felt truly ready to perform the almost impossible combination he'd thrown at her.

"All right," he growled when she'd finished. "Are you ready to listen now?"

Tatiana smiled at him.

"I remember the combination, monsieur."

He caught his own look of surprise almost before it emerged.

She moved to the far right corner for the *chaîné* turns, waiting until his stick began savagely tapping out the beat. Then she danced, pulling the disparate movements together effortlessly into a glowing whole, letting the leaps and turns carry her lightly as a feather.

When she finished, she hazarded a quick peek at his face and caught a gleam of unwilling, astonished admiration. Tatiana kept her answering smile inside as his frown returned. It was a game between Roland and his old friend and she was happy to play it for them.

Martinon barked out another set of movements aimed at tangling up any dancer. Tatiana sailed through it. She bested his combinations gleefully, one after another. After a particularly intricate one, she looked out over the auditorium to Roland as she caught her breath. He grinned happily to her and blew her a kiss, along with a gesture that said, "Superb!"

The next combination seemed to Tatiana full of cheerful mockery and she was pleased to see Martinon abandon his rhythm-tapping stick, allowing her to set her own pace. She watched his head bobbing to her tempo as she covered the stage with gleeful little *pas de chats,* cat leaps.

When she was done, the choreographer asked abruptly, "Do you know the spindle section in Act I of *Sleeping Beauty?*"

At her nod, he turned brusquely, left the stage, and found a seat front-row center. Tatiana closed her eyes for a moment, conjuring up the royal court, the suitors, and the hidden evil fairy Carabosse who concealed in her black cloak the fatal spinning wheel. Then she began the dance of innocent, youthful exuberance that was the princess Aurora.

Roland moved quietly to where he could view Léon's face. For the first time in the twelve years he had worked with the brilliant choreographer, Roland saw a beatific smile appear on the old man's visage. She's done it! Roland exulted. She's won him over.

Roland had to stifle his whoop of delight. His mind raced ahead. Léon Martinon would finally have a ballerina who could bring his visions to life, he thought.

Even this season's creation, *Echo et Narcisse,* would be like nothing Paris had ever seen before.

As he watched his old friend's face, scored with a lifetime of disappointment, soften and light up at the sight of Tatiana's magic, Roland felt a deep rush of gladness. At last Léon was getting what he had dreamed of for so long. Now he would be happy. Roland stole away, knowing he'd done his job, buoyed by a rich sense of satisfaction.

"Well, if I were you, dear Tatiana, I'd simply refuse to do more than six *cabrioles,* if as you say, they don't fit the music," Micheline whispered helpfully. "I've worked with Léon for two years now and I know he'd appreciate your suggestions."

Tatiana gave her newfound friend a doubtful look as they waited for the slight, blond-mustachioed ballet master to end the day's final class. Léon Martinon didn't strike her as the type who'd welcome anything but strict obedience. When she said as much, Micheline shot her a malignant look that disappeared so quickly Tatiana decided she must have imagined it.

"I'll think about your advice," Tatiana assured the chestnut-haired beauty as they watched another group of three dancers pirouette diagonally across the practice-room floor.

"I'm glad," cooed the prima. "Tell me," she inquired in a syrupy voice, "how do you make your hair look so thick and lustrous? What do you use?"

Before Tatiana could answer, the ballet master bowed to the assembled dancers and was answered by the traditional round of polite applause and reverences that marked the end of every ballet class. Each dancer came up to him, bowed gracefully, and backed away.

The ballet master held up his narrow hand to stop the procession and bowed low himself.

"Monsieur le Comte," he said.

Roland swept into the room, a large, glossy box under one arm, and moved directly to Tatiana.

"Come, darling, let's go to your dressing room," he said exuberantly.

Under the envious gaze of the assembled dancers, Tatiana smiled happily up into her lover's face and went away with him.

"You've had a long first day," he observed when they were alone in the tiny room, running a lazy finger along her dewy hairline.

"A wonderful day, Roland," she said jubilantly, "and I owe it all to you."

"Some of it," he conceded with a grin. "But you're the one who turns cynical old perfectionists into believers."

"Léon is a genius, Roland. He showed me the first act of *Echo* and it made me cry; it was so beautiful."

Tatiana mopped her face with a towel as she spoke.

"But what a madman. He worked right through lunch, all afternoon, until my legs felt like they were ready to run away from me and join someone else's body who knew when to sit down. He was surprised when I told him it was three o'clock."

Tatiana smiled sweetly.

"He gave me a kiss to say, 'Sorry,' and sent me off to class. Oh, Roland. I am exhausted," she finished, sinking onto the gilt and horsehair footstool that faced a simple dressing table.

He came up behind her, taking her slender shoulders in his big, warm hands. His bright, golden eyes met her misty ones in the mirror.

"Do you know what I'm dreaming of?" She sighed, sinking back against him. "A long, steaming bath, a light supper, and sleep."

"*Non, ma petite,*" he corrected, massaging her shoulders, "a quick rinse, a big box of something to rouse you, and a night of excitement."

She looked up, bewildered, and saw the gleam of the long, silver box propped up against the table.

"What did you buy?" she asked, a faint sparkle of interest beginning inside her.

"First, the rinse," he insisted, pulling her upright, peeling her clinging practice tunic and skirt from her damp body.

About to protest, Tatiana turned and felt Roland's eyes caress her bare, moist breasts. An answering tingle of heat danced within her. Locking his eyes on hers, he slid his hands inside the sides of her gauzy pantaloons and eased them downward, over her quivering hips, down the pearly curves of her thighs, her calves, to the floor.

Unprotesting, she allowed him to raise her feet in his warm caressing hands, one by one, to remove completely her last garment. He knelt before her, and slowly drew his palms with their long, knowing fingers up her legs again, against the grain of her fine body hair, tickling, teasing her tired skin to trembling life.

"Ohh . . ." she moaned softly as he pressed his heated lips to the pale, tender skin just above the dark curls at the apex of her thighs.

Her hands groped downward to find his head, to press him to her, but he rose to his feet suddenly and gave her a slightly ragged grin. Taking up the towel from where she had discarded it on the table, he dipped it in a tub of steaming water and began wiping the perspiration from her body in long, efficient strokes.

"You taste like a salted peach," he said in an offhand tone, as if he didn't realize how he'd aroused her.

She raised her arms to fling herself against him, but he held her off, saying, "Wait, my sweet. You'll get everything you want."

Puzzled but trusting, she let him wash her with the hot, reviving water while she stood with her blood pounding in her awakened body. With another towel, he dried her from head to toe. Roland stepped back to view his creation, a glowing, rosy Tiane, curiosity and arousal tangled in her eyes.

"Now for the present," he announced, and opened the silver box, shaking out a floor-length, black velvet gown from the great house of Worth.

It was the most elegant dress Tatiana had ever owned. As Roland deftly piled her hair on top of her head in a lovely welter of curls, Tatiana kept eyeing the splendid creation. It had a high neck with a delicate, lacy collar that opened in a tiny V. The tightly molded bodice was lightly sprinkled with brilliants and came to a soft point at the waist. Leg-o-mutton sleeves with their ballooning width made the velvet look wonderfully rich. The sleeves ended in slender lace cuffs that climbed halfway up her forearms. She swayed a bit to make the softly flared skirt with its deep gathers flow luxuriantly about her legs.

"Stay still, *chérie*," said Roland, who was affixing the last pin to her coiffure, though her artless delight touched his heart.

Then he stepped back and gave her a long, appraising look.

"Lovely! You're as delicate and rich as the moon herself, all black and white, all dreams," he told her.

He turned over her hand and planted a fervent kiss in her palm.

"I'm a lucky man, Tiane."

"I'm the lucky one," she corrected, looking at the beautiful Parisian sophisticate in her mirror and back to the dashing, impetuous nobleman who was her escort.

"You've turned my life into a fairy tale, Roland, my darling."

"You haven't seen the half of it yet," he returned. "Come with me, and let me introduce you to Montmartre, where anything is possible."

He flung a heavy, velvet cloak about her shoulders.

Her heart pounding in anticipation, Tatiana placed her hand in his.

"Wasn't I exhausted a moment ago?" she asked wonderingly as they raced through the theatre and down its marble stairs to the street.

"A long time ago, wasn't it?" Roland teased as he flagged down a horse-drawn hansom. "Boulevard de Rochechoart et Trois Frères," he cried to the driver as he helped Tatiana up into the wooden coach with its cracked leather seats and sat down beside her.

He pulled the door closed with a creak as the driver cracked his whip and they took off. In the ice-blue dusk, the streets were impossibly packed with a wide variety of vehicles. Automobiles with their strange mechanical clankings vied for running room with buggies, coaches, carts, and cabs of every description. Elegantly dressed men and women thronged the sidewalks.

Above all the clamor rose the timeless beauty of the theatres, their white neo-classical columns and staircases faintly blue in the misting evening air. Not very different from St. Petersburg, thought Tatiana with surprise, except for the lack of snow. She watched delightedly as the queen of theatres, the block-long Opera, loomed over them for an instant from its own wide square. A true palace for the arts, she thought.

The streets began to change as the opera district fell away. The buildings became less grand, the people more nondescript.

"What is Montmartre?" she asked.

"A hill," he answered noncommittally, but his eyes were dancing. A moment later he added, "See for yourself."

Though the traffic was just as heavy, in fact more so as the boulevards narrowed, Tatiana had the strangest feeling they were climbing up the streets of a rural village. Grass grew between the big cobblestones. Lanes twisted off, offering glimpses of weedy court-yards strewn with chickens and once even a cow. Buildings were smaller and leaned over the alleys as if to confide to each other the latest county gossip.

The inhabitants were an incredible sight. An unshaven man with waist-length gray-threaded hair, leaning on a knobby stick of wood, stood on a corner declaiming poetry at the top of his lungs. A woman in stained and ragged work clothes with a basket of folded laundry on her head walked past him without a glance. Next to her strode two very slender men . . . no . . . women, dressed in conservative businessmen's suits, with their arms about each other's waists. A man four feet high, with pince-nez and checked trousers, gave the pair an interested look as he paused to adjust his bright green muffler.

There were aristocrats in polished tuxedos and top

hats. The beautiful women on their arms wore too many jewels. Like Maman, recalled Tatiana. A young girl with a sweet face who might have arrived yesterday from the farm chatted with a tired-eyed man in paint-spattered linen and a drab, weatherbeaten coat as they examined one of the storm of bright posters plastered anywhere there was an open space on a wall.

"Quite a parade, *non?*" Roland interjected, his eyes bright with anticipation. "And they all meet in the cafés."

She looked about wonderingly, at the fantastical signs above many of the colorful buildings: La Nouvelle Athênes, Le Chat Noir, Le Rat Mort . . .

"Who could eat in a café called The Dead Rat?"

"They eat, they drink, sing, fight, create . . . You will see, *chérie*. We are here."

The driver had stopped in front of a café called La Bouteille Riante. The sign showed a man chasing a laughing bottle. Both were painted mint green except for their overlarge, blood-red, open mouths. Without knowing why, Tatiana shivered. Roland paid the driver and guided her out of the hansom, onto the cobbled street now slick with rain, and up under the awning of the café.

He had reached for the scratched brass doorknob when it was wrenched open from the other side by a lanky, cadaverous-looking man in a ragged coat and rough boots.

"May Satan take me before I see you again, you flint-hearted pig of a woman," he shouted hoarsely.

He stumbled drunkenly against Roland, who good-humoredly steadied him and turned him toward the street. The man's odor was overwhelming, Tatiana thought as she turned her head away to escape the amalgam of cheap alcohol, rotting teeth, unwashed body, and turpentine. Instinctively she clutched Roland's arm.

A rich, husky voice boomed, "First the painting, *mon ami,* and then the bottle."

Roland strode into the strangely lit interior, up to the zinc-plated bar with Tatiana in tow. He grinned at the burly, redheaded woman with huge, freckled forearms.

"What did Triard promise you this time, Zazou? A landscape or a portrait? Or perhaps his next illegitimate child?"

They both laughed. Tatiana was fascinated by the woman's exuberance. She threw back her head and chortled from her apron-covered belly, displaying for all to see her trio of gold teeth.

"Eh, comte, so you came tonight!" the woman said as she wiped her eyes, smearing her heavy makeup. "Your usual?"

Roland waved to a group of people ranged around a table who were calling his name.

"Tonight is special," he told the proprietress. "Bring a bottle of your best Beaujolais, and bring yourself too."

Roland's friends were a strange lot, Tatiana thought uneasily as he made the introductions. In the greenish-white gaslight, their faces had an unhealthy pallor as they clamored for Roland's attention like a pack of barely trained wolves.

"Mes amis," he declaimed, holding up one of her hands, "you remember Tatiana Ivanovna Dmitrova, whom I stole from the frozen clutches of old Mother Russia. Until you have seen her dance, you are blind, deaf, and dumb, knowing nothing but second best. She is what dance is meant to be, the standard against which

all future ballet will be measured. You'll tell your grandchildren you saw her, and they'll hold their breaths, clasp their hands, and beg for details."

Tatiana felt like pulling her hands away from Roland and retreating to the deepest shadows of the café. He was putting her on display, like a barker in a circus. Six faces turned up to her; six pairs of eyes examined and dissected. Inwardly she quailed but forced herself to smile. He was simply very proud of her and wanted his closest companions to feel the same. These are Roland's friends, she reminded herself sternly as he reintroduced them one by one.

She recognized Zazou Picard, who poured the wine. The big café owner's wise, brown eyes met Tatiana's startled ones and offered a kind of solace. Also familiar was the outrageously attired painter Camille Carteret. This time he was wearing a shirt with black and red checks, maize leather pants, a swooping neckerchief of purple paisley, and a puffy jacket the brightest green. He smiled lazily at her with the unconscious sensuousness of a cat. Again at his side was Marguerite, his model. Compared to the rest of them, she appeared normal, buxom, milk-skinned, fresh looking as the daisy she was named for. But it was strange to see a cigarette dangling from her rosy lower lip.

La Maigre was there, thin as a rake with an unnaturally long neck and waxy skin. She winked at Tatiana from huge, heavy-lidded eyes. La Maigre was a popular cabaret singer whose cynical, lascivious lyrics were assiduously imitated by Parisian shopgirls, dreaming of the stage.

Tatiana met two other men. Paul Morais, plump, short, with flat, gray eyes and colorless skin, painted dramatic backdrops for Roland's ballets. The artist gave her a quick, hard look before raising his newly filled glass to his lips.

Seated slightly apart from the rest, giving her a brooding look from his round, pansy-brown eyes, was a crippled artist with beautiful hands. André Bonfleur looked like a dissolute Italian choirboy, his pouting lips and headful of black curls curiously at odds with his gauntness, his oversized clothes, and his withered leg.

Suddenly he whipped out a pad and began drawing. This characteristic response drew a round of laughter from Roland and the rest.

"Ah, your fame is ensured, Tatiana," La Maigre purred. "André has put my face on every market stall in Paris with his endless posters."

There was a short pause in which Tatiana could have responded but she could think of nothing amusing or witty to say to these sophisticated people.

"Here's a toast to Comte Roland de Valois, who froze for us in Russia while I burned for Marguerite," proposed Camille Carteret, giving the model an exaggerated leer.

"Don't feel sorry for me," retorted Roland with a grin. "Vodka isn't the only way to stay warm in St. Petersburg."

"Did the tsar let you pick from his stable?" asked Zazou with a chuckle.

"Tsk, tsk," admonished the amused impresario, "he's too busy polishing his icon collection to watch every door."

Tatiana was puzzled by the smiling looks at her that followed this remark. What were they talking about? She looked from face to face, hoping for a clue, a way into the conversation.

"You missed the exhibition at La Grande Pinte,"

André told Roland, the artist's hand never pausing in its sketch work as he described the glowing canvases.

Roland became all impresario for a moment, asking in detail about the art work, the painter Charpentier's background and current financial status.

"Perhaps I'll have a chat with him," Roland concluded.

Marguerite threw Tatiana a mock-tragic look with an exaggerated sigh as if to say, "These boring businessmen!" The model perked up as the talk turned to a boisterous public squabble between two can-can dancers vying for the same man.

"And you know, *chérie,* the most amusing part was that the gentleman in question is actually in love with his cousin Maurice," La Maigre murmured, looking down at her long, black-gloved fingers making a steeple before her on the marble-topped café table.

"Ah, Montmartre, Montmartre! You wild, fickle mistress. We will drink of your excesses till we die," cried Camille Carteret.

They all drained their glasses in playful homage. Tatiana sipped her wine, feeling like a child at a table of adults. She huddled at Roland's side, trying to look inconspicuous.

Paul Morais's cold, gray eyes fixed on her disdainfully.

"Has Martinon stamped your sugarplum fairy into fairy dust yet?"

In the sudden, uncomfortable silence that followed, Tatiana's clear, quiet voice said, *"Au contraire.* With a stroke of my toe, I bearded the lion."

"Very good!" André laughed, saluting her with his wineglass. She smiled at the ripple of surprised, pleased laughter.

"Drink up, drink up, little one," Zazou encouraged. "I've plenty more behind the counter. You have some catching up to do with these professionals."

Zazou brandished the now-empty wine bottle in the general direction of the drinkers.

Marguerite yawned, ostentatiously showing everyone her pretty, pointed, pink tongue.

"Let's go to the Cirque Nouveau."

Her suggestion was met with enthusiasm, though Yvette, the slight bedraggled girl who'd been trying to catch Roland's attention all evening, slumped her shoulders in despair. Before Tatiana knew what was happening, she was bundled into her cloak and the whole party raced off across the rainy cobblestones to a perennial, Parisian sensation. She found it surprising that this cosmopolitan group should want to see a circus, which she remembered from her childhood in St. Petersburg as a simple, gaudy show with bears and puppets.

When she saw the Cirque Nouveau, she understood. There were thousands of people there, a vast canvas of aristocrats and beggers, artists and thieves, vagabonds and staid bourgeoisie, all stamped with the same nightmare air of desperate gaiety. Shoals of eyes glittered feverishly under the eerie viridian glare of the tent lights. When a pretty trapeze artist faltered, one could almost hear the decadent audience breathe, "Fall! Fall!"

The crowd roared for Cha-U-Kao, a muscular, arrogant horsewoman who performed death-defying acrobatics on her galloping pony, all the while keeping a defiant snarl on her painted face. There was little innocence to the clowns. Their pantomimes were all subtle and mocking, with sinister playfulness.

Tatiana tried to keep her spirits up but she found the show repellent despite her best efforts. She was relieved when, still drinking heavily, the group decided to return to the Bouteille Riante.

At the café, La Maigre excused herself. It was two o'clock in the morning, time for her last act on stage. Tatiana listened politely as the purring voice sang slyly of aged, drunken crones and street urchins, satyrlike old men and laundresses. She felt very tired.

Under one of the tables, a ragged man sprawled, asleep, hugging a sticky, green bottle. Camille Carteret was pawing at Marguerite, pressing drunken kisses to her neck and shoulders. She didn't seem to object but simply leaned her head back and closed her blue-shadowed eyes. Tatiana shuddered and looked to Roland for assurance.

Paul Morais gave Tatiana a long, unspeaking look across the table. Then he began sketching rapidly on the back of a menu. When he had finished, he tossed Tatiana's portrait before Roland.

Tatiana peeked and gasped. On the wrinkled paper, a raw, helpless child stared out at them with Tatiana's features. The girl was clinging possessively to the arm of a faceless man, and her fingers looked almost like claws, so tightly did they grasp the man's flesh. She looked unfinished, incomplete, empty.

Roland flung the portrait back at Morais as tears flooded Tatiana's eyes.

"Pah! You're in your cups tonight, Paul. That's quite a self-portrait."

Morais favored them with a disquieting smile as Roland wiped Tatiana's tears with his silk handkerchief.

"Come, my Tiane. It's time for us to go. It must be near dawn."

In tired relief, she let him wrap her in her velvet cloak and lead her out of the dim café. As she leaned into his warmth, her hand clung to his arm as if never to let go. Morais saw the gesture and nodded once to himself.

Tatiana slept in the cab on the way home, drifting up the three flights of stairs with Roland to his apartment. There she sank bonelessly into a chair and watched him through half-closed lids as he built a fire. When it was blazing, he turned to her, his face all in shadow, with the edges of his ruddy gold hair lit up by the firelight like an unearthly vermilion corona.

He knelt in front of her, parted her cloak, and put his head in her lap. Her hands twined through his hair as she watched the leaping flames, and to her drowsing mind, they were one. Roland, her sun-haired lover.

"Tiane," his lips murmured against her velvet-clad thighs. "Take me deep into the volcano tonight, my black swan, my lovely."

She felt the writhe of excitement in her belly as his hands pushed the velvet skirt higher and higher until there was only lace between his lips and her naked skin. Then his hands were ripping the lace away and he was tasting and pressing her shaking thighs, parting them, bringing her to quivering life.

"Oh, yes," she moaned, wanting the wholeness of them again, where she was all to him and he to her. They melted to the floor.

In his overpowering arms, she could shut the intrusive, sinister world of Montmartre away with its shadowy clamor of doubts and questions. As they arched and undulated, stretched and thrust, gave and received, to her they were two innocents again, feasting deliciously in love's plenteous garden.

For Roland, the rushing build-up of sensation was his own deeply buried coiling of lava, rearing its serpentine neck higher and higher until it had annihilated them both in its fiery breath and they rested in sweet ashes.

Replete, Tatiana floated to sleep, to dream of a pair of newly fledged birds, fluttering and swooping through a gentle rain of iridescent flower petals, down lanes of swaying willows, through clouds and clouds of joy.

Roland remained awake, reveling in all of the freedom Montmartre had given to him over the years, all of the societal shackles the artists with their wild ways had broken for him. Tiane's elemental giving had opened him even farther, and tonight's unbelievable lovemaking had proved that. He felt powerful as a god, as if he could accomplish anything he set his mind to. In his arms he cradled the soft sweet girl who had given him this new strength. On a wave of self-satisfied gratitude, he drifted to sleep.

Chapter Nine

ON EITHER SIDE OF THE VELVET CURTAIN, THE AIR brimmed with intoxicating suspense. As the orchestra tuned up in a flurry of strangely pitched notes, the audience tossed greetings and sophisticated speculations back and forth. The Companie Valois's opening night was always one of the key events of the cultural and social season, and the rumors about this performance had brought out even the most jaded of theatre goers.

Who was this Dmitrova whom de Valois touted about town as some sort of dance goddess? Her piquant little face with its extraordinary tilted black eyes peered out from one poster after another at every city block, it seemed, though she had yet to perform a single step. And those in the know had it that Léon Martinon had

141

been seen actually smiling, more than once, at the end of a rehearsal of tonight's ballet, *Echo et Narcisse.*

"Impossible!" cried anyone familiar with the bitter, choleric choreographer.

But if it were true, if it were true . . . Excitement coursed through the perfumed pulses of titled ladies and livened the assured smiles of their aristocratic escorts as they waited the seemingly interminable minutes for the performance to begin.

On the other side of the curtain, all was controlled chaos. Roland de Valois prowled his backstage kingdom, straightening a wig here, a ruffled temperament there. He had encouraging words for the anxious and reminders for the overly assured. A backdrop was brightened, the timing of the lights reviewed, a snapped violin string replaced.

Roland glanced over to the darkened corner of the stage where Tatiana, dressed in Echo's bright daffodil tunic, was doing her warm-up *pliés* and *battements.* She was oblivious to the bustle around her as she bent and straightened her slender legs in the cloud of concentrated quiet she seemed able to generate about her at will. She emerged for a moment to return Roland's loving kiss but soon was deep in her own thoughts again.

Now, *Giselle battement frappés,* Tatiana ordered herself. One foot whipped out and struck the floor with a quick brush before returning to rest near the other ankle. Over and over she kicked, with a lightness that suggested the fragility of a tragic sylph. Now, *Coppelia grand battements,* she thought, making her leg kick up in front of her with doll-like precision.

Micheline Arnot, in the costume of one of the

supporting dancers, shot her a sneering glance as she passed. Tatiana had learned to ignore the former prima's petty cruelties. However, tonight Tatiana was in a heightened state of awareness and her mind leaped automatically to Paul Morais's perennial mocking expression.

The last few weeks had been wearing, spending her nights with Roland's wild friends. They were like naughty children, mused Tatiana, who, when their parents reject their sandcastles and mud palaces, act all the more outrageous to show how little they care. Roland had explained to her that since the traditional art world had belittled their odd, imaginative paintings, the artists rebelled even further. He adored their exaggerated despairing playacting and Tatiana tried to appreciate them for his sake. Though they no longer shocked her, she remained uneasy.

"Curtain in five minutes," warned the stage manager.

Tatiana's ingrained stage discipline immediately took over, Montmartre and its dissipated inhabitants disappearing from her mind. She felt her way into the lush, gay spirit of the nymph Echo as the orchestra began the overture. Moody crescendos warned of tragedy before the music softened into the romantic theme. Then the curtain rose.

A summery glade in ancient Greece appeared. To the carefree rippling of a single flute, a line of nymphs in flower-hued tunics circled and swayed. They were joined by trios of dryads, each dressed in the costume of her tree: birch maidens in pale chartreuse, spirits of the olive tree in shimmering gray, and cypress girls in deeper green. Naiads appeared, clothed in the liquid blue draperies of their streams. They all danced a paean of joy to the dappled woods suggested so evocatively by Morais's impressionistic backdrop.

A butter-yellow light appeared and there was Echo, her arms full of vivid flowers, bright as a flower herself. Her dance was the personification of never-ending summer. She moved with careless largesse, as if she had all the time in the world. Though the ballerina was actually slender, she managed to suggest plumpness, fullness, the deliciousness of ripe fruit. All her movements were round and complete, exuberant or languorous in turn as the music swelled and thinned. She was a nymph, that happy creature of satiation and forgetfulness.

There was a call of deeper horns, a distant roll of drums. Narcisse, a mortal, strode onto the stage. He was an exquisitely handsome young hunter. All the supernatural beings scattered but Echo, who remained, fascinated, as Narcisse removed his outer robe, unstrung his bow, and lay down to rest after his exertions.

Echo, enchanted by his beauty, tiptoed up to him and stroked his chest lightly. Awakened, he saw the delicious nymph and pulled her to him. They danced together, their overflowing passion heating up the very stage and causing many a flushed cheek in the audience. When he was satisfied, Narcisse shoved Echo from him. Her undulating, sensuous gesture faltered and fell away. Gathering his belongings, he left her alone.

Miserable at his abrupt desertion, Echo tried to recapture the fullness of their loving but now her movements were incomplete, building only to break off. With a last longing reach toward Narcisse, Echo collapsed into a weeping huddle, arms bent over her bowed head, as the curtain fell.

The tumultuous applause ended only when the curtain rose for the second act. It was the Festival of Aphrodite and the nymphs danced joyfully, carrying long bright garlands. Though Echo tried to honor the goddess of love in the same happy spirit as her sisters, she allowed her length of garland to droop as she brooded on Narcisse's cruelty. When he pranced by, ignoring her, she dropped her flowers and entreated him to love her. Narcisse rejected her with all the coldness of utter self-centeredness. Behind him, Echo moved as he moved, in a pathetic attempt to be close to him, but her movements erased the arrogance of his, making the same dance steps soft and giving.

As the celebrating nymphs moved off, Echo and Narcisse were left alone at a forest pool. Narcisse spied his reflection and fell passionately in love with it. His dance was filled with the adoration Echo dreamed of for herself. Every posture of love Narcisse offered himself, Echo offered him. The curtain fell on this strange triangle to the sound of warning tremolos.

As they applauded furiously, the audience of balletomanes marveled to each other at Dmitrova's astonishing ability to mimic her partner's movements while suggesting the opposite emotion. The watchers quieted quickly for the final act, not wanting to miss a single magical gesture of this brilliant new ballerina.

Three nights had passed. Echo and Narcisse remained where they had been. Each still opportuned the ungiving object of their affections but now the moon had turned the pool into a silver mirror. Narcisse danced in frenzy, desperate to reach himself but weak from lack of food and drink.

Echo too had withered. Her tunic's ragged edges were pale and clung to her seemingly thinned body. She pleaded with him to taste the succulent fruits she had found, even to sip water from her cupped hands. But Narcisse was furious because her dip in the pond had disturbed his beloved reflection. With blows and curses, he drove her from him. Echo had to watch, pleading, helpless, as he leaned weakly over the water to kiss his adored reflection, tumbled into the pond, and disappeared into death.

Echo was inconsolable. Gone forever was the round, tantalizing nymph. In her place was a tragic wraith, drifting sorrowfully over the stage. Poignant, pathetic, her misery moved many in the audience to tears. She stooped to pick a white and gold narcissus that had sprung magically from the margin of the pond, kissed it once, and cradled it against her snowy breast as she danced her pain. Darkness fell on the mourning figure.

The light dawned softly and nymphs darted through the morning glade, drinking dew exuberantly from freshly opened flowers. Unseen by anyone, ghostly Echo floated behind, imitating their gestures as she had once copied those of her beloved Narcisse. But the careless fecundity of their movements became a haunted yearning when copied by Echo. The procession frolicked across the stage and off to other glades, to other mornings, always followed by an echo.

As the final curtain fell, there was a breathless silence, the ultimate, spontaneous homage every performer hopes for. Then a roaring, cheering rain of appreciation filled the theatre. Strangers hugged one another. Tears ran unashamedly down people's faces as they demonstrated their complete enslavement to the little ballerina from Russia.

The curtain rose and fell as regularly as waves cover and uncover a beach and still the applause continued. Tatiana saw with a thrill that they were all on their feet. She curtsied gratefully back to her appreciators, her heart as full of joy as her arms were of flowers.

After the twenty-second drop of the curtain, the stagehands hurriedly conferred with Roland, who reassured them, walked to center stage, and signaled for the curtain to rise once again. He basked in the bravos that came his way and held up his hand for silence. The audience quieted, wondering what the great visionary impresario would reveal.

"*Merci,* my friends, from the bottom of my heart. We have all witnessed history tonight."

He was interrupted by another round of cheering, which he encouraged with raised arms for a space before calming them again with a single palm.

"Now you must stop and allow the rest of Paris to adore our Dmitrova. I bid you adieu until tomorrow."

His easy yet commanding presence quelled what might have become a riot. When the curtain closed and the houselights came on, the audience obediently filed out, though complete enthrallment could be read in their jubilant voices.

Tatiana's dressing room was a madhouse. Wellwishers pressed bouquets on her, broke open bottles of wine, grabbed her from all sides to take her hand. Léon kissed both her cheeks, his eyes bright with fulfilled tears. She floated happily on the stream of congratulations, feeling light and giddy as a champagne bubble.

Finally Roland chased them all out, firmly locking the door behind the dancers and designers, the backers and artists. He took her in his arms, holding her to him like the precious treasure she was.

"You outshone even the incomparable Dmitrova tonight," he murmured, covering her face with slow, delighted kisses. "How is such a thing possible?"

"It's you and Léon and sweet, sweet Paris," she cried with an exuberant jounce, flinging her arms out and then around him again.

She released him to whirl about the tiny room, spinning like a demented top. He smiled, delighted as a boy at her intoxication.

"Put on the dress we chose together," he ordered when she leaned against him, panting with her exertions.

"We chose? You were the one who insisted . . ."

He drew the rich, flame-colored damask silk gown out of her pocket-sized closet and held it before her. Her eyes narrowed.

"You know, I think I can wear this thing and feel comfortable in it, tonight," she murmured in surprise.

He threw back his head and laughed.

"*Bien sûr,* mademoiselle. You have earned the right to it."

Yes, she thought when she had put it on, considering herself in the mirror. She was so full of joy tonight that the off-the-shoulder gown with its tiny puffed sleeves and daringly low-cut bodice edged by only a wisp of golden lace looked perfect against her flushed skin.

The closely fitted bodice was hung with diagonal lengths of pink pearls. A similar garland of jewels looped across the lace-bordered overskirt that fell from the right hip to the left foot. Underneath was another floor-length skirt of the same glorious fabric. It had a single flounce from calf to toe bordered with golden lace and tulle.

After she had put up her hair in elegant curls and

fastened the five-strand choker of rosy pearls around her neck, she pulled on pale pink elbow-length gloves and swirled her eggshell velvet opera cloak about her shoulders.

"One more thing, my darling," Roland said.

There was a serious note in his voice that made her pay attention. Out of a velvet-lined case, he lifted out an exquisitely delicate circlet of bronze laurel leaves, veined in copper. Tiny yellow diamonds glinted at the slender tip of each leaf.

"Tonight you wear the victor's crown, Tiane," he murmured, placing the sparkling tiara on her head. "My heart you won long ago, but tonight you have all of Paris at your feet."

"My Roland," she said tenderly. "You may not use paper and pen, but you have a poet's soul."

Glad tears sprang to her eyes. With infinite tenderness he kissed them away.

"Come," he beckoned, offering her his arm. "Your subjects await you."

In the brisk spring night, there was no need to call for a cab. Her fans had one ready. They had also removed the pair of horses from their traces. Replacing them was a crowd of tipsy, cheering students who vied for the privilege of pulling La Belle Dmitrova's carriage. Roland's golden eyes gleamed with pleasure at this grandiose gesture of worship to his star. Gathering her up in his arms, he carried her through the crowd and placed her inside the vehicle.

He leaped above to the dismissed coachman's seat, cracked the discarded whip in the air, and shouted exultantly, "To the Moulin Rouge!"

The legion of fans took up the cry, "The Moulin Rouge!" as they drew her down the crowded boulevards, up the butte of Montmartre, and deposited her with a flourish at the thronged entrance to the famed public dance hall.

"I don't want to seem ungrateful," Tatiana whispered to Roland after he had extricated her with difficulty from the arms of several overenthusiastic fans, "but are they going to be at our heels all night?"

"Once we're inside," he murmured back, "we'll lose them easily enough."

She understood his words the moment they entered. The Moulin Rouge was gargantuan. The stage alone was five times the size of the one she'd danced on. Around it ran a dirt track for the equestrian acts. Surrounding the track on three sides was a wide gallery where patrons promenaded, sized each other up, gossiped, made assignations. Many of the women looked as if they were for sale. A vast crowded bar dominated one side of the gallery while the other two sides were taken up with an immense, packed dance floor, bouncing with the efforts of thousands.

Small pockets of space opened around the nightclub's professional can-can dancers, plump-thighed, small-waisted, insolently powerful twirlers. They kicked their muscular legs over their heads, revealing garters, stocking tops, and even lace panties to their encouraging oglers. The orchestra blared at peak volume. Everywhere people shouted to be heard and the stomping of feet was deafening.

At least in this confusion, Tatiana thought, we can return to anonymity. But it was not to be. No sooner had Roland and she found a table, then one of her fans told the band leader who she was. The musicians struck up the theme from *Echo et Narcisse,* and again Tatiana had to curtsy gracefully to a cheering assemblage.

When the manager asked her to mount a donkey and ride the track about the entire nightclub, she looked to Roland to refuse this idiotic request. He waved her on, obviously elated at the attention "his" ballerina was receiving. Tatiana, feeling she had no choice, assented.

She pasted on her face the smiling facade she'd learned to show her lover's café friends and mounted the gaily caparisoned beast. She nodded graciously to the wild throng who raised brimming champagne glasses to her and cried her name. One hand held on to the donkey's saddle horn for dear life as he stumbled over flowers being tossed at them.

It's a role like any other, she told herself as the faces started to blur into a smear of shouting mouths and protuberant eyes. She had been Echo the nymph earlier; now she was Dmitrova, toast of Montmartre. The thought gave her the courage to complete the entire circuit without revealing either nervousness or distaste.

As gladly as a storm-tossed bird returns to its nest, Tatiana found Roland's arms again. She was soothed to feel his warm, solid body move against hers as he led her into a waltz. The strains of "The Blue Danube" floated around them and he guided her as firmly as he had engineered her ascent to stardom. When fans flocked about, wanting to cut in, he held them off for two full dances. Then he relinquished her with a rueful gesture to an opportuning German prince who had financed most of *Echo*.

Tatiana made polite small talk, ignoring the sexually appraising looks from the handsome, yellow-bearded nobleman. She obediently danced with several more of Roland's acquaintances while he acknowledged the salutes and compliments of the crowd of well-wishers.

But she was relieved to hear him say, to a small russet-haired fellow who was a foremost French architect, "Another night, Marcel. We're running off to La Bouteille."

"Perhaps you are running," responded the dapper little man, "but this celestial goddess shall not sully her blessed toes with crude cobblestones. We shall carry her there!"

She found herself hauled up onto the broad swaying shoulders of several adoring fans. Tatiana shot her lover an alarmed look.

"Let these madmen have their fun," he shouted up to her above the deafening noise of the nightclub. "Your feet can use the rest."

Roland threw her cloak up to her with perfect aim. He looked about as hundreds craned their necks to view the spectacle, and pride filled him. How sweet was the applause after all the hard work. I may not be an artist, Roland told himself, but at least I reap my rewards while I'm alive to enjoy them. He hastened after the bobbing line of fans out into the night.

Ahead, Tatiana shivered as she clutched her lopsided cloak about her. She dared not try to adjust it for fear of losing the precarious balance she'd found on the uneven surface of her admirers' arms and shoulders. Every time they passed a café, one of her bearers would cry out her name and the café would empty of cheering patrons.

These French are crazy, she thought. Most of the applauders hadn't even seen her dance, yet they lined the streets, toasting her. They look for any excuse to celebrate, she realized, not for the first time. Like neglected children, desperate for gaiety.

And there, at La Bouteille Riante, was Camille,

dressed in yet another garish clash of colors, saluting her drunkenly, with Marguerite, La Maigre, and all the rest. Zazou, laughing, assisted Tatiana down from her human conveyance and bussed both her cheeks.

"They say you have wings hiding in your heels," the proprietress said to the diminutive ballerina. "Is this so, de Valois?"

She turned to hug Roland in a bear of an embrace.

"Bien sûr, that's the only explanation," he assented as the café denizens escorted them into the dim, green-lit interior. "But even from me, she keeps them hidden. Only on stage . . ."

"Oui!" came a shout from a red-eyed painter at another table. "On the stage with her! Dance for us!"

Wine-sloshed calls for Dmitrova echoed through the little café and she wearily assented, preferring to dance rather than listen to the yelling. Paul Morais bellowed out the beginning of Echo's theme as Tatiana climbed up onto the little stage, kicking off her shoes and hiking up her skirt. She took up a pose and leaped into the nymph's dance to fecund summer.

Roland and Paul led the ragged chorus as she moved through the steps for the second time that evening. Her body protested this abuse, but doggedly she continued. When she had finished, Tatiana saw the shining worshiping eyes of the little waif whose habit, it seemed, was to be forever tripping in Roland's shadow. The girl looked as though she'd just caught a glimpse of heaven.

Tatiana retrieved her shoes and hurried to rejoin Roland but was stopped by a roar from some of the patrons.

"Non! Stay up there. Don't move!"

They were taking out their sketch pads, favoring her with the distant, evaluative stares of artists. How long can this go on, she thought in sudden despair. Will they never leave me alone? She threw Roland a look of veiled imploring, but he was clinking glasses with Morais, laughing triumphantly. It's his supreme moment, she realized. He will savor every ounce of it.

Tatiana resigned herself to posing for the painters of Montmartre. They had her turn this way and that, assume balletic positions, raise her arms and lower them again. All the while they sketched furiously while Zazou lumbered around, pulling paintings from the walls, making room for the pictures to come.

I'm like a doll to them, Tatiana thought tiredly. A big wind-up doll in a pretty package they can drag around to their hearts' content. She closed her eyes, letting herself feel the heavy ache of her muscles, the weariness that felt like hundred-pound weights settling themselves on her shoulders. The pose finally settled on, a full arabesque, began to waver as tremors of exhaustion shot up and down her supporting leg.

Timidly she began, "I must—"

"Don't move a muscle," ordered Berengère, a bulky, disheveled painter who always seemed about to drop from drink. He hadn't even looked up from his work.

Like a rescuing angel, André Bonfleur appeared before her, took her hand, and led her from the stage.

"Forgive them," he whispered to her. "They forget everything but their art."

In a loud voice, he announced, "Put away your pencils, *mes amis*. Do you want to extinguish Paris's newest star on her first night out?"

André tucked her hand firmly under his arm and limped to Roland. Behind them, Zazou called huskily to her can-can dancers to fill the empty stage. In a moment, the platform was filled with a storm of frills and plump, kicking legs.

"My dear comte," said André, "you must take more care with this magical child of yours. They've had her standing on one foot up there for twenty minutes."

Roland stood and reclaimed Tatiana's hand from André.

"Forgive me, my darling," he said as he cradled her pale hand in both of his strong ones.

He raised her hand to his lips and gave it a tender, worshipful kiss that she felt throughout her body.

"Has there ever been a woman so exquisite?" he asked André in a low voice.

Roland's arm came about her, holding her close to him. André smiled wistfully at the two of them and limped back to his seat. Roland began making his good-byes.

Zazou, hanging up a dazzling drawing of Tatiana, complained, "But the night is young!"

Roland silenced the chorus of remonstrations with one raised palm. A luminously sensual smile lit up his face.

"But the night is ours."

Tatiana felt a shock of excitement bring her body tremblingly alive. She looked up at him, and he cupped her flushed cheeks in his palms, giving her a kiss that was a promise.

Amid a hail of good-natured rejoinders, the pair made their escape. The moon was full outside, bathing the lovers in soft silver. Floating on a cloud of voluptuous anticipation, they walked the mile and a half home. Roland carried Tatiana in his arms for the last few blocks.

He held her as he climbed the stairs, locked them

155

inside his apartment, walked into the bedroom, and laid her quivering form on the coverlet. The moon smiled through the window, showing him her softly panting mouth, her black eyes liquid with love.

She is mine, he exulted, as he bent down to her and took her unresisting mouth with his. He cupped a satin-covered breast with one hand and felt her body melt into his in response. Anything I want, Dmitrova will give me gladly. She has no resistance, no boundaries.

He removed each piece of her clothing, looking eagle-fierce down into her eyes as he did so. They were wide pools of acceptance, depths he could plumb to his heart's content. Her swaying body seemed to beg, Faster! Faster! But he would not be rushed, tonight of all nights. When she was completely naked, he sat up again to view his handiwork.

"Roland . . ." she protested imploringly.

"Let me look my fill, Tiane. I could stare at you forever, at your spun silk skin, your pure little breasts with their rosebud tips, your—"

"Please," she begged, "come to me before I die of this wanting."

She was molten silver, he thought as he gave in to the demands of both their bodies. All formless, inchoate wanting, the very stuff of creation, until he gave it form, taught her delight. She gave him herself to mold, and he would shape her against him again and again, making them one.

How powerful, how dominant he was tonight, Tatiana marveled as Roland's ecstatic demands swept through her, ripping away her will like paper dissolving in flames. He showed her needs she never knew she had, and satisfied them with a drive to mastery that utterly overwhelmed her hesitations. His fingers, his mouth, his tongue, seemed to be everywhere, tender, knowing, irresistible. Gladly she gave herself up to his loving so that they flew, free and wild as thunderbolts, through the driving storm of their own passionate making.

whole overturned it upon both their feet by during the dance. Dance is easy to this method. The sister of the give to wait for us to know at each the same the wall a the garden the world each other my the next training

Chapter Ten

THE SUN WAS ALREADY HIGH IN ITS ASCENT WHEN Roland snapped back the antique gold silk draperies from the drawing-room windows. He turned with a flourish and gestured toward Tatiana.

"Come, my darling. Look. Another glorious day before another glorious evening," he proclaimed.

She was leaning back against a teal-blue velvet chaise with her eyes closed. One hand rested on the hot cup of chocolate in her lap. She opened her eyes and smiled wanly, trying to look enthusiastic for Roland's sake.

"Now, Tiane," he reproved, a frown catching his brow in a net of disapproval. "How can you feel the excitement in the air, the coming of spring, if you wallow on that lounge?"

He bounded over, removed her cup, and picked her up in his arms as if she were no heavier than a feather pillow. Carrying her to the edge of the heavy old glass, Roland forced her to look at the busy city beyond. Age had long distorted the clarity of the windowpanes. The odd view of an elongated boulevard with twisted carriages and contorted horses rushing by at a mad pace made Tatiana dizzy. Her skin, already pale, grayed, and she lifted an unsteady hand for Roland.

"Tiane! So pale! What you need is a deep breath of Paris," he ordered.

"If you say so," the young girl said faintly, "but at least from the other windows, Roland."

Pivoting about, he marched her over to a set of windows and flung open tall, thin-latticed panes of glass. The silent shelter of a tiny churchyard with an adjoining cemetery met Tatiana's glance and calmed her frantic heart. She leaned forward eagerly, drinking in the quiet order below.

The bare willow trees with long drooping branches seemed to embrace the grim but neatly manicured gravestones. Her eyes flew to her favorite monument. A tiny angel with its face lifted heavenward seemed to smile beatifically at Tatiana. Fresh dewy violets, held together by a lacy white doily, lay in the angel's fist.

"The peace of it, the utter peace . . ." Tatiana mumbled aloud. "I could almost wish . . ."

"What, dearest?" Roland asked, cocking an eyebrow.

He spun her to him, away from the pensive scene. Automatically she lifted one leg in a balletic pose and raised the other onto her toes. He caught her lips with his.

"My beautiful ballerina," he breathed into her ear while raining kisses on her face and neck. "Do you dance for me?" he asked provocatively.

Tatiana blushed.

"Haven't I danced for you nearly every night . . . since the season began?"

It was a question charged with both intimacy and irritation, which Roland apparently chose to overlook. He winked at her, patted her on the derrière, and turned his attention back to the busy boulevard, never seeing the clear signs of weariness and pain in Tatiana's slow measured steps back to the lounge. She settled herself onto the comfortable padded chair, sighing deeply and stretching out the kinks in her legs.

Wasn't she the one capable of incredible endurance? Hadn't her whole life been spent in developing the utmost strength and agility in her body? Yet here she lay, every bone creaking, every muscle screaming, while Roland never seemed to tire. He sparkled endlessly, she thought ruefully, like a newly uncorked bottle of champagne. He was as fresh for the day's work as he was for all-night partying . . . day after night after day after damnable night. He was inexhaustible and she was as limp and tired as an old rag.

Perhaps she was to blame, she mused. Her success in *Echo et Narcisse* had so violently imprinted her name and image on the public that demand for more performances was inevitable. Wasn't it a stroke of luck for Roland and Léon, she thought with unaccustomed cynicism, that unlike so many other dancers and artists of the theatre and cafés, she had more than a single skit in her?

The welling bitterness surprised Tatiana. Why else

had she come to Paris but for the opportunity to dance and to be with the love of her life? She sipped from her cup, the warm drink easing her tense body and the tangle of her emotions.

Dance . . . she had. Léon had rescheduled the entire season so that she was to perform three or four times a week. With barre classes in the mornings, rehearsals and fittings every afternoon, and Léon hammering at her every second, she hardly knew when she was on or off stage.

Now, a scant six weeks since her arrival in Paris she was prepared to dance in Léon's version of *Coppelia*, the grand *pas de deux* from *Sleeping Beauty*, the mad scene from *Giselle*, a new piece of Léon's entitled *Saisons* in which she interpreted each of the seasons in four solo vignettes, as well as *Echo et Narcisse*.

True to form, fulfilling all of Léon's hopes and Roland's predictions, Tiane Dmitrova had become prima ballerina assoluta. The critics were ecstatic. They raved at how she brought to life every balletic conception, answered any choreographic demand, delivered all emotional nuances. They compared her to the fleetest of racehorses, the most magical of swooping falcons, the most delicate of fairies. She made dancing look like a lark.

It always had been, the girl thought wistfully. It could be still, if dancing were all she cared about. But there was Roland. She needed to be with him as surely as she must have air to breathe and food to eat. She gazed helplessly at the alert masculine figure at the window.

With each deep intake of air, he seemed to expand with energy and good will. Flushed with feelings of love for the man, Tatiana resolved to take a firm hold of herself, wishing away the dullness, the aches, the resentment. She would live up to all of Roland's expectations, including his damned enthusiasm for the café life.

She glided up from the lounge, trailing her satiny peignoir behind, and became very industrious at the breakfast tray. Joining Roland at the windows open to the boulevard, she offered him a croissant replete with fresh country butter and apricot jam.

"Sweets for my sweet," she murmured.

"Merci, Tiane."

He took the flaky morsel from her and held her close beside him.

"What better place to be than Paris. You agree, my love? The amusements we'll find today will outweigh those of yesterday when Berengère sketched the caricature of you . . . your beautiful face topping the body of a great Russian bear with toe shoes."

He waited for a response from Tatiana, grinning broadly and gently squeezing her shoulder. None came.

"Well, it was worth a laugh or two, you must admit, *chérie.* And then, when Bonfleur came to your defense, stamping his good leg while dragging the bad one halfway across the café, to rip the sketch from Berengère's hands, only for the big man to lunge at poor André with a palette knife . . . it was well worth the bottles of absinthe I had to buy each one to get them to shake hands again. You know, if I can get those two to collaborate on the backdrops for your huntress ballet next season . . ."

Roland continued on while Tatiana drowned in the effervescent morass of his monologue. She tried to inject a smile or a chuckle at the right moments, but she found her hands were trembling. It took all of her will to control her nerves.

Unexpectedly she yawned. She stiffened and looked with alarm at Roland. Had he noticed? No, he was oblivious, busily entrenched in repeating the details of a haute couture gown he had bought for Tatiana and wanted her to wear that evening after her performance.

"B-b-but, Roland," she stammered in distress, "Léon says—"

"No, no, Tiane, not Léon Martinon," he interrupted. "I said the Café Lion's Mane. That's where we're going tonight. The whole gang wants to give you a birthday party, darling. Doesn't that sound like fun?"

Against her will, tears formed in the dark pools of her eyes and her lips quivered.

"I can't, Roland," she whispered, despairing of yet another night of drunken adventure in Montmartre. "Léon has put his foot down. He says my art is suffering. And Roland . . ."

She gazed up at him, her eyes pleading her case.

"He's right. I've been burning the candle at both ends for too long. Can't we postpone the party? I just need a night or two of complete rest. We can go to another party next week."

"Oh," Roland said in clipped tones, not hiding his disappointment. "I don't think the date can be changed. They've dreamed up some kind of special surprise in your honor."

"You know when my birthday is. They don't even have the right date," complained Tatiana petulantly. "Your friends are crazy . . . and dear . . . but couldn't they wait a couple of months until my real birthday?"

"You don't understand, *ma petite*. They've cooked up this mad scheme to celebrate your coming of age, your great triumph in Paris. You know Camille and Paul. Once they've gotten an idea . . ."

Tatiana flopped down wearily into a chair, grasping at its arms as at a lifeline.

"I'm not going, Roland. I must think of myself for once."

She raised her arms toward him.

"Please, my love, say you understand. Besides, there'll probably be another extravaganza tomorrow night or the next. They wouldn't miss us anyway. There's always such a crowd."

Roland walked out of the window's glare. Gently, he touched Tatiana's face and saw for the first time the lavender shadows beneath her eyes, the faint lines of worry creasing her forehead, the downward curve of her petallike lips. He frowned, stunned at the toll Paris had taken on his brave little ballerina, and he was angry at his blindness. He raised her and tenderly embraced her.

"Hush now. Everything will be all right."

She melted in his arms, relief flooding through her. Roland understood. She was filled with gratitude and love for this wonderful man. Her mind rushed to plan the quiet intimate evenings they would have here in the apartment . . . dinner before a roaring fire, perhaps a leisurely stroll near the churchyard. They might read aloud to each other. She would dance for him alone. It would be heaven.

". . . you do need your rest," he was saying. "Léon will have my head if I harm his prima."

He paused to think as he nestled Tiane against his chest. The comte's eyes lit up with the fire of inspiration.

"Here's what we'll do," he began briskly. "I was

going to take you for a final fitting at Madame Paquin's salon, but the gown is already lovely. I'll cancel the fitting. That'll give you two hours between your rehearsal with Christophe for the *pas de deux* and tonight's performance."

He released her and paced the room, his mind a whirl of activity.

"I'll leave strict orders that no one may disturb you for any reason—"

"Oh, no," Tatiana laughingly interjected, "make sure someone comes for me if the theatre catches fire."

"Of course, darling," he said, sweeping her little joke aside. "Then you'll be so rested for the performance, you'll be eager to go to the party afterward."

He clapped his hands, proud of his solution, and grinned brightly. But the echoing smile on Tatiana's face froze and withered to a grimace.

"It won't do, Roland," she said in a small hurt voice. "It's not enough."

The promising vision of the cozy couple by firelight had evaporated.

"No?" Roland asked, his brows forming a sad frown.

He stood pensively, as though searching for some other answer. Roland shrugged his shoulders and smiled implacably at her.

"So it must be, then."

She felt rooted to the ground. If she moved, she might yield to him and this time she couldn't.

He walked back toward the pale slim girl.

"I can see I've been thoughtless, dragging you along with me, night after night to entertain my crazy associates. I forgot the fragility of my little Russian flower."

He stroked her long hair, fingering each tress as if it were a silky petal.

"I see now it's been too much for you. You really must have your rest."

He kissed her face as a tiny unsure smile hesitated on her lips.

"Yes, Roland."

"So," he continued solicitously, "after tonight's performance, I'll put you in a cab so you can go home and directly to bed. I'll go on from the theatre to the party. We can honor La Maigre instead. Her new act at the Moulin is sensational." Almost as an afterthought, he added, "I'll give everyone your regrets, darling."

He went to kiss the top of her head but she flung herself from his condescending embrace.

"What do you mean you'll go without me?" Tatiana cried. "If you go, I won't see you all night. You won't get home till dawn."

Her voice descended to a piteous whine.

"All I wanted was for us to have a quiet evening at home alone together."

Roland stared at her, bewildered by her outbreak.

"But, *chérie,* that would be a waste of both our evenings. You"—he stressed the next word—"obviously need the rest. I have the party to attend. It's only logical we separate."

More tears coursed down her cheeks.

"That's not why I came to Paris," she bleated.

Roland's exasperation grew by the minute.

"Why are you going on like this? It's just for one night."

"And how many nights after that?" she demanded.

"Tiane," he stated coolly, "you're overreacting. I repeat. It's just for one night!"

He grabbed at his watch and examined the time.

"I must go," he said crisply. "I'm already late for an

appointment. I'll stop at the theatre and tell Léon you'll be late today. I think a little rest right now wouldn't hurt you at all."

He left the room quickly without kissing her good-bye. He hated displays of possessiveness.

Tatiana stared at the closing door. She wanted to call him right back and scream at his selfishness. Angry and hurt, she strode to the wide windows facing the boulevard and shut them sharply. She wouldn't watch him drive off. She hugged her shoulders, feeling alone and cold. With a cry of despair, she hurled herself toward the chaise and hid her face in her hands, hating Paris.

The drawing room was dark except for the gilded hands of the mantel clock which gleamed the passage of time. Tatiana sat, transfixed, her hands clenched on the elegant thin arms of a Queen Anne chair, as the hours slipped away. The thirty-minute chimes began their brief melody.

The girl jerked to attention. It was four-thirty in the morning. She had been sitting there, alone in that chair, in that apartment, for five hours. Footsteps sounded in the foyer. Tatiana smiled grimly. Roland had returned.

The dapper comte tiptoed into the drawing room. His arms were filled with his coat, newspapers, posters, and a bottle of wine. His shoes dangled from two extended fingers. Without lighting the lamps, he made his way to the central table and, careful to make no noise, laid down his treasures. From the dark, a low disembodied voice emerged.

"You're home early."

Roland jumped.

"Tiane, is that you?"

Quickly, he lit a lamp. The yellowish glare cast hazy shadows about the room but there was no mistaking Tiane. She still wore the gown she had put on after the ballet. Now it was badly wrinkled. Her upswept chignon was disheveled with wild wisps emanating in every direction. Her simple makeup was smeared by tears left to dry on her face.

"I waited for you," she stated, accusation unmistakable in her voice.

"I don't understand, darling."

His innocence dripped with each word.

"You mean after all that foolishness this morning . . . and this evening when I begged you to come with me . . . you decided to stay up the whole night anyway?"

He threw up his hands and shook his head.

"You should have come to me at the café, Tiane. We had a marvelous time. La Maigre was in rare form. She was so drunk she even confided her real name to me. It's Susan Smythe. She's English, not a French girl at all."

Roland paused, casually lighting a cigarette.

"And Breton was there tonight with a paean composed to you, my love. When he found out you hadn't come, he was so heartbroken, he—"

"Not another word, Roland de Valois!" hissed Tatiana.

She had risen from the chair and in her haste knocked it down. Her jaw was clenched tight and red angry blotches dotted her pale complexion.

"You've made yourself crystal clear. You left me for that . . . that drunken orgy. It made no difference how I felt."

Defiant now in the face of her unreasonable attack,

169

Roland retorted, "What the hell did you want me to do?"

"I thought . . ."

A torrent of tears came unchecked. In an instant, Tatiana flew to Roland, wrapping her slim arms around him for comfort.

"Oh, Roland, I love you so. But don't you see? Ever since we arrived in Paris, it's been one round after another of your artist friends following us to the theatre, joining us at restaurants, insisting on taking us to the cafés, the circus, the clubs . . . Must we be with them every second of the day and night? Can't we have time, just the two of us, to be alone together?" she implored.

Roland pushed her from him and held her at arm's length. He looked at her with stern eyes, the green flecks stagnant, the brown wooden.

"You're acting like a child, Tatiana."

He released her as if touching her repulsed him. Irked, he gathered up his paraphernalia from the low table.

"Here we are in the most exciting city in the world. You are the toast of the town. Life is all around us . . ."

He punctuated each condemningly sarcastic remark with a slap of papers against the wine bottle.

". . . and you want us to ignore it, to sit at home before the fire, you with your knitting and me stroking my beard, waiting for the hooded man with the scythe."

Tatiana cringed at the sting of his words.

"You don't understand," she cried piteously. "I only want—"

Roland raised his eyebrows so abruptly she was frozen to silence. His message was clear. She knew he no longer cared. With a muffled shriek, her fingers pressed white against her mouth, she rushed from the room, slamming the drawing-room door behind her.

Roland threw his armload to the floor.

"Damn her possessiveness," he muttered.

Yanking on his shoes, he grabbed his coat and headed out the front door for the solace of the streets.

Chapter Eleven

"TIGHTER," TATIANA DEMANDED. "PULL THE RIBBONS tighter."

"But, mademoiselle, you must be able to breathe," protested the wizened seamstress. "What if you faint on stage?"

"And next you'll be telling me how to point my toes?"

The ballerina's voice was heavy with sarcasm.

"As you will, miss," the old woman mumbled, her fingers busy over the rainbow of satin lacings below Tatiana's bosom.

"I know what I'm doing," she muttered, less for poor old Lucette's ears than for her own.

Dipping her toes in the resin box, she signaled her readiness to Léon to begin the final dress rehearsal for *Coppelia*. He nodded to the conductor who led the orchestra in the saucy opening strains. The corps took their places in the village setting and their gay folk costumes caught the sparkle of the stage footlights.

In the wings, Tatiana awaited her musical cue. For a brief moment, she closed her eyes. Her shoulders sagged slightly and she seemed to exhale her last breath of air. The weariness and frustration of the last hours weighed her down. Her feet felt as though they were encased in bricks.

"Tiane!"

Léon came pounding across the stage and into the wings.

"Tatiana Dmitrova!" he shouted.

Startled, she looked up, realizing the music had stopped.

"I missed my cue," she acknowledged to the white-maned dance master.

She stood her ground bravely. Léon, usually a gentleman in her presence, looked ready to breathe fire and smoke at her.

"Pay attention," he gritted through clenched jaws, "or you'll be seeing the spires of St. Petersburg sooner than you imagined."

Tatiana's face was a patchwork of embarrassment and chagrin. Léon had every right to reprimand her, she told herself. Either one was a professional or one was not.

"I'm ready, Léon," she whispered. "Really ready."

Martinon turned on his heels without another word and furiously snapped his fingers at the conductor. Once again the music swelled through the empty theatre. Tatiana came trippingly on stage as Swanhilda, the flirtatious and beautiful peasant.

174

In her flimsy folk costume of ribbons, satin, and tulle, she practiced her pretty wiles on all the village lads, including Franz, her favorite, whom she hoped to make jealous. She twirled among them, cast her long ribbons about their hands, kicked her legs high. Tatiana floated along automatically to the familiar melodies, smiling and dancing promises to each of the boyish peasants.

"No. No! NO!" cracked Léon at the top of his lungs. "Put some heart in it, girl. I didn't alter the story line for you so that I could be made a laughingstock."

Tatiana stopped in midpirouette, almost twisting her ankle in the process. Her face was a question mark of surprise. Were her feelings so transparent? Snapped out of Swanhilda's world, she became aware of Léon's twisted sneer and, far worse, Roland was there, a mask of disappointment prominently displayed.

The two men were whispering confidentially. Roland's eyebrows worked up and down. There was no question in Tatiana's mind that they were judging her and her performance was coming up short. She colored and raced from the stage, feeling ill.

Having had nothing to eat since yesterday's lunch, she had nothing to give back, but her stomach churned violently and her throat constricted convulsively. She waved away a small curious band of dancers. She needed no one's help; she could be self-sufficient too, just like Roland.

She heard herself say aloud, "I'll show him."

Then she was at the resin box, bending to repowder her shoe tips. When she straightened, her inky eyes were shooting devil-may-care fire and a secret smile appeared on her lips. Pushing curtain panels out of her way, she strode on stage. Instantly, those assembled came to rapt attention.

"Maestro," Tatiana called out in total command, "if you please . . ."

The perky music picked up again, and Swanhilda, the ultimate coquette, began her assault on the country bumpkins of her village. At once pert and saucy, she seemed to promise more than it was humanly possible to give. With melting eyes, she tempted each corps danseur with flicks of her hips, teasing tosses of her head, impossibly lyrical arm movements, and always the willowy legs sure in their leaps, jumps, and spins about the stage.

"Bravo!" roared Léon. "That's it . . . that's it. Keep it up. *Fantastique!*"

He sank into a seat, blissful content bathing his lined visage.

"What depth," he confided to Roland. "Considering the life she's been leading, I don't know how she does it. And I thought she was losing her touch."

He smiled proudly as if Tatiana were of his own creation.

The corps ballerinas glanced uneasily among themselves. Their costumed partners actually seemed to be caught in the snare of this wild prima. The men were deviating from their set steps, following Dmitrova as if she held some demonic sexual power over them. Swanhilda enticed, lured, pitted peasant against peasant.

Roland, too, was dazzled by Tatiana's irresistible talent, taken in by the charm of her acting and consummate skill of her balletic art. The blatant quality of her flirtatiousness, even if she were merely dancing a role, made him feel uneasy and nervous. She was too good at it, and he was shocked to feel an unfamiliar pang of jealousy.

Roland took in the assembled company in a single glance, sensitive to the women's unsureness and acutely aware of the men's primitive response to Tiane's overt allure. His eyes focused on Tiane and devoured the captivating ballerina as she danced the thin line between art and reality.

Then, as she claimed the stage hers, she shot him a look so challenging, so direct, he could not mistake its meaning. No man present, on or near the stage, was her master. His sunny eyes glazed gold with passion. He forgot she was a dancer, at one with her role. He only saw her as a woman, his woman, and felt the hot need to claim and possess her flash through him.

He fought his way to the stage, blind to the chairs he knocked over and the dancers he pushed out of his path. The music screeched to a halt. He grabbed at the peasant siren, half wanting to break her spell, half wanting to make it last forever and trap him alone in her web.

Caught in Roland's grasp, she seared him with ebony fire deep in her eyes. Pleasure rippled through her as he met her bold scrutiny. Her victory was complete. Gone was any vestige of common sense or impartial judgment. Gone was the real world about them. It only mattered that they were together. It only mattered that they were one. Roland lifted her roughly to him and, oblivious to the gasps of the company, carried her off stage.

A protesting roar erupted from Léon, who had jumped to his feet.

"Bring back my ballerina!" he commanded.

From the depth of the wings, Roland shouted back hoarsely, "Get another one."

Léon threw up his arms and marched off toward the lobby, muttering, "Everyone is a temperamental artist . . . even the management!"

Outside the theatre a light rain was falling. Tatiana, still wearing nothing more than her thin costume, began to shiver within Roland's viselike embrace. He hailed a passing carriage, and the driver immediately responded, his eyes round as saucers at the exotic couple. Roland gave his home address and quickly loaded his treasured armful into the cab.

"Angel. Temptress," the inflamed man breathed onto the girl's shiny tresses, chilled earlobes, soft skin.

He buffeted her with hard kisses and caressed her scantily clad body with a desperate urgency. His touch, usually so tender and expert, was rough and clumsy, as if all he wanted was to brand her his. He pulled hard on the ribbons at her bosom, and when the laces wouldn't give, he yanked them from the flimsy costume. He tore at the bits of skirt at her hips and tugged at the netted hose she wore, shredding them from her legs.

Naked, Tatiana leaned against the cold leather seat, her body assaulted by the clash of temperatures and textures. Against her back, the tautly stretched hide chilled her skin, which recoiled and constricted at every minute movement. The front of her was scorched by Roland's headstrong raid. Her breasts seemed to engorge and her belly heat from within, even at his glance.

Hot blood surged throughout his body, vitalizing his loins, sharpening his need for Tatiana. His only pleasure lay in this tantalizing slip of a woman. She was inhuman, supernatural . . . a sprite . . . a nymph . . . a siren . . . an enchantress . . . all woman.

He grasped her small firm breasts, kneading the nipples to aching quivering peaks between his fingertips. Tatiana gasped in excitement. His mouth searched out and claimed the tender rosy flesh, leaving his hands free to roam down her torso, past the soft curves at her waist, between her supple thighs. On his knees before her, he bent to taste her secret juices. Finally, he bowed his head to her feet, cupped her toes in the palms of his hands, and reverently kissed each one.

A shattering sigh ripped through Tatiana and she closed her eyes as Roland slowly made his way up her body. Finally he was hers, smothering her with the attention she had demanded. He arched against her, biting at her lips, her neck, and her breasts. Ecstatic, she responded to him as he covered her with his body, wrapping her arms about his neck, raking her nails along his back and through his shirt, making her mark on him. He was hers as much as she was his, and Tatiana wanted him to remember her claim.

They were alone in their own private world, glorying in each other's domination and surrender. When the cab reached its destination, the driver had to rap sharply on the roof of the carriage before the lovers came alert to their whereabouts. Roland looked up and cursed under his breath.

"One moment," he yelled. To Tiane, he growled, "Come."

He wrapped her naked body in his thick overcoat, leaving the remnants of Swanhilda's garb on the carriage floor. Sweeping Tatiana into his arms, he emerged from the cab, his eyes boring into those of his beloved. Without stopping, he threw several franc notes at the cabbie and ploughed straight ahead up the narrow stoop, disappearing into the depths of the building.

"Ah." The driver smiled, rolling his eyes at the size of his tip. *"Toujours l'amour."*

Roland carried Tatiana upstairs to his bed. Tearing his clothes off, he joined her under the heavy feather quilt, mounting her quickly. She was open to him, churning with her own hungers. Legs and arms intertwined, mouths and tongues spurring their passion, they fought for union, ferocious to possess one another. They clung together, desperate to prolong the moment. Victory . . . victory . . . then it was over . . . too soon . . . and still they clung to each other, afraid to let go. Tears rolled down Tatiana's cheeks, wetting Roland.

"Sadness now, *ma chérie?*" he murmured.

"Only that we argued, Roland," Tatiana answered. "Promise me, my love," she cried, her eyes bright with renewed hope, "promise me we'll never disagree again."

"I never meant it to go so far," confessed Roland, kissing away each tear.

She stroked the taut brow, the firm chin of her lover's face.

"Is it possible to love too much?" she asked, her chin trembling like a child's.

"Hush, my darling."

He enveloped her in his warm embrace.

"With love there can never be too much."

He held her, calming her shivers, and she crowded close to him as if to climb within his skin. Roland frowned. He possessed her body and had given his, but he owed her more.

"Tiane," he said quietly, "I want to apologize. I was bullheaded . . . a fool, dragging you along to all my

favorite haunts. I never thought . . . I forgot you don't
know Paris and love her as I do."

He sat up, staring at the window and Paris beyond.

"Just tell me what you want to do, where you want to
go, and we'll do it."

The girl sat up too and threw her arms around her
hero. The last shreds of tension and fear fled from her.

"You make me so happy, Roland. We'll have such a
good time . . . just like when we were on the train."

"Well," he asked, "what do you say? We have the
rest of the day, all of tonight and tomorrow . . ."

Tatiana searched her mind. Visions of the journey
from St. Petersburg to Paris flooded her thoughts:
private dinners in their compartments, frolicking in the
wintry forests when the train was snowbound, in each
other's arms staring at the stars, dancing for him alone.

"It doesn't matter, Roland," she said, smiling and a
little nervous. "I just want to be with you."

Roland fought back a sting of irritation. It wasn't her
fault, he kept reminding himself. How can she make a
suggestion when she doesn't know the city? His jovial
spirit returned. He would just have to show her everything.

"I have it. The Gallerie Chateille is having an exhibit
of Maurice Garnolle's latest works. He's even more
avant-garde than Morais—just blocks of color, I hear.
And nearby there's a tiny Russian restaurant I've been
meaning to take you to . . . between evenings in Montmartre."

He looked at her pointedly with an arched eyebrow
and a slow droll grin. She caught the barb and laughed.
All that craziness was past, she felt sure. Life for
Roland and her would really begin tonight.

"Yes, yes, Roland," she cried with genuine pleasure.

Like children playing dress-up, they chose each other's clothes for the evening. Roland designed a coiffure for Tatiana's hair and she bravely shaved him. Roland offered to let her drive the motorcar but Tiane demurred.

"Perhaps one Sunday, later in spring," she promised.

Hand in hand, they left for the gallery, starting early so they could stroll the long distance uptown. Tatiana wore her Russian furs, but it was Roland's presence that kept her warm.

The walk of four miles was a complete success. Tatiana began to understand Roland's fascination with Paris, its living history and vibrant people.

At the Gallerie Chateille, she was bombarded by huge canvases dominated by modernistic chunks of pigment. She had never seen anything like them before and wandered off alone into another room to gawk at one canvas that filled an entire wall. It was entitled *Angels and Demons*. She was twisting her head, trying to figure out which were which when a familiar high-pitched sneering voice grated at her ear.

"Charlatans! All of them! Damn Garnolle and his money-bag cronies."

She turned around, sick to see Berengère, as disheveled and drunk as ever. Fresh daubs of paint were smeared across his shirt, and from a deep pocket in his overalls, he extracted a lurid green bottle of absinthe. Staring at the painting, he took a long slug of the insidious liquid, swilling it in his mouth. My God, Tatiana thought in alarm, he's going to spit on the canvas.

"Roland!" she called in agitation.

The comte jauntily appeared, a look of happy surprise on his face. Tatiana rushed to his side. He patted her hand and saluted the distraught painter.

"So, Berengère, come to sneer at Garnolle's success, have you?" Roland teased.

"I want to leave," Tatiana whispered in urgent tones to Roland.

"Just a minute, dear."

Roland left her and walked forward, putting his arm around the unkempt, unhappy man who continued to mutter garbled curses at the complex abstracts.

"Come along with us, Georges. Tiane and I are going to stop at La Vieille Moskva for some stroganoff. She's homesick, old pal. Help me cheer her up, eh?"

Tatiana felt a roaring in her ears and shook her head violently. What was Roland talking about? Why was he winking at her? He was ruining their evening before it had begun.

The shaggy painter squinted in her direction, waved a limp hand, and Tatiana found herself waving back. Berengère took a deep rasp of a breath and turned back to the nattily dressed nobleman.

"You're a kind man, de Valois . . . and clever too. To hell with Garnolle and Chateille."

He linked arms with Roland and Tatiana as if they were a band of conspiring art critics.

"You know," he confided, "I even tried to bribe Chateille into exhibiting my drawings. I promised him a portrait of his wife. Free!"

The man laughed, his foul breath suffocating Tatiana.

"There was your mistake, *mon ami,*" replied Roland amiably. "Madame Chateille is his mother; he has no wife. You couldn't have insulted him more if you tried."

183

The men broke into hearty guffaws and Berengère affectionately squeezed the arms of his friends. Tatiana cried out in pain.

"Did I hurt you, Russian fairy child?" mumbled the artist. "I'm too rough . . . a big galoot. You go on with your lover. I'm all right now. De Valois knows how to jolly me along. Go on now, lovebirds . . . I insist."

Tatiana was too embarrassed to say anything and merely hid her head against Roland's shoulder as Berengère shuffled off in the opposite direction.

"Poor Georges," Roland was saying. "He's really a damn talented illustrator. I must find a place for him. I think I'll ask him to design next season's program. His pen-and-ink drawings will look sensational, don't you think, Tiane?"

She didn't reply. Raw emotion scourged at her heart. Did Roland care so much more for a silly old painter than for her? Here he was, fitting that scruffy, ill-smelling vagabond into his life, leaving her less and less room. At the same time she was immensely proud of Roland's seemingly selfless generosity and wisdom and she hated herself for the smallness of her own spirit.

"Having a good time, darling?" he inquired. "Too bad Berengère couldn't join us for dinner. What a grand time we'd have had. We might even have gotten him to draw a portrait of you, my sweet."

"Do you need another caricature of me, Roland?"

The petty words came out in a rush before she could stop herself.

"I thought this evening was for us alone."

Roland stopped midstride.

"You don't think I planned to meet Berengère at the gallery with the avowed purpose of spoiling your fun," he said coldly.

"No, no, of course not. Forgive me, my love," she appealed hurriedly. "I just want our night to be as perfect as our day was."

She went on tiptoe to nuzzle his cheek and offer him a conciliatory kiss.

"M-m-m-m," he purred provocatively. "You're making me hungry."

They both laughed and proceeded on to the Russian restaurant. Inside was the arresting sight of a steaming silver samovar. Tatiana suddenly ached with memories of her homeland.

"Oh, Roland," she cried, "I must tell you about my grandmother Sofia. She would polish her samovar till it gleamed like a—"

"De Valois! Over here! Is that you, slumming in the expensive district for once?"

Her mouth still open to finish her little story, Tatiana winced. Not again, not now. Were they to be intruded upon everywhere they went? She bit down on her lip and clenched her teeth tight. It seemed as though all of Montmartre were dogging Roland's steps.

With sinking recognition, she saw the five musketeers —Morais, La Maigre, Bonfleur, Carteret, and Marguerite—all converge on Roland like sharks around their prey. She glanced quickly at Roland, hoping to see disappointment or at least dismay register on his face, but he was smiling broadly. He beckoned to his chums.

"Look, Tiane. This is great. Now we can have a real party."

There was a great deal of backslapping and handshaking. La Maigre, of course, bussed all the men soundly. Only André Bonfleur noticed the downward curve of Tatiana's lips.

"Bad timing, Mademoiselle Dmitrova, oui? It is the story of my life, *n'est-ce pas?*"

She attempted a smile for the crippled artist's sake, staring for an instant at his withered left leg and mud-brown eyes. Tatiana felt naked under his scrutiny and, again, ashamed. She looked to Roland for forgiveness but he was already engaged in a heated debate with Morais and Carteret over the value of top billing and immortality. Tatiana looked away, unable to bear the sarcasm, unable to see the fun. Her evening was ruined; that was her reality.

Although the food was deliciously authentic, Tatiana ate little and drank less. Roland ate mountains of piroshki, drank oceans of vodka. As the group argued about the check, Tatiana observed them.

To herself, she muttered, "I don't understand. In Russia, the best people eat French food. Why is it in France, the worst eat Russian?"

"Wait, everybody," La Maigre shouted. "Tiane said something."

Twelve eyes stared in anticipation.

"Nothing," Tatiana replied, coloring deeply. "I—I was just talking to myself."

"A dangerous habit," quipped Morais.

But La Maigre had heard quite clearly and repeated it loudly for the benefit of the assembled party. Cheers and hoots greeted Tatiana's aphorism. Roland laughed loudest of all.

From the next table, a man wearing a classic beret leaned over.

"May I quote you, mademoiselle?" the man asked with mock civility. "I'm working on a short piece for a new magazine. I call my poem 'Ode to Pernod.' Your line would fit in nicely."

"Brava, Tiane," Roland cheered, saluting her with his glass. "The toast of the town and the life of the party too."

Bonfleur eyed the miserable girl, but whether with sympathy or pity she couldn't tell. He lifted her hand to his lips and brushed her glove in parting.

"You really wanted an answer to your question," he said perceptively. "It wasn't a joke at all, was it?"

Stricken, she nodded. He could see into her very soul. Why André Bonfleur and not Roland de Valois? She yanked her hand from his gentle grasp as if it were on fire and turned to her lover.

"A carriage, Roland. Please. My head is splitting."

"Of course, *ma petite*. Au revoir . . . *À bientôt* . . . *Demain* . . . yes, tomorrow . . . I'll be there," he chorused to his friends.

The comte in the highest of spirits put her in a taxi. For a moment, he seemed to hesitate at the door. Tatiana thought he might just repeat his actions of last night, packing her off to the lonely apartment while he went on with his friends. But he crawled in next to her, placed his arm nonchalantly around her, and whistled a merry tune.

"So silent, my love? Won't you sing along with me?" he prompted.

"No, I won't. I can't."

They both knew their brief conversation had nothing to do with making music but spoke volumes about their relationship and the growing divergence of their lives. The remainder of the ride home was spent in empty uncomfortable silence.

Chapter Twelve

TATIANA HELD HER IMPLORING GESTURE TOWARD Narcisse just long enough for the curtain to glide shut. Then she dropped her arms and raced backstage, praying Roland would have arrived while she was dancing the second act. He'd never missed any performance of the company before. When she didn't see him in the throng preparing the stage for the last act, she felt a sour pang of panic. The stagehands and dancers, even Léon, all had the same woebegone expression. We're like puppets whose strings have been cut, she thought.

Tatiana huddled against a discarded heap of canvas backdrop, her feelings snarling within her. She was furious at Roland for shirking his professional responsibilities, especially on a night when she was performing. But deeper than this anger was her fear that Roland had abandoned her. It couldn't be true. Even if things had become so strained between the two of them, he wouldn't desert his company, would he?

Tatiana wrung her hands as she remembered the unspoken war that had raged between them now for weeks. In the mornings they parted wordlessly, Roland for his many appointments, Tatiana to rehearsals. Until tonight, he had attended every ballet faithfully, but after each performance, she would refuse to accompany him on his jaunts to Montmartre. Occasionally they made love in the early morning, as he prepared for bed and she rose from it. Their passion waxed as intensely as ever, but their anger prevented anything more than a temporary truce.

Tatiana shivered as she remembered the unfeeling stare he'd favored her with only this morning. She'd asked a simple question about the orchestra and Roland had looked through her as if she wasn't there. This trivial question had remained unanswered as so many more important questions did these days.

"Well, I tried to warn you," came Micheline's gloating voice, breaking into Tatiana's reverie. Sneering at the Russian girl's puzzled, vulnerable expression, the former prima continued, "With me, Roland did the same thing. Told me I was his moon and stars and then, after a few weeks, pffft!"

"I don't believe you," whispered Tatiana brokenly.

"Don't worry, dearie. There're plenty who're waiting to take his place. They all want to sleep with ballerinas."

With a negligent wave of her hand, Micheline wandered off, leaving Tatiana smarting. Desperately Tatiana told herself, You know she only wants to hurt you. It's only jealousy . . .

The subdued murmur backstage swelled as Roland sauntered in, exuding a ripe odor of absinthe. Léon rushed up to him.

"Where've you been, son?" he demanded frantically, his posture an odd mixture of parental concern and professional disquiet. "It's been terrible back here. *Sacré bleu!* Half the props are missing and the orchestra came in late again!"

Roland threw his arm companionably around the old man's shoulders.

"Ah, you remember how it was, Léon, when you were young," he confided in slightly slurred tones.

Tatiana's lips thinned to a white line. Out of the shadows behind him came her cutting voice.

"But you're not so young anymore, are you, Roland? Life passing you by?"

He spun around to find her, the little Russian who was driving him crazy. It was like living with a damp, clinging cloud. She depended on him for everything, and complained, always complained. The words he had been holding back for weeks emerged, loosened by the liquor he'd consumed.

"What would you know about life? You're so busy hiding in your silly dreams . . . anyone tries to give you a taste of reality, you scream and run."

How dare he act superior, she thought, when he had walked in halfway through the ballet, and semidrunk to boot?

"At least I'm responsible enough to be at the theatre for a performance," she retorted, biting off the words.

"I suppose I should be grateful that you don't act as immature onstage as you do off, you whining, insecure, dependent child."

His barbs hit home, redoubling Tatiana's fury.

Through clenched teeth, she said, "And you, of course, are the perfect mature sophisticate, yes? The world revolves around Comte Roland de Valois's slightest wishes."

She made him a disdainful curtsy.

"Who could resist his zest, his sheer good-natured bonhommie? And if anyone tires of the party, well, she can certainly be ignored. After all, no one's feelings make the slightest bit of difference to the great Roland."

"Very pretty," interrupted Léon, coming up to stand between them, "but the audience is getting restless. Certainly you two can continue this later?"

"We'll finish it now," said Roland, shoving the old choreographer out of the way.

Tatiana, trembling with anger, didn't even notice the interruption.

"Your feelings are coming to mean very little to me," Roland agreed coldly, "since you wallow in them so luxuriously. How could a mere sophisticate such as myself appreciate the depth of feeling you can call up in the blink of an eye?"

"You are over an hour late, Roland," she said, enunciating each word with care to avoid shouting them.

His casual shrug was the last straw.

"Where the hell have you been?" Tatiana exploded. "I need you here when I dance!"

"You need, you need, you need. That's all I ever hear from you!" he shouted.

The company had silently gathered about the sparring couple, mesmerized by their loud, public quarrel. With ill-concealed grins and wide eyes, they followed every exchange intently.

"Is it too much to ask for the man I love to be at my side?" she demanded.

"Every second of every day? You want a watchdog, a faithful shadow, not a lover."

"I want you to be with me," she screamed, "not with that pack of filthy, drunken degenerates you call your friends!"

There was a taut silence.

"You'd better apologize, Tiane," he warned, his eyes dangerously flat.

But she was beyond caution, beyond reason.

"I can't go on like this any longer, Roland. Choose. Either them or me. You can no longer have both."

His eyes widened in disbelief. That clinging, possessive little brat. How dare she give him an ultimatum?

"Either I give up my friends of twenty years or you leave me? Well, be my guest, *ma cherie*. Leave. Leave with my blessing."

It was as if he had stabbed her through the heart with his indifference. An anguished sound somewhere between a sob and a wail escaped her lips. She gathered up shreds of strength.

"You . . . you can't mean that . . ."

For answer, he turned and walked away from her.

"Oh," she said in a high, cracked whisper.

For an endless moment she stood alone, as if incapable of moving. Only her eyes darted frantically from face to face, as if begging for a different conclusion. Her searching eyes lit on the carefully constructed pool on the stage where Narcisse would soon drown. It was only silver cloth stretched over a hole in the stage with cushions for the dancer to land on below. But to her desperate gaze, it was a spot where she could plead once again with her self-centered, uncaring lover. As if in a dream, Tatiana made her way onto the stage and knelt in Echo's pleading pose.

Thinking that her professionalism had finally surfaced, in relief Roland signaled for the rest of the company to assume their positions. As the orchestra hurriedly broke into the ballet's tragic theme, the curtain rose, bringing the audience's growing complaints to an abrupt halt.

Tatiana shuddered as her lover turned away from her yet again. He must love me, he must, she thought as she tried to reach him with the perfect beauty of her dancing. She flung her body into an endless turn, careless of where she might stop. It did not matter. Only love mattered.

The uncontrolled passion of her dance fired the audience to ecstatic heights. They cheered after every overly extended arabesque, every wild spin. Léon watched from the wings, a horrified expression on his face. Tatiana was taking chances no ballerina should dare to take. He turned on Roland.

"How could you say such things to her just before she performed?" he hissed at the younger man.

Roland shuddered as Tatiana barely avoided smashing her leg into a wooden backdrop.

"What should I have done?" he demanded hoarsely. "Let her tie me to a post like a gelded stallion?"

Léon sputtered, "I know, I know, but . . ."

He gasped as the overwrought girl on the stage leaped far too high and came down awkwardly on an unstable ankle. At his side, Roland winced savagely, his whole body tense with worry. He knew she'd almost broken her foot.

The audience was enthralled. They applauded her brilliant-looking daring with large gusts of cheering.

194

"Fools!" hissed Léon furiously. "Don't they know she could kill herself out there?"

Tatiana's stricken heart throbbed at a new wound every time Narcisse rejected her. When he drove her from him, she abandoned the choreography that directed her to watch him helplessly from a rocky outcropping. Instead she continued to plead, pulling at his arm, trying to save him from the silver water. He would not die. She could not let love die.

The young man dancing Narcisse shot her an alarmed look and lifted her away from the audience.

"What are you doing?" he whispered as he lowered her onto the high rocks.

But his words did not penetrate the pounding dread flooding through her. He was blind, she thought despairingly. So blinded by his own self-love, he would destroy them.

With a baffled expression, her partner returned to the choreography, making pleading gestures toward his own watery reflection. He leaned over to kiss himself, lost his balance, and plunged to his "death."

"No! Roland!" Tatiana cried hysterically, and leaped from the four-foot-high papier-mâché construction. As she hurtled down toward the glittering cloth, the trapdoor beneath slid closed. She hit the floor with an ugly, smashing sound.

There was a concerted gasp on both sides of the curtain. The orchestra stopped in an awkward thrust of notes. People stood, craned their necks to see the broken body, lying far too quietly, facedown, on the rumpled silver fabric. One leg bent strangely at the knee. The buzz of shocked speculation swelled.

Roland strode onstage and the curtain closed quickly behind him.

"Mesdames et monsieurs, there will be a short delay. Please take your seats." After a tiny pause, he continued, "If there is a doctor in the house, would he please join me backstage?"

His apparent calm reassured the audience and they obeyed. As he rushed to Tatiana's crumpled body, remorse pounded through him. He had heard her cry his name before she leaped. He knew how fine-tuned were her sensibilities, how vivid her imagination. He knew and yet he had thrown her out of his life onto the stage, callously, publicly . . .

He knelt, cradled her head and legs with his own body, and gently turned her over. Her skin was cold and moist. He had to keep his hands from shaking. Inwardly he cried, Please, Tiane . . . please be all right. At the sight of her unconscious, ice-white face, he stifled a groan. The company around him gasped. Helplessly Roland smoothed the tousled hair from her forehead.

From amid the chorus of worried whispers came a welcome voice.

"I am Dr. Louis Guilbert, monsieur. Allow me to examine her."

Gratefully Roland relinquished his limp burden to the big, capable hands of the doctor. Plump, pewter-haired Guilbert inspected the bruised limbs, frowning at one of the knees. When he probed the small swelling near her ear, Tatiana groaned and her lids fluttered open.

All was shadowy, liquid, before her eyes. Voices drifted like fishes in and out of her consciousness.

A man she'd never met boomed, "Nothing time won't heal. She is a very lucky girl. No bones broken.

Only a scrape or two. And that knee. A bad sprain. She should rest it completely for several days. No dancing, do you hear?"

Where was she? Who was this girl he talked of? A face peered down at her out of the murk. It was Roland. Roland! A sob escaped her as their last encounter returned to Tatiana in all its cutting cruelty.

"My love," he said in a voice that shook. "You're going to be all right."

His hands reached for her.

"Don't touch me," she hissed, and flinched from him.

The movement caused a sharp pain to jolt through her temple.

"I never meant to . . ."

She tried to stand, to run. Guilbert held her back.

"You must rest, mademoiselle," he said firmly. "You cannot even finish tonight's performance."

"Let me go," she cried, wresting her arm from him.

Her head pounded abominably.

Roland tried to reason with her.

"Tiane, listen to—"

"I hate you, you pitiful excuse for a man. Get away from me!" she burst out.

Roland recoiled as if slapped.

"As you wish."

He raised himself from his knees and slipped out between the curtains to inform the audience that the performance was canceled and that their tickets would be refunded. As he stepped back behind the closed curtain, he reminded himself that she was only a hurt child who'd taken a frightening fall. She didn't know what she was saying. There was no point in his taking offense at her unreasoning words. Roland resolved to be patient. But the doctor was shaking his head and Tatiana was nowhere to be seen.

"Where is she?" Roland demanded.

Léon answered, "She ran from us like a crazed thing."

"We've got to find her," Roland said. "She's hysterical."

But a search of the theatre, the dressing rooms, turned up nothing.

"She's in no condition to be alone," Roland said, his eyes dark with worry as they scanned the empty seats without seeing them.

At his side, Léon said, "She's wandering the night streets in nothing but that torn little costume, all bruised, with a bad knee, and thinking God knows what terrible thoughts."

He took a deep breath.

"Poor little Echo."

There was no moon to light the way of the slight figure in shredded toe shoes who bolted down the crowded boulevard as if chased by hungry demons.

No, no, he won't hurt me again . . . like knives, like arrows of biting acid . . . can't bear anymore . . . run . . . run, little Tati . . . run from the words . . . the eyes cold as death . . . the empty hands . . . home . . . no—not the apartment . . . where . . . run . . .

Her thoughts made screaming circles in her mind, driving her on. She didn't notice the chill air of early spring, her own exhaustion, even the throbbing pain in her leg. Her hysteria lent her superhuman endurance that would later exact its toll.

Astonished faces flickered by as theatre goers, cozy in their thick coats and well-bred facades, eyed her disdainfully. In a moment of clarity, she realized how she must look to them, hurtling past in a bloodstained tunic and toe shoes, her face naked with pain. Let them look. I don't care, she thought dismissingly, redoubling her efforts to outrun her agony. Her breath tore in and out of her dry throat as she left the opulent opera district behind.

Run . . . flee the words with hooks that tear, the sneering mouth that once whispered love soft as pillows . . . run.

A smiling face loomed out of the gaslight illumined darkness. It was an odd face, neither male nor female but painted gaudily as a clown, topped with a green pompommed hat. Another face, with a black beard thick as a rug and wet red lips, gave her an interested glance. His companion, three-chinned, with her white hair curled tight as sausages, laughed heartily and gave his back a wallop.

Tatiana slowed, feeling a strange sense of kinship with these Montmartre "grotesques," as she had always called them in her own mind. They lived life in the raw, their feelings of the moment displayed for all the world to see.

Tatiana was jostled by a sword blade of a man with a pencil-thin mustache. She watched as he grabbed his female companion's arm, spun her to him, and slapped her face resoundingly. Tatiana stopped to hear the brightly dressed woman let loose with a torrent of abuse, gold hoop earrings bouncing in the lamplight. He slapped her again before forcing her to come away with him.

The pair was also watched by a drunk in wrinkled clothing, leaning against a pockmarked wall. He saluted their retreating, gesticulating forms with his half-empty bottle.

"Don't let 'em get away with it," he slurred. He broke into giggles and stumbled back into a café.

"Yes. Don't," Tatiana called, her voice a croak in her punished throat.

She stared up at the sign above the café that depicted a dead rat. The danger, the decadence of Montmartre's underground no longer affronted her. It was what she craved—to lose her beaten, discarded self in a sea of drink and noisy laughter.

She pulled open the door and stepped into the smoky, raucous interior. The sickly sweet odor of absinthe mingled with the sour smell of spilled wine. People stood three deep at the bar, shouting orders at a harassed, rumpled bartender. On the stage, a grinning poet-songwriter sang loudly to a few tables ranged around him. The patrons raised glasses and sang the chorus with him.

". . . and on the ground, a red herring—dry, dry, dry."

The rest of the habitués paid him no attention, lost as they were in argument, seduction, or buffoonery.

At a table near the door, a man in a once fine suit of English tweed was shouting, "And I say, the proletariat will no longer endure their degraded lot. Before the year is up, they will rise, as inevitably as the dead from their graves on Judgment Day, and scourge their oppressors. Ah, now here is a perfect example."

The speaker, a chunky, balding man with a moon-round face, grabbed Tatiana's ice-cold arm and pulled her to his side at the crowded table. The six other men evidenced various degrees of surprise but made no move to stop him when she didn't protest.

"Look at her! Dressed in rags, starving-thin, despair in her eyes. A typical victim of our class system, gentlemen. And she's freezing. Here, mademoiselle. Drink this."

He handed the shivering Tatiana a glass of wine, which she gratefully gulped down, welcoming its musty bite. Encouraged by the empty glass, the other men vied to keep it filled and soon Tatiana felt a glowing cloud expand inside her, stealing through her veins, bringing soft relief from memory and cold aloneness. When one of the men offered her a bottle that was almost full, she accepted eagerly, clutching its glistening green neck like an anchor.

"Imagine this waif in a Worth gown, with jewels to match," her savior continued. "How is she different, but for an accident of birth, from any comte's wife or mistress? And yet she is left to rot in the gutter, at best ignored, at worst trodden on."

Their sympathetic glances warmed her as much as did the wine. Never mind that they cared for the wrong reason. Alcohol was blurring such distinctions, leaving her thankful to the point of tears.

"Could any red-blooded man, her father, her husband, her brother, stand by and watch her wither? I tell you, they will storm over the barricades and this time, nothing will stop them!"

"Let's hear from your working-class heroine herself," cried the man who'd given her the bottle.

They looked at her expectantly.

"If we would all love each other . . ." The warmth in her belly made it so clear. "That's the answer, don't you see . . ."

"Here's one who won't be taking potshots at aristocrats," said the questioner with a dismissing wave of the hand.

He turned away, unimpressed by her fragmented message.

"What I want to know is, wouldn't England or Prussian Germany invade to protect the upper classes? After all . . ."

The men fell to discussing international politics, leaving Tatiana stranded at the table like a forlorn seashell after the tide has receded. She raised the mouth of the bottle to her lips to wash away the hovering sense of abandonment engulfing her again. When one more swallow didn't erase Roland's punishing face, she was about to take another when a sudden crash almost made her drop the bottle. Someone had thrown an ashtray against the mirror covering the wall to her right and the shattered glass barely missed her.

As an overwrought man was dragged out of the café by friends, Tatiana found herself staring back at a host of bleary-eyed harridans gaping at her from triangular shards of mirror left on the wall. She screamed at the horrific vision and backed away from haunting splinters of herself, cradling the bottle at her breast. She turned and ran from the café into the safe blackness of the night.

Instinctively she sought the dark side streets, escaping from the revealing lights of the boulevard. It was very cold. Her body covered with a thin film of perspiration, Tatiana shivered violently as she ran her dizzy, weaving pace. Her knee ached miserably, slowing her progress with pain.

She started at a scraping sound behind her, then another. A thrill of fear shot through her. Someone was following her. Tatiana tried to run faster but the footsteps kept pace with her. She felt as though she were stumbling through a childhood nightmare, unable to run away, unable to scream. The horror in the darkness gained on her.

A bony hand grabbed her arm with a grip like iron. She whirled around to find a grinning face, gaunt, gap-toothed, with bulging, staring eyes. Transfixed by terror, she looked helplessly at a stony death's-head.

Its grating gravelly voice said, "I've been watching, waiting for you."

Her thin scream was lost in the frozen air. He clamped his icy palm over her mouth and began dragging her panic-stiffened body toward a dank alley.

"No, you may not have her, foul scum," rang out a mellifluous voice.

Her captor released his prey and turned to face his challenger.

"Who . . . who are you?" Tatiana whispered, shaking from head to toe.

"I am the poet of shadows, my lovely, the knight of alleyways and dark, uncertain stairs."

She barely made out a tall handsome man, thin with hunger, whose clothes, though faded and torn, had once been quite fashionable. He wore a strange hat, wide brimmed, with a long plume that drooped, broken, over one side.

The first man gave a frustrated snarl and pulled out a wicked-looking knife from among his rags.

"Wear this, my bedraggled lily," said her rescuer, throwing her his much-patched cloak, "whilst I dispatch your plagued dragon."

She huddled in the welcome warmth while he crouched, whipping out a blade of his own. The two men stalked each other, circling warily, vagrant starlight glinting on their sharp weapons. With an animal howl, her captor leaped at her rescuer, seeking to sink his blade home in the man's stomach. The two men fell into a desperate huddle, grappling, punching, stabbing.

Tatiana could no longer tell who was who as she stood, mouth agape, transfixed by their raw violence. There was a thrust, and a grunt that sounded almost surprised. Then one body disengaged itself from the other, falling like a heavy sack.

Her rescuer straightened, grinned, and picked up his fallen hat, shaking the dust from it with dramatic flicks of his wrist. Settling it on his head, he walked toward her, his knife blade dripping.

"And now, sweet maiden, I have slain your marauding beast."

"You killed him?" she choked out.

Airily he replied, "Oh, yes. He's quite dead."

He doffed his hat and gestured toward the ground, bowing.

"A gift for my wordless, eloquent compatriots, the maggots."

He held the blade, still bloody, out to her. She took a step back, clutching the collar of the cloak closed with one hand and her bottle with the other.

In the musing voice of a well-fed philosopher over a glass of port, he continued, "Does it not beguile you? That marvelous instant when man becomes wormmeat, with a single poke of the knife. One of the loveliest faces of Mother Nature."

He was mad, she realized, shuddering. He lived in a bizarre, private world she couldn't begin to comprehend.

With an abrupt about-face, he straightened, put on

the fawning expression of a courtier, and made obeisance before her, holding out his still-wet knife.

"I have paid the price you demanded, have I not, Lady Death? The victim lies at your feet, awash in his sacrificial blood. Your kingdom is secure once more. Now I claim my reward."

He advanced on her until the knife blade was an inch from her throat. Tatiana looked up into his crazed eyes, gleaming with unmentionable plans for her, and shrieked. She spun around and raced out of the alley. Fear lent her strength, but even when her pursuer gave up the chase she sped on. It was only when she realized she was among the bright, garish lights of the boulevard that she slowed, coming to a halt at a fantastical doorway. She leaned against a wall, her chest heaving, as she gaped at the strange café.

The entrance was painted to look like the huge, open mouth of a devil, with flame-licked teeth lining its inner rim. From under red horns, slitted eyes glared down on the patrons. The cynical, all-knowing face seemed to say, "Let me swallow you up, little one. There is no hope in my house, no past and no possibility. There is only pleasure, the pleasure of the lost. I am home for the homeless. Where else will you go? Why else are you here?"

A ribbon of devilish laughter seemed to drift inside the door with her, winding itself around her aching throat, cackling victoriously in her ear. "Now choose, chooooose . . ." came the farewell whisper in her confused mind.

For there were two rooms in La Bouche du Diable instead of the usual one. The room to her right shone with bright white light, so glaring it made her blink. The floor was painted with clouds and the waiters were costumed as angels, complete with long white robes, wings, and halos that bobbed comically as they rushed about bringing drinks, and occasionally something more substantial, to the tables. On the walls hung portraits of the Grand Inquisitors, a crusader with many infidel deaths to his credit, and martyrs in the throes of torture.

Tatiana started as a trapdoor opened in the center of the floor and a man whose skin was painted the dead green of a cadaver laboriously climbed out onto the clouds. The waiters dropped whatever they were doing and forced him with kicks and blows to return back down under again. The café's patrons, clearly familiar with this event, interrupted their animated party-going to cheer the rejection of a "soul" from "heaven."

Tatiana began laughing hysterically. She took a desperate swig of her bottle and fixed her swimming eyes on the room's small stage, where a group of can-can dancers had begun their act. They were dressed as skeletons with wide, feathery angel wings. Their skin-tight costumes, painted with bones and darkness, revealed a shocking amount of detail about their plump, muscular bodies. The air rang with lewd comments and requests.

It was all too boisterous and playful. Tatiana turned with relief to the deep soft red light of the second room that bathed its black leather booths in an intimate ruby glow.

No sooner had she taken a step over its threshold than a waiter in a devil costume took her hand and announced, "Welcome to hell, lost soul."

At this signal, the patrons raised their glasses solemnly and repeated his words in a ragged chorus, most not even looking up. The waiter, his barbed tail draped over his arm in place of the usual napkin, led Tatiana to a deserted corner booth, frowned when she ordered nothing, and moved on. She slumped on the cold black leather and stroked the moist petals of the blood-red lily in a smoky vase that decorated her table and all the others. It was quieter here. Customers drank deeply, many saying nothing unless they wanted more liquor. In one booth, a man snored, one cheek resting in a puddle of wine on the black table.

Along the wall to her left unfolded a mural of a dinner party presided over by His Satanic Majesty, drawn in deliberate imitation of Leonardo's *Last Supper*. The diners included such celebrated sinners as Attila the Hun and Bluebeard. The opposite wall was all mirrors, with glass that subtly or intensely distorted whoever stood in front of them.

Onstage, a man in monkish robes was singing of the putrification of the grave in a honey-thick voice. With a shiver, Tatiana looked away only to have her eye caught by a luridly detailed painting that hung over the bar. A naked, snowy-skinned woman writhed in the hairy embrace of a creature with the lower torso and legs of a goat, the wings of a bat, and a snake-fanged face.

In an uneasy moment of awareness, Tatiana felt alarm begin to build within her. What was she doing in this poisonous place? Roland had refused to take her here, even when Marguerite had pouted . . . A sob broke from her throat and she drowned the ones behind it with swallows of wine from the bottle under her cloak. She bolted down more wine, praying for blurred peace. The room began to swing in dizzy confusion.

It was good, the wine. Good . . . kind . . . warming. She swayed, waving the bottle before her, humming a tune only barely recognizable as Echo's theme. All her demons were gone, struggling in vain to reach her through a bank of alcoholic cloud. It was funny, she thought, giggling. In hell, her devils couldn't get her. Couldn't . . . get . . .

"Selfish bastard," she muttered to herself. "Damn him."

Her head was swimming as she unsteadily raised the bottle for another drink.

A man in the next booth leaned over and said thickly, *"Alors, ma petite.* Didn't anyone ever say to you, don't drink alone?"

"No. Never," she affirmed with great seriousness.

"Come 'n join us. There's plenty room."

In her blurred vision, they looked like a circle of hounds, hairy and warm, huddled together.

"Why not?" she slurred, and got to her feet with great difficulty.

It was like crossing an ice-bound river without skates, negotiating the few feet between her booth and theirs. But finally she was part of them, raising her bottle in time to the incoherent song they were singing, resting her reeling head on the bulky arm of the man nearest her. What did anything matter, her mind muttered. She was with her friends. Having a good time.

"Hey, whatsa matter with him? He's not drinking."

Tatiana waved her bottle at a man bent over a sketch pad at the shadowed far end of the booth.

"Don't worry about him," said a companion with exaggerated slow exactitude. "He's always drawing."

She was at the point of offering him her bottle but changed her mind when she noticed how little wine there was left. She took another swallow.

The pianist began playing the theme for the can-can

and the dancers from the other room climbed up on the stage. Now they wore bat wings but otherwise did the same provocative act.

One of her companions began pounding on the table, yelling encouraging words to the women on stage kicking their legs high. Tatiana gave him a hard shove.

"You call that dancing?" she demanded. "They're ridiculous. No form, no control, no—"

"And what do you know about it?" he shouted. "They look good enough to me."

"You have the taste of a blind pig," she snarled, flaring with the quick rage of drink.

The insulted man raised his heavy hand to strike her but his friend, who had initially invited Tatiana to join them, grabbed the raised fist.

"Cool down, Jacques. Look at her. She's jus' a girl with a big mouth."

How dare he belittle Dmitrova? Tatiana raged to herself. She threw open her cloak, let it drop, and leaped up onto the table. The room whirled sickeningly as the men tried to protect their drinks from her staggering feet.

"I can do better than those cows onstage," she shouted in answer to their shocked exclamations.

She tried to steady her body as one might pull on the reins of a runaway horse. Her high-kicking legs sent their bottles flying to shatter on the floor. Like love, her mind shouted at her. Kick it, it breaks into a million, stabbing pieces.

Waves of vertigo made the table loom up at her and shrink again. She saw her leg high in the air, her hand groping to grasp it, but neither limb seemed to belong to her. She knew no sensation but pain as flames from the red floor seemed to leap up and engulf her.

209

She tried to fly, to soar above the splotched tapestry of sweating firelit faces. Where were her wings, the wings of dream that had always carried her past . . . Gone. Reduced to ashes. Leaving her to the agony of memory.

The room tilted wildly, a roaring conflagration. Greedy hell fingers reached for her, to pull her down into an inferno of pain. She was falling, falling . . .

"Look out!" André Bonfleur shouted, his sketch pad dropping to the floor.

He rose from his seat and rushed to her. He was too late. She hit the table headfirst with a sickening thud. André's frantic face appeared above her. She had one last thought before she yielded to the red dark she had been courting all the long night. Why André? Why isn't it Roland holding me, here at the end of the world?

Chapter Thirteen

IN SEMICONSCIOUSNESS, TATIANA STIRRED. SOMETHING rough and scratchy grazed her bare skin. She tried to shift her body, only vaguely aware of its unresponsiveness.

Soft light flickered before her. Dim thoughts, too slippery to be anchored down, swam through syrupy layers of fluid and vapor and flitted past her.

Abruptly her eyes opened and focused on what seemed to be a garden riotous with flowers and smiling faces. She closed her eyes. The vision was gone and she knew nothing.

Later, she struggled up from her dreamless state again. Her head pounded with dull constant pain. Her mouth was dry and her tongue felt bloated and huge. She tried to speak out but the hammering in her ears was too loud and her lips wouldn't meet to articulate anything but moans.

She blinked, barely able to lift her lids. A somber woman in dark shadows seemed to stare at her. Only a spark of candlelight reflecting in her eyes gave the woman a sense of life. It was too much for Tatiana. She sank back into the void.

It was light again and a fresh warming breeze danced about her. She breathed deeply and evenly, inhaling a thick sweet scent of jasmine. She turned toward the beguiling fragrance, willing it to pervade her dull senses and awaken her. With every breath, she seemed to grow stronger. At last—it seemed an eternity—she was revived.

Tatiana looked about. She had no idea where she was, except that she was lying on something. Frightened, she went to sit up but her body was immediately wracked with pain. Vivid images of her two falls hurtled into mind and she carefully drew rough covers about her for solace and escape.

She began to take an accounting of herself. She was more alert now that the pain in her head had subsided. She stretched slowly, pampering her body. A wrist was bruised and slightly swollen and there was a large bump on one hip. Not too bad, Tatiana judged, considering the punishment her body had undergone.

But when she bent her legs, the left knee exploded in shards of agony. Tatiana clutched at the wounded area, a shriek rising to her lips and tears rushing to her eyes. As gently as possible, she laid the leg straight again, flexing her feet to relieve the pain. Her right ankle immediately telegraphed a series of urgent twinges to stop that movement too.

Self-pity overwhelmed Tatiana. She hugged herself

tightly and the tears fell freely. She was alone, unloved, lost and at the mercy of whoever had taken her in. Why couldn't she have been swallowed up by the pond on the stage? she wailed to herself. Bitterly she recalled the room of demons. Better to have been left a broken heap on the floor of Parisian hell. She fell back against thin pillows and sobbed herself to sleep.

It was still light when she awoke, not the white light of morning but a more subtle golden hue. She roused herself soberly, drained by the prior anguish of first full consciousness. Now she devoted herself to discovering her whereabouts. First she determined she was on a makeshift bed, a couch of sorts, raised slightly higher than usual, as though on a platform.

Everywhere else in an orderly jumble were stacks and stacks of artist's canvases. Some were completed. Others were in the midst of creation. Still others were being resurfaced with thick slabs of gesso burying old unsatisfactory works.

On the walls hung a few framed pictures. With a shock of recognition, she saw the idyllic garden and the portrait of the woman of her dreams. It hadn't been delirium after all, Tatiana realized. She had just been drifting in and out of consciousness.

A large easel dominated the center of the room . . . no, the girl corrected herself, the studio. Several high tables sported tubes of pigment, jars of oils, different-length brushes, and an assortment of palettes. There was very little evidence of the person who lived here beyond a discarded moldy loaf of bread, a case of empty wine bottles, a couple of dingy shirt collars strewn over the back of a shabbily upholstered arm-chair, and an incongruous basin garishly painted with cavorting nymphs and shepherds.

With great care for her wounded knee, she hoisted herself into a sitting position and leaned back with an arm tucked behind her head, propping it slightly forward. She turned her face toward the open window so that the gentle breeze might fan her skin. The stirring air played with her hair, tousling it into softly flowing waves about her shoulders.

"Stay as you are. Don't move."

Tatiana twisted and tensed, wincing as darts of pain shot through her. The imperious commands had come from somewhere in the room . . . and from someone who had been watching, spying, on her. Vulnerable, she clutched the worn sheet to her breasts, realizing at the same moment her torn costume was gone and in its place a man's shirt.

From behind the wooden easel on which sat a canvas of huge proportions emerged a stern André Bonfleur. His gaunt prominent features were belied by the unruly mop of dark curls which threatened to spill over his forehead into his eyes and by his cherry-red cherub's mouth defiantly fighting back a small smile. He limped toward the bed on its dais.

"So, you have returned to the land of the living?"

His question wasn't out of place considering how he'd found her. And now, to find he had cared for her . . . where was Roland? Her catapulting thoughts played havoc with her weakened mind. She tried to calm herself.

"I'm in your debt, monsieur," she said formally, lowering her eyes. "I must have been a great bother to you."

"Nonsense, mademoiselle. I consider you my latest example of 'good works.'"

214

He struck a pose often seen on park statues.

"Voila! They will remember me as Saint André."

Tatiana couldn't help laughing.

"And you, my dear," he said, pausing to stare at her, "you shall be known as my Lazarus."

The implication of having been brought back to life from hell's door was not lost on Tatiana. But the embarrassment she might have suffered was replaced by shocked gasps. André hauled the easel around to face the bedridden ballerina.

"I don't often do this—show my model a half-finished piece of work. But under these rather extraordinary circumstances . . ." he said.

There, on canvas, Tatiana had been captured. He must have painted me while I slept, she thought. She should have felt outraged, that he used her so in her helpless state. But she only wanted to cry.

The painting had exposed her. She stared at her ravaged suffering soul, curled in repose like a baby. The face echoed a turbulent swirl of muted blues and grays streaked with reds and violets above her recumbent figure. The confusion of nightmare and dream in her world was unmistakable. Was she so transparent or was it only that demon of an artist who could see into her and pull her inner torment outward?

Another horrible thought crossed her mind. The painting was too complex, the layers of pigment too thick. How long had he been working at this canvas? How long had she lain in bed, drifting and sleeping in unconscious limbo? She looked to Bonfleur for the answer and, afraid to learn it, buried her face in her hands and wept.

André was at her side in a moment, coddling her.

"No, no, Tatiana. What will the neighbors think . . . that I beat my models and starve my little pet orphans?"

His well-intentioned quip only provided fresh grounds for more tears. André was right, Tatiana conceded. She was an orphan, far from home, devoid of loved ones and destitute.

"There, there, *ma petite*. You've had too many shocks, including this painting. Just lean back in my arms like a little baby and Père André will take care of you."

There was something soothing, albeit ridiculous, about Bonfleur's mothering. But Tatiana felt magic in it too. Seemingly out of nowhere appeared a bowl of hot delicious broth which the artist fed to her as though she were indeed a helpless baby. He even hummed a tuneless old lullaby, and like a spell of enchantment, the song swept away her tears and her fears.

Soon she was laughing at an absurd story about three poodles and an abbé, made even funnier by André's impersonations. So warm and relaxed was she that she didn't notice how much her eyelids drooped. She dozed off, her face still wreathed in smiles.

"Now you shall really rest," he whispered at her sleeping form.

He adjusted the covers, searched for his hat, and went out into the haze of the late afternoon. He hailed a carriage at the outskirts of Montmartre which deposited him within minutes at the home of the Comte de Valois.

Roland, wild-eyed, answered the door, flinging it open with such force André was almost bowled over.

"Good God, man," the artist exclaimed, trying to regain his footing. "You look like death warmed over."

The nobleman clawed impatient fingers through his unkempt hair and rubbed three-day-old stubble with his other palm. His eyes were red and deeply hollowed.

"Haven't slept," muttered Roland.

"Have you eaten?" André asked with genuine concern.

"Only drunk," came the reply.

"That, I can tell. Let me in, de Valois. We have business to discuss."

"Not today, Bonfleur," Roland said gruffly. "I'm in no mood . . ."

"I'd like to sit down," persisted André. "My leg is hurting. And Roland . . ."

He paused to give the distraught man a cool penetrating glance.

". . . you'll want to hear what I have to say."

In resigned silence, Roland gestured to André and led him to the drawing room. Pouring a cognac for each of them, Roland swallowed his in one deep gulp. André set his glass down.

"She's safe. I've got her," he stated simply.

Roland looked up quickly from his goblet and stared hard at his friend. He replenished his cognac, gulping it down again.

"Thank God."

The warm kick of the liquor and intense relief washed over Roland. Safe. Alive. His worst thoughts were banished from his mind.

"You found her?" he grunted.

Bonfleur nodded.

Roland averted his blurry eyes. He couldn't let André see how confused . . . guilty . . . glad he felt that it had been the artist who found Tiane and not himself.

"Where?"

"Drunkenly dancing on top of a table at La Bouche du Diable," André said calmly.

Now Roland met André's serious expression and the two men exchanged looks charged with meaning. Both had witnessed the ballerina's hysterical behavior at the theatre. Only André had been present at Tiane's lowest moment. Again Roland turned to his cognac for surcease. André's message was too clear. What was to be done with Tiane?

"You know I love her," the haunted man growled.

André gave him no breathing space, sharply asking Roland, "Enough to take her back?"

Roland turned away and began pacing the length of the room. The last three days had been sheer hell. No, he corrected himself. More like the last three weeks. Their relationship had soured like rotting grapes on the vine. He couldn't deny the wealth . . . the welter of feelings he had for this child-woman, but he couldn't wade through them all. It would be like choosing an exotic coffee only to find it brewed as thick as molasses.

He stopped in his tracks and regarded the artist, who seemed to have an endless supply of irritating patience. The answer was clear to Roland. He wanted to say to André, I love her but I can't live with her. Instead, he lurched toward the window and stared out at the busy boulevard.

"I want to see her," he grumbled.

André stood up, took a quick sip of the fine aged cognac, and limped over to Roland. He put a hand to the taller man's shoulder.

"No, *mon ami*," he said gently. "Neither one of you is ready to forgive or forget. Tiane has been devastated . . . physically and emotionally. And you, old friend

. . . I think you must ask yourself what it is you really want."

Again Roland was embarrassed by a wave of gratitude and relief.

"Damn it," he shouted testily, pushing André away. "How can I know until I've talked to her?"

André became cold, formal and sardonic.

"She can't take another round like that elegant display backstage the other night. She needs time, at least a few weeks."

His voice softened cajolingly.

"I'll be in touch with you."

Roland glared at André with suspicion. A few weeks alone with Tiane, he thought darkly. That's all the time he'd need to take advantage of her. She was a beautiful captivating woman. Any man would want her and Bonfleur would have her all to himself. Could Bonfleur actually steal Tiane away?

Surly, he boasted, "I could have her back anytime I want."

The words were out of his mouth before he could mold them into something less oafish. He took another swallow of the fiery amber liquor. Tiane had done this to him, turning him into a small jealous creature.

André drew himself up to his full height and gave the comte a withering glance.

"Is that what concerns you?"

Shaking his head, the artist walked from the room and left the apartment.

In a storm of sullen self-righteousness, Roland grabbed up the near-empty bottle of cognac, emptied the remnants into his glass, and retreated to his post by the window. Damn André for coming. Damn him for reminding Roland that Tiane was still in his blood.

Tiane, he cried to himself, it wasn't supposed to be this way, to end like this.

André returned to his atelier by early evening, having stopped along the way to purchase some fruit, cheese, a rasher of bacon, an extra-long baguette, a bottle of vin blanc, and, with his last sous, a bouquet of flowers.

At the creaking click of a key in the door, Tatiana awoke from her nap. She tried to rise from bed but found herself still too weak from pain.

"What a baby I must seem to you, Monsieur Bonfleur," she said sadly, "as helpless and useless as a newborn."

"First of all, mademoiselle, as you are accepting my hospitality, you must be Tatiana and I, André."

"André," she echoed.

"And second, you aren't helpless because you're going to help me devour this meal," he said, displaying his wares. "And last but by no means least, you're not useless, because after dinner you shall pose for me with these flowers."

Tatiana's eyes grew wide with astonishment and with hunger.

"Yes sir," she said like an obedient child.

He handed her a glass of wine, which made her feel dizzy but dulled the still bothersome aches. She watched André in fascination, wondering if the man had more than two arms and hands. He seemed to eat, feed her, gesticulate as he talked, pour more wine, and keep sketching at the same time.

Once during dinner, they were interrupted by raucous knocking.

"Hey, Monsieur l'Artiste, when are you coming to

the café tonight? I have a new singer I want you to hear . . . and draw."

It was the raw scratchy voice of Zazou Picard. Tatiana froze in fear. André patted her hand and put a finger to his lips indicating silence.

"Not tonight, Zazou," he called out.

"What do you mean 'not tonight'? Isn't my rotgut good enough for you, Monsieur Bonfleur?"

André winked at Tatiana.

"I got a commission, madame. You know, a painting for real money."

"Ooh-la-la," cried Zazou in a high rasp. "Bonfleur selling out for the all-mighty franc. Wait till they all hear this one."

Her heavy steps resounded down the stairs. André and Tatiana burst into laughter. Finishing their meal, André showed the girl his sketches of her. They were of all sizes, at all angles on the sketchbook pages, and of all shadings. They showed Tatiana sleeping, drinking, frowning, smiling, pensive, sitting, lying down, full face, profile, dark, light, shadowed, realistic, impressionistic.

"But André, all this in a night and a day?" she gasped.

"No," he said with caution. "You've been here three days."

Three days, she thought, unable to grasp the loss of time. She had dance commitments. Roland would be expecting . . . Her mind stopped abruptly at Roland. It had been three days. Did he know where she was? Had he come to see her only to find her asleep or unconscious? Where was he now?

André took her hand and tilted her chin so that she had to look at him.

"Roland knows. I've spoken to him."

Wildly she searched the resolute face for more information.

"Did he . . . is there a message?"

She half hoped and half dreaded André's answer.

"No," he said softly.

So, she thought, that is that. The beautiful dream had ended. Her eyes filled with tears.

"Excuse me, André. I'm about to make a nuisance of myself."

He handed her a worn handkerchief from his pocket and stepped over to his easel.

"I expect you are," he agreed, and began laying out his paints.

When Tatiana awoke the next morning, she felt strangely refreshed, almost reborn. Had the tears she shed over Roland begun to cure her feelings of helplessness? A fresh warm wind blew through the open window, bringing with it the irresistible odor of a country onion soup.

The girl's stomach growled in anticipation. If I'm hungry, Tatiana posed pragmatically to herself, I must be better. Gingerly she tested all her sore spots. The swellings were down and the bruises had begun to change from livid purple to a dullish blue-green.

She was able to sit up without causing further pain. Looking about the room, her eyes fell on a portrait of Yvette, the sweetly sad café can-can dancer. Tatiana thought about the young girl, who, though barely twenty years old, seemed like an old woman. How many times had Tatiana watched the dancer timidly prowl behind Roland, anxious to steal just a moment of the great impresario's time to beg for an audition with the ballet company?

How pathetic Yvette had seemed, with her gaunt body veiled under layers of petticoats, a perpetual handkerchief daubing her nose, and her pleading eyes at odds with the garish stage makeup she wore. Roland had paid no attention to her. Only André, with his keen eye for character, had listened to Yvette's little dream.

In her portrait, André had captured the fragile hopes of a young girl made brittle and old before her time. Tatiana was taken by the subtle play of light and shadow, warming her skin yet showing its sad decay at the same time.

The same pattern seemed to emerge from a self-portrait not far away. Unmistakably the artist, André had depicted himself before a canvas, hair wild as ever, eyes sharply focused, even the deformity of one leg apparent in the odd flowing line of his trousers . . . and the smock, full and loose, freely spattered with reminders of other pictures already painted.

Tatiana froze. She knew that shirt well. She was wearing it. A deep crimson blush heated her cheeks. André had obviously seen to her every need, even removing the tattered wisps left of her costume and replacing them with his own shirt.

Hot with shame, she thought for the first time of her impulsive actions. She could have awakened to consciousness to find herself at any itinerant stranger's mercy. Cold faceless memories crept forward of an alley in Montmartre and her struggle with the wild antics of two insane men. If it weren't for André . . . The grateful prayer stuck in her throat.

Only a few months ago, hadn't she felt the same way

about Roland? And now? She lay back down in bed, surrendering to her feelings. She still loved him but she hated him too. It was his fault she was here . . . his fault he preferred his Montmartre cronies to her . . . his fault she was hurt and couldn't dance . . . his fault she thought of André's studio as a safe haven . . . his fault she wasn't in Roland's arms right now.

He had flung her away and so she would stay away, out of sight. So much for the meteoric rise and disappearance of Tiane Dmitrova, prima ballerina assoluta. Her chin quivered but she thrust it forward with resolution.

The studio door swung open. Bonfleur gamely limped in with a steaming tureen in both hands, a fresh bouquet of flowers tucked under one arm, and a net bag hanging from the other.

"Thanks to Zazou we eat this morning!" he proclaimed in fine spirit.

Tatiana sat up quickly, smoothing the tangle of hair about her head and wiping away defiant tears.

"So the patient improves despite herself," he said perceptively, noting the war of emotions on her face. "See what Saint André has brought his poor maimed pigeon today."

He peeled off the lid from the huge soup bowl. One sniff of the rich onion broth with its thick chunks of bread and cheese was sufficient to quell even Tatiana's black mood. Bodily needs came first, her stomach reminded her forcefully. She ate greedily.

André laughed but Tatiana didn't mind. He had been so kind to her, never admonishing her for her mad dash to oblivion or her subsequent tearful spates. He had housed her, clothed her, fed her. Let him laugh, she thought, and joined in. In short order she gulped down a second bowl with remarkable ease.

"That's much better," he said, nodding his approval. "Now, Tatiana, it's a perfect day outside and one not to be wasted."

Unbelieving, she asked, "You're leaving me?"

Childish fear suddenly took hold of her while André bustled about gathering brushes and knives, pigment and palettes.

"If you want dinner tonight, I must sell a painting."

Remorse struck her. Not every Parisian lived like Roland. She thought how much she must already have cost André.

"And anyway," he was saying, "you're coming with me. You can help me today. So, here, catch."

He threw the net bag to the bed.

"No, no," Tatiana cried. "I . . . I don't think I can walk."

"Pah," the artist retorted as he sorted and pitched old canvases about the room. "You're talking to an ex-medical student. I've examined your bruises."

He stopped and turned to look at the protesting girl. His meaning was explicit. When he brought her, unconscious, to his studio and changed her clothes, he had seen her nude . . . with the cold clinical eye of a doctor or an artist.

"You're on the mend, Tatiana. Trust me."

Tatiana stared back into the calm chocolate eyes of the artist, finding reassurance without condemnation in his gaze.

"You can't run away from your problems," he added. "You tried that the other night without much success, *oui?*"

She nodded, mesmerized by the truth of his words.

"Are you thinking you might just spend the rest of your life reclining on my couch?"

Tatiana colored, stammering, "I . . . I . . . don't know. I haven't been thinking . . ."

It was André's turn to nod.

"You're welcome to stay here—for a while—as long as you make yourself useful. Remember our conversation last night?"

"Yes, André."

Tiny tears appeared in her eyes and she strove not to let them fall.

"You're right. I want to be a help to you," she said fiercely. "I owe you so much already."

He waved his hand in denial, then pointed to the bag beside her. She opened it and pulled out a serviceable day dress. It was clean though shabby. Darning was obvious though it had been done in small delicate stitches.

"You may thank Yvette later," André stated, back again collecting his equipment.

Gingerly Tatiana tested each step between her make-shift bed and the model's screen in one corner of the studio. She found she was more stiff than sore. Once behind the screen, she donned the smock and washed in a basin of water. The dress fit well enough and the boots buttoned tight enough to stay on her feet.

Again Tatiana was smitten with shame. She wasn't used to being on the receiving end of Montmartre's generosity, something she didn't think even existed here. Bonfleur and Yvette, with little to spare, even Zazou with her leftover soup, had given freely of themselves to a veritable stranger. She emerged feeling chastened and eager to prove herself of some value.

Almost finished gathering his supplies, Bonfleur cast a harried eye at her and stopped in his tracks.

"You could be a country lass of thirteen with your hair down, natural color in your cheeks, that simple dress. Yes, a girl fresh with the best of naivete and wise with the innocence of a child. I will paint you like that."

His remarks satisfied Tatiana. She had done something right.

"Here," he ordered, "take this box of paints and my folding stool."

Together, going slowly down the flights of stairs, they set off into the village streets of Montmartre. André was right, Tatiana admitted to herself. Her body was resilient. She was healing. If anything, she felt light-headed from the tangy spring air breezing about and was glad of André's staid pace.

Tatiana soon discovered Montmartre by day was a different world from its nighttime frenzy. It exuded a shabby friendliness instead of nightmarish decadence. From every open window, the fragrance of newly baked sourdough emanated. Small dogs raced about the cobblestoned byways and children played with wooden hoops and crudely carved hobbyhorses.

Flowering vines disguised the crumbly walls of apartment houses and small dwellings. Behind each one, Tatiana could just make out the first growth of vegetables shooting up in tiny backyards. From one small house, a heavy door creaked open and a woman wielding a broom swept several cackling chickens from inside her foyer out onto the street. Further along the winding roads, artists displayed their paintings along garden railings and small storefronts.

Then, before Tatiana's delighted eyes she saw a beautiful ruin of a park dominated by a windmill.

"I've never seen anything like it," she breathed, "except, perhaps, in a dream. No, no, André," she added in excitement, "I've seen it in your paintings."

"Yes. La Moulin de la Galette," explained Bonfleur. "It's truly beautiful, with a character all its own."

He took her into the gardens, no longer fettered by human design. There, yellow-green grass grew long, too long to mow. Flowers, once confined in rigid rows, dotted the lawn in uncontrolled splendor. There were splashes of pink and red poppies, yellow and white daisies, orange and purple lilies. Even the white-latticed gazebos, in which people danced and ate, were interlaced with morning glories.

There were young people everywhere with the bloom of health on their cheeks and a sparkle of merriment in their eyes. Even the elderly leaning on their canes seemed infected with a sprightly joy. The more daring girls challenged each other to a contest of high kicks in the manner of can-can dancers to the chagrin of their mothers.

"This is Montmartre, too?" Tatiana wondered.

"Even so, Tiane. There are two sides to every coin, *n'est-ce pas?*"

They stopped before one latticed arbor, empty except for a wicker chair. André looked up at the sky, consulted the sun's position, and trod determinedly to his left a few paces.

"There!" he announced. "Help me with my easel, Tatiana. Good. And now, if you will take your place in that chair . . ."

"But I want to help you, André. Can't I set out the paints or keep your brushes clean or—"

"You can be exasperatingly dense, *ma fille*. Now, go sit down."

She frowned.

"Then I'm only a drudge to you after all."

"Tatiana," he repeated, "you are modeling for me."

She balked and violently shook her head.

"Oh no, André. I couldn't. People will stare at me."

"But you're used to that, dancing on stage," retorted Bonfleur.

White-faced now, she could only whisper, "That was before."

"I see," André said, nodding noncommittally. "And this is 'after.'"

Tatiana pleaded with her eyes.

"You may be interested to know," he said, removing his jacket, "that in the art world it is the painter who is the star. People, should I be lucky enough to attract any, will watch me rather than my model."

He stared hard at her.

"I know about pain, Tatiana. I would never cause you any." Then he ignored her completely as he began to set out his paints in vertical globs on the palette board. First came the hot colors of yellow, orange, and red; then the earth tones of ocher, sienna, and umber; finally the cool-hued greens and blues.

Meekly, Tatiana climbed the short steps into the open summerhouse. She sat stiff and uncomfortable, moving to the right or left as André ordered, stretching a leg or an arm, tilting her neck and head as necessary. Finally she got the pose just right.

"I'm only doing this, André," she muttered tartly, "because I respect you. Because I can't figure out how you carried my dead weight up all those stairs with that leg of yours. But most of all because I wish to help pay for supper tonight."

André threw back his head and laughed and Tatiana

had to join in. When he looked back at her, she was relaxed.

Her eyes scanned the intimate scenes all about her, the groups of friends, the families, the lovers. A great sigh of undisguised empathy escaped her lips as she saw lovers strolling, lovers sharing cups of chocolate, lovers lying next to each other on the lawn. Roland, her heart called out, where are you?

The quality of womanly yearning she had been suppressing now emerged and spread about her like a sacred halo.

"That's it. That's it." André smiled. *"Fantastique!"*

Chapter Fourteen

OVER THE NEXT SEVERAL DAYS, TATIANA IMMERSED HER-
self in the world of art. She went everywhere with
Bonfleur . . . on routine stops to his paint and canvas
supplier, to his agent, to his poster producer . . . on
endless jaunts to the Moulin de la Galette where she
would pose for him, to tiny crumbling churches, to the
humble abodes of Montmartre's own proud inhabitants.

André painted washerwomen at their boring, bone-
wearying tasks. He sketched the sadly adultlike antics
of truant children. He drew thickly muscled draymen,
well-to-do dandies, dapper soldiers on leave. He was
most fascinated by the young women of the country
and city who flocked to Montmartre looking for the
elusive, seductive spices of life. Too often, their star-

filled eyes became blurred and dimmed by life's grim realities and the cutting edge of laudanum.

Through André's art, Tatiana began to see the totality of life. It was not as she first thought or had been brought up to believe. Life was not a set of extremes. In her mother's world, one either danced or one did not. One either played the patronage game or one starved. One either reached for the richest prizes or one was nothing, like a peasant.

From the vast panoply of life peopling André's canvases, Tatiana became aware of the nuances, the gray areas where class and culture met, mingled, and re-formed. There were still the excessive dreams and tumultuous nightmares; many of the artist's subjects were proof of life's highest successes and its worst degradations. But above all, Tatiana started to understand the ordinary everyday world with its cumbersome routines and sweet moments.

The goal was survival, André's canvases seemed to tell her. Give vent to the exhilarating sensations of victory. Feel the heavy weight of painful sorrow and loss. But survive to know them again another day. Tatiana saw the message as clearly as though he had written the words instead of created the image.

One fair afternoon as the sun slipped away into twilight, André slapped down his palette knife and wiped his brow.

"Enough for today, Tatiana. The light is gone but the heat remains. I'll finish up in the studio."

Bonfleur had chosen an obscure corner of the old park to paint the girl this time. He had rented a bicycle and posed Tatiana so that she stood next to it but looked away in the distance at a flock of migrating birds flying in the sun-dappled sky.

Tatiana steadied the unpredictable huge front wheel and walked toward the easel.

"May I look?" she asked respectfully.

While waiting for an answer, she poured turpentine into a battered tin cup and began to dip the paint-thick brushes and knives into the sour-smelling fluid. André smiled to himself.

"There's a change in you, you know? At one time, you might have scampered over and squealed your insistence to see my progress yet hide it from any other viewer."

Tatiana blushed, protesting, "I never did that, André, although I might've wanted to. You're teasing me."

"But you see, my wise one, we are both right. You have given up your tears and you interpret my words correctly."

Tatiana looked at her friend with grim eyes, judging herself.

"It wasn't so long ago that I only heard what I wanted to hear and saw what I thought was there."

She paused in thought while the two of them worked side by side in companionable silence.

"You know, André?" she began. "When I first met you and then when I first came to stay with you, I thought of you as an artist, not a person. Wherever you went, there was a sketchbook. Your studio seemed like a place of work, not a place to live. Your eyes always seemed to be balancing and weighing the worth of a possible subject."

"And now?" he prompted.

"Now I see you as a person first, my dear friend, who happens to paint with a ferocious talent."

Bonfleur shifted to his stronger foot, burying his

head among the paint tubes he sorted, blushing with quiet pleasure at Tatiana's compliment.

"Your sketchbook is a lifeline, isn't it," she continued, "your eyes like a cipher. Your atelier is filled with creativity and individuality. You and your work are one, André. What an accomplishment."

Her voice was tinged with bitterness and self-doubt. Bonfleur set down the last tube of pigment. He took her trembling hands in his.

"And you think less of yourself still? After my supreme tutelage?" he mocked.

In a small voice André had to strain to hear, Tatiana said, "I always considered myself a dancer. Life was dancing. Even love was dancing. Now that has been ripped from me. What is left to me, André? What can I become?"

Her eyes glistened with the approach of tears.

"Now," André commanded. "Come. Look at this painting. Tell me what you see."

She looked from the artist's kind gaunt face with its merciless gaze to a miraculous scene of hope and beauty. White fleecy clouds flecked with shadows of sunlight and spring dotted a perfect aquamarine sky heightened with natural shadings of peach and violet. In the center of a grassy meadow stood the supple vibrant figure of a woman. She dominated the painting with her strength and vision.

More than the line of her body, it was the overwhelming impression of clear-sightedness which gave life to this woman. With feet firm on the ground, with hands sure in their grip of the fragile bicycle, her eyes beamed ahead to the soaring birds. Somehow André had imbued passion and determination into the woman's gaze. The darkly flowing hair, the long graceful hands and fingers, the healthy pearl glow of the skin, and the black piercing eyes were unmistakably Tatiana.

"I . . . am . . . this person?" stammered the girl.

She thought back to the other pictures André had done of her: the neophyte's first frightening success, the mad wraith dancing on tabletops, the unawakened child caught in sleep between life's dream and nightmare, the woman consumed by loss staring out an open window into the dark, the young girl on the brink of womanhood wondering and yearning. And now this woman, healed and whole.

"It's how I see you, what you can be," he explained.

Her chin quivered slightly.

"Without Roland," she murmured, half in question and half a statement.

"Regardless of Roland," replied her friend.

Tatiana stared at the painting. She liked what she saw.

That night as Tatiana removed Yvette's tired dress and put on André's old smock, a new spirit enlivened her.

"André," she called out from behind the screen.

"Oui?"

His voice seemed far away. He must be in the little alcove he annexed as his private room, she thought. Tatiana had never been in it, either by design or invitation. She respected Bonfleur's privacy as he did hers.

She had come to think of the alcove as his magician's lair, never knowing what might come out of it next. It could be a complete gourmet dinner, case after case of empty wine bottles, assorted props with which she was meant to pose, even a violin he played once.

"Before you leave for Zazou's tonight," she went on, "I'd like to discuss something with you."

He came out in his drinking clothes.

"No sketch pad tonight?" she inquired.

"I proclaim this my night out, actually my night off . . . from good behavior."

Worried, she frowned, "On my account?"

"No, *mon amie*. Blame it on my leg."

He smiled a little crookedly and she knew he must already have consumed a bottle in his room. She also knew she couldn't stop him.

"You will be careful?" she asked shyly.

She glanced quickly at the crippled leg. Although liquor might kill the constant aching reminder of André's bad limb, his limp always seemed even more exaggerated by the effects of drinking.

"I promise to return and paint you till one of us turns old and gray," he said, smirking, and saluted her.

"Before you go, André . . ." She paused, searched for the proper words, and finally blurted out, "I must have some other clothes. I can't subsist on Yvette's castoffs and your shirts. I need my own clothes."

Tatiana's declaration couldn't have had more effect than if she'd thrown ice water in his face. There was a long silent pause while Bonfleur sorted out her sobering words. He sat down, his hands limp at his side. Finally he looked up at her. With each minute, she was resembling his vision more and more.

"Does this mean you're ready to see Roland?" he asked seriously, cautiously.

She sat down opposite him and stared straight ahead, beyond him.

In a quiet voice she answered, "Yes."

"The moment has come," he said aloud but for

himself. "The little dove's wing is healed. She's ready to fly away."

He shook himself out of his reverie and rose. He walked toward Tatiana, the limp very apparent.

"I shall find Roland tonight and tell him."

He turned and went out the studio door. His unrhythmic footsteps echoed down the stairs.

Tatiana's eyes shone with sympathetic tears for her friend. Letting go was the hardest task of all. She knew.

Early the next morning, too early for someone with the breadth of hangover André possessed, the artist prepared to withdraw discreetly from his studio. Roland was coming.

"I'll be at Zazou's," he told Tatiana, "playing nursemaid to my poor ravaged body. I just haven't decided which to tend first: my head or my gut."

He gave her a brief hug and groaned, putting a shaky hand to his throbbing head.

"You'll be fine," he mumbled. "I'm the one we should pray for."

André left as Tatiana smiled tremulously at him. Her heart began to flutter and the calm she wished to possess seemed alarmingly out of reach. She would not let her nerves claim her, she declared to herself.

Determined to present herself to Roland with all the aplomb of her newly developing maturity, Tatiana looked about the studio. She would straighten some of the jumble, she thought. If the studio looked its best . . . if she looked her best . . .

Her hands flew to her hair. She had adopted the popular style of wrapping her long locks into a tight corkscrew atop her head. It would never do for Roland to see her like that. Her eyes fell with dismay onto the decidedly ordinary, in truth, quite shabby dress she wore. The way she looked, Roland could easily mistake her for any one of Montmartre's common female horde.

She dashed to the narrow mirror André had installed for his models, only stopping to gather up a comb, a second used dress, and a thin shawl Bonfleur kept on the premises. Harried, she glanced in the mirror. One hand was already unbuttoning her blouse and the other tore at the pins which kept the topknot erect.

She stopped abruptly.

"There's nothing wrong with the way I look," Tatiana said aloud, scanning her reflection.

She had spent the last few weeks wearing these dresses, happy to have them, happy they were clean. She had been unconcerned about other people's opinions of her and, she decided firmly, she wasn't going to start worrying now.

"Roland will have to accept me the way I am."

With careful deliberation, she rebuttoned the blouse, smoothed the hair back into place, and recinched her belt. She looked hard at herself. It wasn't just her style of clothing that had changed. Her face seemed different. Her eyes might have lost some sparkle but her gaze was surer. As for her body, she observed, it was still dance worthy, although for all the thick soups and bread André forced her to eat, the skirt seemed a little tight at her waist. She nodded at her image, satisfied.

Tatiana walked back to the couch and sat staring out the window into the heart of Montmartre. She thought back to the last time Roland and she had been together, had fought. There had been no understanding then. Roland had accused and blamed her and she had retorted in kind.

Forgive and forget. Was it possible between them anymore? She knew she was willing to forgive Roland. These weeks with André had shown her Roland had not been off the mark. In many ways, she had acted like a spoiled child, fueled by her mother's dreams, her own talent and success, and, yes, by Roland's magnanimous gestures. But now she had learned what it meant to be responsible and she thought she might be ready to try her wings.

Her heart pounded loudly, though, at the likelihood of forgetting. With a sudden rush of worry, she wondered whether Roland would be willing to forget her. Her thoughts exploded at the harsh premise and she could only feel the crush of fear overwhelm all other senses.

A world without Roland. It couldn't be. Hadn't she known from the first moment he held her that he was the love of her life? She frowned and her jaw tightened. Could she really consider a world without love?

Tears filled her eyes. Brusquely she willed them away. She had no time for such indulgence, she told herself. Roland was on his way.

At that moment, Roland de Valois rounded the corner and paused. He looked up the street toward Bonfleur's atelier and covered his brow with an arm to diffuse the sun's glare. He started forward again, his gait more measured.

Tatiana stared, unable to tear her eyes from his familiar form.

"But the light's gone out of him," she gasped in wonder.

She strained to see him more clearly, closer. The dapper clothes were the same. His stride, full-legged, still claimed the ground beneath him as his own. But there was a joylessness, a dullness to him, as if he were going through life automatically. She couldn't quite put her finger on it. It was like he was missing some part of himself.

Tatiana nodded slowly to herself. Roland had changed too, then. She felt a ray of hope spring within her. Forgive and forget, she repeated to herself. But how to get on from there? She turned away from the window as Roland disappeared from view and his footsteps could be plainly heard in the stairwell. She stood, feeling calmer and a little sad, and waited for Roland's knock.

Roland glanced upward. The square spiral of rickety banisters leading to Bonfleur's atelier suddenly reminded the comte of an open web. A vision of Arachne, the legendary Greek woman for whom all spiders are named, weaving her snare of deceitful beauty, flashed before his eyes.

"Bah," he grumbled disparagingly.

He was perspiring and wiped beads of sweat from his forehead.

"It's the sun," he said, trying to convince himself. "It's only April and already the heat is oppressive. It makes one's mind wander and play tricks on itself."

He had to laugh at himself. Tiane as the clever spider woman . . . the notion was ludicrous. She was no more capable of setting a trap for him than a child was capable of outwitting a general. Mademoiselle Dmitrova was a dreamy girl, capable of great feeling, great flights of fancy, great moments of fury. Like all women, he thought, her scars were of the heart, painful but invisible.

He pictured her as he assumed he'd find her. Pale but whole, her bruises all healed, she'd be reclining on a divan. She'd offer him her hand and the moment would be fraught with emotion. Their eyes might exchange tenuous feelings and fragile hopes. When their fingers met—for of course he would be the gentleman and take her hand—a shock of familiar intimacy would jolt both of them. She would cry. Haltingly she'd tell him how much she wanted to come back to him . . . The scene would play itself out like a cliché.

He paused at the first landing. He had to admit he wanted her to return . . . for the ballet. The Companie Valois wasn't the same without her. As for himself, to live again with her, to fight the same battles, to endure the pouting, to wait for the short-lived ecstasy of their lovemaking, was he ready to undertake it all again? He didn't know.

Roland started up the second flight of stairs. He thought back to the last few weeks without the moody ballerina. True, he'd never felt more relaxed, more carefree. It was like being on holiday. But at the same time, he was constantly nagged by a sense of loss. He seemed to float through the days and nights, hardly aware they had come and gone. The intense satisfaction was missing from sure-fire punch lines, fine wines, sensational performances, the successful completion of a business deal. None of them touched him deeply anymore.

He rounded the next landing and kept climbing. Maybe when he saw her, Roland thought, he'd understand and know what he wanted. When he saw her, he'd decide the terms for taking her back. Roland kept a steady eye upward.

Finally at the third story, he stood before the door. In the midst of cracked and peeling paint, André Bonfleur had inscribed his artful signature. All that was on the other side of that pathetic door belonged to Bonfleur. All but Tiane, Roland thought. With unnecessary force, he brought his fist to the wood twice.

Tatiana answered immediately. The door opened, the young woman stepped back, and Roland entered the homey art studio. They stared at each other as if needing a third person to reintroduce them.

Haltingly she said, "You . . . you look well, Roland."

It was the polite thing to say but hardly the truth. Up close—she could only be nearer if she were in his arms—he looked tired. Perhaps his nonstop schedule was finally catching up with him, Tatiana thought in surprise.

Roland was caught completely off guard. Already the clichéd meeting he had foreseen was altered. The girl stood firm and strong before him, captivating, in an aura of glowing light and self-possession. She was as poignantly beautiful as ever but there was a new unmistakable presence of authority about her. He was stunned. How could she have matured into a woman in a matter of a few weeks?

"I hoped to find you better," he began.

"And so you have," Tatiana completed.

She was overwhelmingly aware of his nearness. With one or two steps she could hold him, be held by him, erase all the mistakes they had made. But she waited for some cue from him.

Roland fought a mad urgency to grab her and kiss her, brand her again with his mark. But something had changed. Not the stakes, for they were the same. No, Roland realized, it had more to do with which of them had the upper hand. Until he stepped into that room, he'd been convinced it was he, as usual. Now he was no longer sure. So he waited, feeling tense and awkward.

Tiane broke the silence.

"I want to go to the apartment," she said bluntly.

An unexpected surge of gladness charged through Roland, exciting and revitalizing him. With dawning recognition, he felt how intensely he had missed her. Go cautiously, he warned himself. Don't let her know how much you care. He chose his words precisely, carefully.

"I want you there, Tiane," he said calmly, almost indifferently, while his heart raced with joy, "but things must change. We can't go on as before. I won't spend all my time coddling . . ."

Tatiana listened and then stopped listening. Undeniably, she loved Roland. But she wasn't a child and it seemed Roland could see her no other way. As much as she yearned to share her life with him, she couldn't go back to the old disagreeable pattern.

He was right on one count, she mused. Things had changed. She had changed. She had to interrupt him, to stop this embarrassment.

"I don't think you understand," she said softly. "I mean I want to get my clothes."

Roland shook his head in puzzlement. Nothing he planned was working. At every juncture, she switched the rules. For the first time, the reality of losing her gripped him.

"You're not coming back?" he cried.

She reached out a tentative hand to soothe him, explain away the hurt. Her heart tugged at the obvious longing in his voice.

"No, Roland."

She withdrew her hand, a little unsure of her new strengths.

"I'm not ready yet."

Her face was an echo of his own confused yearnings but Roland only saw it as typical of her childish uncertainty.

"Not ready yet," he mocked her. "Not ready for what, Tiane? To come back where you belong? To the ballet? To my home? To me?"

Fueled by his own words, Roland's anger raged unchecked. How dare she refuse him. His eyes roamed about the studio.

"Just where are you planning to stay?" he demanded.

He gestured wildly at the clutter of canvases and paint pots.

"You choose this squalor over the home I've given you?"

Unbelieving, he paced the length of the studio, sneering at Bonfleur's bric-a-brac as if they were worthless scraps. He flung aside the curtain that separated André's alcove from the rest of the atelier and glanced in. Men's and women's clothes, a hip bath, rusty shaving paraphernalia, books, and an unmade bed greeted Roland's gaze.

Tatiana felt the heat flush across her cheeks. This was a Roland she had never seen. He must be mad, she thought, to invade another man's privacy. She hesitated, then stepped forward to stop him.

"No, Roland, you mustn't . . ."

He turned on her and the explosive danger in his face scared her. Mute, she backed away.

"Where do you sleep?" he demanded in deceptively quiet tones.

Tatiana didn't answer. She couldn't answer such a ridiculous question.

"Have you been struck dumb," he shouted, "or are you hiding something?"

The girl stood there, numb. She could only shake her head and raise her hands toward him in supplication.

He looked past her, around her, suddenly mesmerized by the paintings on the walls and at the easel. Tiane was everywhere, Bonfleur's Tiane as the artist saw and knew her. There she was in muted light with a book. Here she capered about in rosy tones with scampering kittens. Again it was a dewy Tatiana caught in the first step out of the bath. And now she gazed up with intimate satisfaction from a rumpled bed.

Roland, in shock, tore his eyes from canvas to canvas and back to Tatiana.

"In his bed?" he exploded. "You're sleeping with Bonfleur?"

He crashed about the room like a wounded bull.

"No, please, stop," Tatiana whispered. "It isn't anything like that."

Her mind was whirling. After all they had been to each other, how could he believe she would sleep with another man?

"You were mine," he said fiercely. "I loved you, took care of you, gave you everything. And what is my reward?"

Roland was so worked up, he hardly cared whether he spoke fact or fancy. All he knew was that she had defiled their love and nothing could repair it.

"One silly fight and you run off like a child, straight into the arms of the first man who'll have you."

"You can't believe . . . I didn't . . ."

She looked at him entreatingly.

He stared at Tatiana and saw guilt in her expression, in her stance. Convinced by his own story, he saw her as a complete stranger. He'd never known her. She'd never touched him.

"You're not ready?" he repeated. "Hell, I'm not ready. I wouldn't take you back now if you begged me."

His words stabbed at her heart. It was her fault their love was dead. Beyond his anger, she felt the sharp jabbing hurt, the sense of betrayal, the emptiness. She brooded, letting the emotions fill her, feeling them for Roland and for herself.

She felt the waves of agony surge . . . crest . . . recede. She looked up at Roland. The emotions wouldn't come. They weren't honest or real. They were calculated to assuage Roland's hurt, to give backbone to his anger. She smoothed her skirts and continued to appraise the man she had loved.

She stepped toward him with her own fire now ablaze. He's pulled the last string on this marionette, she thought determinedly.

"Perhaps we loved each other, Roland, but nothing else you've said is true."

"You're here, aren't you?" he scoffed.

"Yes, thanks to a good friend," she answered emphatically. "But I haven't slept with André. And if I had, you still don't have the right to tell me who my friends or bed partners may be."

She pushed him into a chair.

"You made it abundantly clear I didn't own you and now you must understand you don't own me."

He wrenched out of the chair.

"That's fine with me."

Roland slammed out, racing down the stairs and out of her life.

Tatiana's legs gave way and she sank to the floor. She stared at the closed door.

"It's over," she said vacantly, repeating the fateful words until they mixed with her tears. "How could he be so blind?" she wailed. "How could he make up such nonsense?"

The door opened quietly. André Bonfleur had returned. At the sound of his thumping gait, the miserable girl looked up.

"I still love him," she cried at the artist.

Bonfleur dropped to the floor beside her, tucking his crippled leg beneath him. He took the young woman in his arms while she wept out her unhappiness.

"Hush, now, my dear," he comforted her. "Sometimes people who love one another can't live together. Perhaps in time . . ."

He sat quietly with her until the storm of tears abated.

"You know, *ma chérie,* you can stay here as long as you wish. I can't offer much . . ."

"Oh, André," Tatiana whispered, "dear, kind, sweet André. I'm so grateful to you. You are such a good friend. You've taught me so much."

She got up from the floor and offered a hand to André.

"But it's not right. I've imposed long enough. After all, you're in the business of art, not hostelry," she said, laughing.

André rose, leaning awkwardly on Tatiana's arm for a moment.

"What will you do, then? How will you support

yourself? Not," he cautioned with a mock frown, "by dancing on tables?"

"No, I promise."

She smiled and grew serious.

"I'll find my own apartment and maybe I will dance again . . . but not ballet with the Companie Valois."

She winced. It was painful to say the name. André patted her arm, sensitive to her sorrow but proud of her growth.

"One more sketch?" he asked. "Before I lose my most profitable model?"

She smiled tremulously at André with the love of friendship.

"This won't be the last," she pledged.

She walked to the center of the room while André poised himself on the edge of the couch that had been Tatiana's bed. With the old professionalism stirring in her blood, the dancer began a series of limbering stretches. Satisfied smiles wreathed both faces as each practiced his or her own incredible talent.

Chapter Fifteen

CHEZ CLAUDE, THE CAFÉ WHERE YVETTE WORKED AS A can-can dancer, was a bleak, unscrubbed little place. Quite different, Tatiana thought, from the rich, buoyant clutter of the Bouteille Riante. Tatiana kept a politely interested look on her face, not wanting to hurt Yvette's feelings. The undernourished girl had very kindly offered to ask her boss to hire Tatiana. One has to start somewhere, Tatiana thought, trying not to allow the café's general atmosphere of neglect depress her.

Though all nightspots shared the same forlorn air during the daytime, Chez Claude seemed empty of charm or even life. The few sunbeams that had managed to penetrate the dust-clogged windows did little to enliven the scattered, cheaply varnished tables and hard little chairs, the chipped, unwiped bar counter that displayed neither bottles nor glasses, or the single dark unframed print tacked crookedly to the stained wall.

Yvette led the way to the bar, where a bald, big-bellied man with long drooping gray mustaches was scowling down into a cash-register drawer.

"Monsieur Claude?" she said in her flyaway voice.

He looked up, his hard little eyes annoyed.

"Excuse me for bothering you, but I was wondering if . . . well, now that Genevieve is so sick, there's a spot open for a dancer here and . . . This is my friend, Tatiana Dmitrova. She's looking for work and . . . and she's very good."

Yvette gave her impassive employer a pleading look from her big, sea-gray eyes.

"Do you think that, perhaps, my friend could have the job?"

"You know something?" Monsieur Claude asked in heavy, viscous tones. "I'm sick and tired of you girls. I'm thinking of closing the act completely."

He banged the drawer shut and Yvette flinched.

"I've had nothing but trouble. And this one, Genevieve, she lasted less than six months. It's always the same. Drink, laudanum, and then they cough their lungs out. You girls are all alike."

"Oh, but . . . but Tatiana's not like that at all. You'd never have to worry . . . ."

Tatiana winced at the way her frail little friend was cowed by the rotund man's bullying.

He snorted his disbelief.

"That's what they all say. They'll be on time, they'll never miss a night, and then—"

"I am available starting tonight," Tatiana inserted

firmly, cutting off Claude's whining diatribe. "I have trained with the Imperial Ballet in Russia for ten years. My last role there was a costarring one. Recently I danced with the Companie Valois here in Paris."

"So you're a little ballerina," he sneered. "Floating around the stage on your toes and catching rosebuds. You think that silly fluff prepares you to dance here?"

"Monsieur Claude, do you want me or not? I haven't all day to discuss it."

She was hard-pressed to remain polite.

There was grudging respect on his face as he answered, "All right. I like your attitude. I'll give you a try."

He eyed her up and down.

"You'll fit into Genevieve's costume. The show starts at ten o'clock sharp. Be here at nine."

He turned to Yvette and quenched her happy smile effortlessly.

"You brought her here," he barked, "so you show her the routine. She'd better be good or you're both out on the street."

"Yes, Monsieur Claude. *Merci*, Monsieur Claude," breathed Yvette, smoothing her washed-out blond chignon with an unsteady hand as she turned to go.

She didn't say another word until they were back outside on the boulevard. Then she turned and gave Tatiana's hand a squeeze.

"Oh, you did it. I'm so happy. I really thought he wasn't going to take you."

Tatiana gave her a grateful hug.

"I was afraid he really meant it about closing the show. What a bear! He must be awful to work for."

"Yes," agreed the gaunt, pale dancer, "but I have no choice. He gave me a job when no one else would.

251

There are hundreds of girls like me, and very few jobs. I'm lucky to have it."

Tatiana saw the shadow of fear that never completely seemed to leave Yvette's waiflike eyes loom large.

In a voice calculated to cheer up her newfound friend, Tatiana exclaimed, "Well, your luck has rubbed off on me and I'm very grateful. Now that I've got a job, the next step is to find a place to live. Do you have any more rabbits to pull out of your magic hat?"

"If you'd like, you could move in with me."

There was veiled pleading in the sad eyes.

Tatiana said gently, "How kind of you to offer. But for me, part of learning to be independent is having my own place."

Yvette gave her a soft, resigned smile.

"If I hear of any vacancies, I will . . . oh, how could I be so stupid? In my building there is a room for rent this very minute. It would be perfect, Tatiana. It's cheap, and so close to work."

"Wonderful. Let's go see your landlord."

Tatiana was amazed at the low price Yvette arranged with the landlord until the two girls climbed up four dark flights of stairs to view the apartment. When Tatiana saw the tiny room, its walls peeling, its single window opening onto a fetid alley, she had to hide her dismay. The only furniture consisted of an ancient sagging couch that gave up clouds of dust when the two girls sat down on it, a rickety table and one stool, and an old wardrobe with its door fallen to the uncarpeted floor.

"Oh, you're lucky," said Yvette, smiling as she inspected the room. "You've got a wardrobe. I hang my clothes on nails in the wall."

She got up to inspect the minuscule grate that Tatiana doubted would do much to warm the room.

"The fireplace looks like it's in good condition. So many of them are clogged."

Yvette stole a glance at her friend's face and sat down on the stool. Her voice was warm with sympathy.

"It must be quite a comedown for you, a great ballet star, reduced to living like this."

Tatiana realized her face was an open book to the street-wise can-can dancer. It was hard to hide her shock at the squalid conditions of the room.

"Listen," Yvette continued. "It's not that cold anymore. You can use some of my things. I'll bring my blanket up, and I have a—"

"Yvette, I can't take your blanket. You are a darling to offer, but you don't have to worry. I have some things of my own."

"You mean, at . . . at your other place?"

Yvette, like most of Montmartre's inhabitants, had heard of the explosive breakup of de Valois and his prima ballerina.

A sad calm look settled over Tatiana's face. It has to be done, she thought. The last step.

"I'll be back in an hour or two. Maybe you can help me sell some of my old furs."

"Oh, that'll be easy. I know a man who's in the business."

Yvette was a rare person, Tatiana thought warmly. Almost penniless herself, she gave eagerly, even if it beggared her in the process. As the two women hugged each other farewell, Tatiana read in her friend's fervent embrace sympathy for the difficult visit ahead. The Russian dancer determined at that moment she would buy Yvette something special, both practical and extravagant, once the furs were sold.

The last person Roland expected to find standing at his door was Tatiana. In her much-mended, ill-fitting dress and tattered shawl, she looked like a laundress down on her luck. Except for her poise. No working girl would show such self-possession. How could she look at him so calmly after all the things he had called her, things she had richly deserved?

Tatiana looked up into his face, where amazement was giving way to anger, and said in a remote voice, "I've come for my things. I hope this a convenient time?"

Nonplussed, he stood in the elegant little entry as she moved past him, in the direction of the bedroom. He stalked after her, only to be taken aback again. Working briskly, she was pulling garment after lavish garment out of her polished mahogany wardrobe and making two piles on the bed.

Anger flared inside of him when he realized what she was doing. Everything she had brought from Russia went on one side while all of his gifts to her, her Parisian clothing, landed on the other heap.

How dare she reject everything he had given her, and so matter-of-factly, as if their tempestuous life together had meant nothing to her? She ought to be cowering, hunched over in shame and raw regret at her own irremediable destructiveness and betrayal.

Instead, while he seethed, she opened her white velvet jewelry case and eyed the pieces inside with all the passion of a pawnbroker considering yet another lot of dubious heirlooms. The sapphire necklace he'd given her on the train landed atop a black Worth gown. The tiara he'd had made for her first night onstage followed it.

He took one step toward her, about to shout at her to take everything and leave him in peace, when she looked up from a bejeweled Russian cross and stopped him with a glance. It was a weary glance, detached, resigned, that said, "Oh dear, must you take us through that again?"

His mouth snapped shut. He would die before he gave her the satisfaction of knowing how much it meant to him. He beat back his fury like a wild man, refusing to let her see how deeply she was hurting him as she filled two valises with her Russian belongings and carried them, along with an empty carpetbag, into the living room.

Every ballet print she took from his walls, every photograph and knick-knack of hers she removed from tables or shelves, made him feel more alone. She was turning his apartment into a wasteland and he couldn't watch. Roland spun on one heel and marched back to the bedroom. Plucking the tiara from the heap of scented, glimmering gifts, he returned to her. She was standing at the front door, about to open it.

Thrusting the delicate circlet at her, Roland growled, "Here. Take it. Take it all."

Mutely she shook her head. Poor Roland, she thought. It's still unfinished for him. He knew the affair was over but he couldn't accept it. The realization gentled what would otherwise have been a cold, flat statement. She searched for words.

Finally she said simply, "They're not mine anymore."

She closed the door behind her softly.

Roland was left holding out the rejected tiara. Inside him there was a strange feeling of something breaking, slowly and painfully, falling to pieces. For a moment he stood irresolute, the diamond-frosted wreath quivering in his hand like a trapped, shivering butterfly. Then he flung it from him, not even noticing as it hit a wall, bent in two, and fell, ruined.

The apartment was stifling, enervating. Everywhere he looked, there were empty spaces, taunting him. The walls seemed to murmur, "not mine anymore . . . not mine . . ." When a rearing wave of restlessness rose within him, he yielded to it gratefully, hurling himself out of the apartment to somewhere, anywhere.

He found himself at the theatre. Roland shouldered past the startled doorman without a word of greeting, took the stairs three at a time, shoved open the door to his office, and slammed it shut behind him. He threw himself into his lush leather armchair and glared at the piles of correspondence awaiting his response. He would get some work done, damn it, and the hell with could-have-beens and improbable dreams.

Roland took great satisfaction in tearing up his notes for a tour of European capitals he had planned for Tatiana. He sent cancellation letters to several trains and hotels, each one he wrote making him feel slightly better.

He turned to reworking his next Paris season, crossing Tiane's name out night after night. Alarm grew in him as he watched the column of thick black slashes obliterate his entire offering for next year. She was to have dominated the company, his prima. Without her, he would have to build all over again, from the ground up. He could not imagine going back to the Michelines, the Linettes, the other mediocrities he had once considered his stars. There was no one, no one who could fill Tatiana's shoes.

The rage that heaved and bubbled just below the surface of his mind came scalding out again, making the sinewy hand holding a fountain pen grip it so tightly that it broke. Blue-black ink spattered over the just-completed letters, the yet-unopened correspondence, the ivory-veined, honey-colored marble desktop.

Wiping at his hands ineffectually with a handkerchief, angry as only a dominant beast can be who has been goaded to the edge of his endurance, Roland stormed out of his office, bent on finding Léon Martinon. If there were a dancer who could take on the challenge, Léon would know.

Halfway down the hall, Roland felt a faint, insistent tugging on his sleeve and looked down to find Émile Aubisson, his blond, effete ballet master, smiling up at him.

"I'm busy right now," Roland told him. "Is it important?"

"Oh, yes, Monsieur le Comte. I would not disturb you otherwise. Could you come in here for just a moment?"

He pulled an unwilling Roland into the practice room where a lovely little white-blond dancer stood ready at the barre.

"I've been watching her bloom for months now," Émile murmured, "but I waited until I was sure she had everything before I called her to your attention. I promise you'll adore her extension."

All of a sudden Émile was such a damned irritation,

with his breathy voice and constant habit of stroking those swooping golden mustaches. They were bigger than he was.

"Make it quick, will you?" Roland said.

Émile glided over to the nervous girl, patted her shoulder reassuringly, and said, "This is Paulette Ardoinne, Monsieur le Comte. She is seventeen years old, and she will dance part of Act I of *Sleeping Beauty*."

The ballet master, proud as a new father, gave a nod to the pianist and the audition began. What the hell was he talking about? Roland snarled to himself after less than a minute. The girl had about as much feeling as an omelet. Irresistibly Tatiana's version for her audition with Léon played across Roland's mind.

Every fault the little blonde made stood out in stark contrast to Tatiana's emotion-charged interpretation. He was blind to the new girl's impressive technique, her poignant sweetness that would leap across any set of footlights and touch an audience. She had one, irremediable flaw. She was not Tatiana Ivanovna Dmitrova.

"Stop. I've seen enough."

The dancer, pianist, and smugly humming teacher all stopped in their places, identical expressions of surprise on their faces. The blonde's soft, chocolate-colored eyes gazed at Roland with melting helplessness.

Unbearably irritated, Roland shouted, "You call that dancing? I've seen cows do better stepping over a bucket."

The girl's eyes filled with tears. Émile's mouth dropped open.

"Whoever told you you could dance," Roland sneered, "must've been looking at you out of the wrong end of a bottle."

There was a kind of acrid satisfaction in being cruel, in seeing plump tears begin to spill down the dancer's cheeks. She, at least, cared about what he felt.

"But, but, Roland," sputtered Émile, formality forgotten amid his shock and dismay. "She's a little jewel. You can't just—"

A black look from his employer cut short whatever admonition Émile had been about to bestow.

Roland made for the door, flinging back over his shoulder, "Don't bother me with garbage again, little man. I won't overlook it next time."

The wooden stairs took the punishment of Roland's slamming heels as he hurried to pin down Léon. The choreographer's disgusted voice reached Roland long before he reached the stage.

"Imbeciles! Spawn of donkey! Are you dancers or legless cripples? We will do it again, and this time count. Count! One, one-two, three-four, one, one-two . . ."

Was Tatiana the only ballerina who could take direction? Roland demanded of himself, watching the performers stumble through the sequence yet again. He strode to Léon's side, near the left wing of the stage, and exchanged a frustrated grimace with his old, stick-pounding friend. When the group on stage had finished, Léon took a deep breath, preparatory to another one of his well-known blasts. The dancers gave one another resigned glances, bracing themselves.

"You're fired, the lot of you," came Roland's hard-bitten voice. "Collect your things and get out. If you can't take the simplest orders, why are you standing on a stage?"

His bitterness poured itself out on the defenseless figures before him.

"We don't have to tolerate rank incompetence . . ."

"What?" Léon cried. "You're firing my dancers? You want fleas and dancing bears up there?"

Roland stopped in midharangue, deflated suddenly by Léon's amazement.

"Damn, what's the good of it anyway," he muttered brokenly to the silver-maned choreographer. "She's never coming back."

"Ah."

It was a dry sound, full of pain. Léon's stick fell from his hand. He looked all his age and more.

"I was afraid it would end this way."

The resemblance between the two men was striking at that moment. Their melancholy expressions looked identical, as a ghostly, infinitely graceful figure in a nymph's moon-hued tunic waved farewell in both their minds, and turned away. They were strong men, formidable men, who took the deepest, most secret longings of humanity and made them real, using only the power of their imaginations and the strength of their spirits.

But the dreams were all blighted now. Roland's desolation rose up in him like a scorching, relentless whirlwind of sand, withering all feeling, all hope.

"I can't . . ." he whispered, and then he was gone, rushing out the front door of the theatre to the dubious solace of the bottle.

Léon and his dancers confronted each other in the long silence that followed.

Finally, with a deep, heartfelt sigh, the choreographer said, "All right, children. Back to work."

The well-used, comfortable-looking chair covered in bright chintz hit the floor of Tatiana's new apartment with a resounding thump.

"Mon Dieu, monsieur, please be careful," called out Tatiana to the disappearing back of the drayman who hustled down the four flights of stairs for another load.

"It's no use," Yvette told her, "they're all like that." She moved toward the dusty couch, saying, "We might as well be comfortable until—"

"No, don't sit down yet," ordered Tatiana. "I'm starting with that filthy thing."

Taking a rug beater out of a long parcel, she began flailing the couch, coughing and waving as the dirt she released swirled about her head in filmy clouds.

"Mademoiselle," came a strained voice, punctuated by coughing. "I'm leaving the rest of your things just outside the door."

There were several more choking coughs. The hurried sounds of his footsteps and accompanying sneezes were the last they heard of the drayman.

"You look like you're going to make rain." Yvette giggled as she ran to help, picking up the stained cushions and hitting them on the floor.

She flung open a window while Tatiana fanned the door to disperse what seemed like three generations of dust. When the air cleared, Tatiana pulled out a deep crimson velvet drape and deposited it with a flourish over the indistinct olive gray of the sofa.

"What do you think? Could I entertain royalty?"

"Oh, it's beautiful," Yvette exclaimed, stroking the worn though still luxurious, rich fabric. "I couldn't imagine why you wanted me to convince Girot to throw it into the bargain."

She rubbed her cheek against the covered couch.

"You did such a good job on that old skinflint, Yvette," Tatiana remarked as she swept the floor with decisive though ineffective strokes. "I was thinking maybe you should go into the pawnbroking business yourself."

She shot her friend a playful look.

"Here, let me do that," Yvette offered. "You start hanging up your clothes."

Yvette scoured the floor with the skill of long practice, her face falling into its habitual unhappy lines as she recounted an experience she had.

"I learned about that business the hard way. Once I had a lover who gave me a real ruby set in gold just before he left me. I wanted to keep it, but I was too hungry for such luxury."

Yvette unconsciously punished the floor with her broom.

"I took it to Girot. He worked me over so well he had me believing it was a fake. Out of the kindness of his heart, he said, he'd give me the price of a meal. *Cochon!*"

She worried the broom in the musty corner near the couch.

"I found out later from my ex-lover the ruby was genuine. He had stolen it from some grand lady at the opera. I went back to Girot and told him I'd turn him in for fencing stolen goods. He said he'd take me down with him but finally gave me a little money to keep me quiet."

Yvette propped the broom against a wall and sighed. The floor was spotless.

"You learn after a while, Tatiana. The world is full of cheats and liars. For a girl like me, with no family, no protector—"

"But I think you've done very well," Tatiana exclaimed. Smiling at Yvette's surprised look, she continued, "You've got a room, one steady job, and you've just acquired a second. I'm officially hiring you as my interior designer. Now, where do you think this little rug should go?"

Tatiana held up a cream-and-coffee patterned secondhand carpet with rich ivory tassels only slightly stained. She pitied the poverty-stricken, victimized little dancer and was determined to bring a note of cheer into her bleak life.

The unsure yet eager way Yvette took up the game spoke volumes about her sad existence.

"Why, right by the couch, my dear madame, where . . . where you can place your feet on it when you rise in the morning."

"And these prints of Taglioni? On the east wall, do you think?"

"Oh, let me see," Yvette breathed, abandoning her sophisticated role.

She examined each of the six pictures with shining eyes.

"Where did you get these?"

"I brought them from Russia. And these as well."

Tatiana pulled a set of black, highly lacquered boxes from her satchel. The two girls studied the fanciful pictures painted with jewellike brightness on each lid.

"The perfect spot for them, as well as the only one, madame," Yvette said merrily, "is on this table, but I would strongly suggest a bit of dusting first!"

Little by little, with much play and examining of treasures, they set the tiny room to rights. The sun was setting when Tatiana called a halt and pulled out the pâté, bread, and wine she had purchased earlier in the day.

"Ohhh," said Yvette when she saw the food. "How marvelous! But I can't eat your pâté. It's terribly expensive."

Tatiana realized that the French girl was serious.

"But then you force me to eat it all and I will get terribly fat and Monsieur Claude will fire me on the spot and I will have to go to work for a drayman who will make me drag heavy chairs up stairs and . . ."

Yvette began laughing helplessly at her friend's dizzying tirade.

"*Alors.* I must save you from such a terrible fate."

The simple meal was quickly dispatched amid much happy teasing and mutual congratulations as Tatiana and Yvette surveyed the richly cluttered, homey nest they had created.

"One more swallow," Yvette said, holding up the bottle.

"It's all yours. I should be a little sober my first night on stage. Speaking of stages, I think you'd better teach me the can-can. We have to dance in two or three hours."

"Well," said Yvette, "you probably know most of the movements so I'll go through them fast."

She stood and dusted crumbs of crusty bread from her lap.

"First, there's the splits."

She pulled her much-mended forest-green skirt above her knees and launched herself swiftly to the floor in split position, her arms arced above her head.

She rose quickly, saying, "And there's the high kicking."

Yvette flung her right leg straight up so that it was perpendicular to the floor. She left it there casually as she talked, using it to demonstrate the hand-to-foot grab, the twirling "round the world" of the lower leg, and the sudden kick that could knock off a patron's hat.

Tatiana was amazed at how astonishingly limber Yvette was. The Russian girl recognized the basic dance movements but realized they had been pushed to their utter extreme. It was part of the can-can's charm, she thought. To an observer, the dancer's body seemed completely elastic, not subject to the normal limits of bones and sinews.

"Now, here's how they go together."

With those words, pale gaunt Yvette became an outrageous, robust-looking flirt. A lusty, inviting grin on her face, she sauntered, flipped her skirts enticingly, displayed her legs over and over, each way more daring than the last, and ended by turning her back, uncovering her derrière, and flaunting it at an imaginary audience.

Yvette met Tatiana's unbelieving stare with a short, self-deprecating, very French shrug.

"C'est le can-can. You've done the movements but the timing, the whizzing tempo, are different."

"Something like this?" Tatiana asked, rising from the velvet-shrouded couch and repeating Yvette's routine perfectly.

"Mon Dieu! I've never seen anyone pick it up so fast," Yvette said, and shook her head wonderingly.

"Well, remember, I've seen it in the cafés many times."

"Even so . . . And you will remember it all?"

"As you pointed out, I already knew the movements. Don't worry. Monsieur Claude won't fire us."

"There's just one more thing," Yvette murmured,

returning to sit on the couch and inviting Tatiana to join her.

"The can-can is a . . . well, it is a dance of invitation, you know? Crude . . . of the earth."

Tatiana patted her friend's thin hand.

"I'm a pretty good actress, Yvette. It will be fine."

"But ballet is so light, so beautiful."

The French girl gave a long, tremulous sigh.

Softly, wistfully, she added, "A ballerina's home is in the air with dreams, not on the earth at all."

"Why, you love ballet, don't you?" Tatiana cried.

With a flash of realization, she finally understood why Yvette had hovered about Roland, almost haunting him, waiting for a moment to be recognized.

Yvette hung her head, her cheeks pink, and mumbled, "It's all I've ever wanted in my whole life: to be a ballerina."

Tatiana asked gently, "Have you seen very much ballet?"

Yvette's words poured over themselves in an eager tumble.

"At the carnival, when I was a child, there was a beautiful lady with stars in her hair. She seemed to float across the stage. I don't know why, but she took a liking to me. Maybe she saw how I worshiped her. Maybe she felt sorry for me. She showed me a few steps and after that, I kept my eyes and ears open. Anytime there was a chance to learn, I took it."

For a moment Tatiana saw the eager child Yvette had been.

"I've sewn up ripped costumes at the opera," she continued, "just to watch the dancers pass by. Once, when my work was done early, I sneaked backstage and watched a whole production. I'll never forget that. And then, of course, a friend of mine, Blanche, was an opera dancer. She taught me a lot. I still practice, every night before I go to bed, no matter how late it is. Someday, I know my chance will come. I have to be ready."

Tatiana's heart was deeply touched by the impoverished girl's dedication to such an improbable dream. Yvette's eyes shone like stars in her thin face, and her whole body trembled with the fervor of her inner vision.

On an impulse, the former ballet prima said, "Show me what you know."

Yvette was only too happy to comply. Tatiana watched carefully as her friend moved from *plié* to *attitude,* from arabesque to pirouette, all with surprising lightness and control.

"Do you know *glissande?*"

"*Bien sûr,*" came the gay reply as Yvette demonstrated.

"And *fouettés?* How many can you do?"

"Let's find out," the French girl cried, beginning a long, precise set of turns renowned for their difficulty.

After the tenth one, both women began calling out the numbers. It was "nineteen!" before Yvette collapsed onto the couch, laughing with a triumphant pride Tatiana would never have believed her capable of.

"Why, you're really quite good," Tatiana told her.

Yvette's eyes grew very wide.

"You need a bit of polishing," Tatiana continued, "since you've never taken formal classes. If you'd like, I could help you with that."

Yvette clasped her hands to her breast like a school-girl, a hopeful smile on her delicate lips. Then her face fell.

"But . . . but you're Dmitrova. You'd bother with the likes of me?"

"It's the very least I can do in return for all your generosity. Perhaps after a few weeks, I can write you a letter of introduction to Léon Martinon. I think he just might take you." To the French girl's disbelieving stare, Tatiana added, "You're good, Yvette. You have a lovely quality of movement and you're a natural mimic. You went from lusty flirt to ethereal fairy in one blink of an eye. Trust me."

"I trust you. I do. It's just that I've dreamed of this moment for so long that I . . . I . . ."

She flung her thin arms around Tatiana and hugged her.

"Thank you," she whispered.

Yvette released her benefactor.

In an effort to return to normality, she said in a voice made husky by unshed tears, "We'd better go. You don't want to be late your first night."

"No. We'll have to dress fast."

"I'm dressed."

Tatiana bit her lip. She had forgotten Yvette only had two dresses and Tatiana was wearing one of them. She jumped up from the couch and went to her wardrobe, pulling out a delicious shell-pink wool gown trimmed in black braid that Yvette had particularly admired that afternoon at the secondhand clothing store.

"Have you noticed that I've managed to ruin the dress you loaned me?"

Tatiana pointed to several paint stains on the skirt

she was wearing that no amount of turpentine could erase.

"I bought you this one to replace it. I hope that's all right."

"I love it!" Yvette exclaimed. "You didn't have to do that."

"Well, since I did, let's get dressed."

The two girls readied themselves, chatting away like old friends all the while. The night was chilly, and Tatiana was glad she'd given Yvette something warm to wear. When they seated themselves at one of Chez Claude's rough tables, they were both rubbing their hands to warm them.

A sullen bar-girl brought them the bowls of thin soup, potatoes, and glasses of wine that were part of their salary. Tatiana took a sip of the wine and managed not to choke at its sourness. Yvette downed hers with a flourish.

Tatiana glanced around at the grim, threadbare patrons whose subdued conversations and listless postures contrasted strongly with the frenetic artists of the Bouteille Riante. Here were poor people who expected to remain poor, who scratched out a shabby living from dawn to dark and came to their neighborhood bar to let their tired muscles unclench. Those empty faces would not be an easy audience to dance for, Tatiana thought.

The quiet was so lulling, Tatiana was startled when two ragged women began shouting at each other over a last potato. When the taller one clawed off the other's dust-caked hat and stamped on it in a rage, several patrons laughed. A thin man in a loud checked suit insinuated himself between them and held up a coin.

"Who'd like this for an hour upstairs?"

Argument forgotten, the women began fawning over him, preening themselves like two starving cats.

"To sink so low . . ." murmured Tatiana.

"When your last few sous won't pay the rent and this soup is your only meal, it happens. I know. I've done it myself."

Tatiana patted her friend's hand, a sad sympathetic smile on her face.

Monsieur Claude's snarl interrupted them.

"I don't pay you to hold hands. Go on. Get back there and get ready."

The tiny, airless dressing room was filled to overflowing with the six other dancers. As Yvette pushed her way past each one, she introduced Tatiana to them.

Yvonne pulled up thick black tights as she muttered hello.

Veronique peered at them through a cloud of the cheap, musky scent she had just enveloped herself in to hide her heavy odor of sweat. Solange, her frizzy hair an astonishing shade of orange, stopped rubbing talcum powder on her thick upper arms long enough to shake the new girl's hand. Colette and Nicole were too busy squabbling over a tin of pancake makeup to notice the newcomer.

Only Marie-Claire, her little cat face sly, seemed polite enough to say, "I'm sure you'll be able to fill Genevieve's shoes."

Tatiana smiled, nodded, and wriggled through the press of underfed bodies to a spot at the long mirror. How sad they looked, she thought as she waited for Yvette to bring the costumes. There was a dead look about their eyes, as if they knew all too well that they weren't going anywhere.

Yvette and she hurried into their tight blouses with

scoop-necked black bodices and tiny white puffed sleeves. They pulled on three calf-length skirts each, lined with white ruffles, and fastened feathers into their hair. Over the black tights, each snapped a garter into place. Yvette loaned Tatiana some stage makeup.

"It's a cross between Coppelia and a milkmaid," Yvette instructed her. "Bright cheeks and very bold eyes."

"How's this?"

"Redder lips. Then you'll have it."

They hurried to join the other girls lining up behind the back curtain as the pianist began to play. Tatiana closed her eyes for a moment, feeling her way into the role of a lusty, good-humored girl, proud to display her voluptuous, inexhaustible body, avid to impress and excite men, athletic, daring, and wanton. I'm not deep, but I'm sensual and talented, Tatiana told herself, squaring her shoulders and tossing her head like a boxer before a bout. I'm the best around.

The introductory music ended and the line of dancers pranced out down the center of the stage, flicking their skirts and yelping like cowboys herding cattle. The line split into two at the front of the stage and the dancers lined up along both sides, facing each other. They began eyeing the customers, sauntering back and forth, flipping up their skirts teasingly. When Tatiana searched for a single man to focus on, she discovered that not one customer was watching the act longer than a bleary second or two between swallows of wine.

I'll make them watch, she vowed to herself, deep in character. She allowed her hips to roll suggestively as she raised her skirts teasingly high and dropped them suddenly. A little shimmer of excitement shook her shoulders and breasts. Her tilted black eyes glittered with restlessness. Her lustrous, moon-white skin begged to be touched. Her carmine-lipped smile promised everything and gave away nothing. When she cried out the can-can dancer's little "yooh!" it was an explosion of sexual energy that could not be contained.

As she lined up with her fellow dancers to begin kicking, one beefy, red-faced customer looked up, began to peer into his drink again, and stared up at Tatiana, astounded. More faces looked up and forgot to look away. There were nudges, comments, men who hushed up their companions as they drank in the new girl's irresistible allure. She made them forget their troubles, this nervy, vital dancer flinging her legs over her head as if it were the easiest thing in the world.

I've got them now, Tatiana saw. It was exhilarating, tossing her body around and boisterously demanding male attention. Different in every way from her real life, the can-can was sheer, releasing, good-natured fun.

As Tatiana reached up to grab her foot before spinning on one leg, she caught a jealous snarl on her neighbor Veronique's garishly painted face and barely managed to avoid being tripped. When they were both facing away from the audience, Tatiana, still in character, contrived to dig her elbow solidly into Veronique's ribs.

"I'll break your foot the next time," Tatiana hissed.

She giggled to herself as she realized what a crazy thing she had said. She had no idea how to break a foot, let alone one the size of husky Veronique's.

But apparently the threat had been effective. There were no further attempts to sabotage her dancing, though Tatiana intercepted several more angry glances as the customers ignored all but the new girl. Monsieur

Claude himself stared at Tatiana, even dropping a glass, an event unknown at Chez Claude.

The music built to a climax, signaling the final tableau. The object of every pair of eyes in the café, Tatiana sank emphatically into a perfect split, her arms rounding triumphantly over her ebony head. The customers broke into a wave of cheering and stamped their feet resoundingly. Still in character, Tatiana blew lusty kisses at her new fans.

She almost ducked when a coin came flying at her before she realized it was meant to reward her. Smiling, she tucked it into her bodice. She was answered by a rain of money, slapping against flesh and cloth, jangling onto the floor. The dancers broke ranks to scramble for the coins and Tatiana found herself laughing for the sheer joy of it, holding out her arms to the audience. When she saw the curtain begin to close, she turned her back, raised her skirts, and shook her derrière impudently before running off to hug an astonished Yvette.

Chapter Sixteen

THAT WELL-OILED BALLET MACHINE, THE COMPANIE VALOIS, was coming to a screeching, grinding halt. Roland, once the invincible unflappable administrator, had become a wedge of frustration and obstruction. Previously content to let Monsieur Lupin figure the accounts, Léon Martinon direct the choreography, Jacques the doorman deliver morning coffee, Roland now rampaged through every office. He examined the most minor of details; he upset the most standard procedures; he cast a pall of uncertainty over his dancers.

Léon could be heard frequently muttering, "He makes problems where there aren't any." And when Roland beleaguered his choreographer too much, Léon would look daggers at him and say, "You are our biggest problem, Monsieur le Comte. You know what's eating you up as well as I. Take care of that and life will go on."

But life wouldn't go on for Roland. He seemed to be stuck in a rut of wallowing emotions. His relationship with Tiane Dmitrova was over for good—he had seen to that. Yet she haunted him, every step of his waking hours. As for slumber, that reliable state of forgetfulness, it had abandoned him too.

He roamed Paris like a ghost seeking surcease. At most, he slept fitfully for an hour or two in the early morning . . . if he could bring himself to stay that long in his wretchedly lonely apartment.

His only comfort was Montmartre, which seemed to beckon to him now with hypnotic urgency. His friends watched with sympathetic alarm as he demanded and attended party after party. His gaiety was forced and desperate. Only Roland's long-standing friends could remember him like this, once in his youth, many years previous.

They knew he was trying to drown his sorrow with the cafés' finest—or worst—drink, and they knew he wasn't succeeding. Surly and sullen, miserable and driven—that's how one always felt at the end of a love affair, Carteret was quick to remind Roland at every occasion.

One night, Roland sat at a table in La Bouteille Riante, surrounded by his closest friends and a dozen bottles of absinthe. He choked down another glassful.

"Disgusting stuff," he growled, swirling the dark green dregs in the bottom of his glass.

"But good for the soul," La Maigre added, her glittering eyes seeming to penetrate the comte's veneer of contempt.

"Is that before or after the soul's left the body?"

quipped Morais, busily drawing a caricature of Roland sucking absinthe from a baby's bottle.

"In your case," André Bonfleur said dryly, "the point is moot."

A round of laughter broke out around the table from all but Roland.

"Absinthe comes from wormwood, you know," La Maigre continued. "Remember my song about the corpse left too long near a wormwood tree?"

She sang a verse, and at the chorus everyone joined in. Roland only glanced up darkly, then stared again at the mysterious pattern of curling arabesques the liquid made in his glass.

"I heard it was used, long ago," he said in a dull voice, "to chase away moths and fleas."

The carousing died down. Breton, the poet, and La Maigre looked askance at one another. The three artists present, Bonfleur, Morais, and Berengère, exchanged knowing glances.

"Eh, de Valois," prompted the shaggy Berengère, "remember Chateille and his infamous gallerie?"

The group perked up, hungry for gossip.

"His mother, that venerable vessel of sanctity, has foreclosed on her own son! It seems she found out he had a wife tucked away somewhere in Normandy."

"Was the wife loose?" asked Zazou, winking, as she replaced empty bottles with full ones.

"Only her lips, like yours, you old blab." Roland grinned in a liquored blur.

Zazou Picard stopped, bottle in hand, and planted her feet firmly. She frowned and stared grimly at Roland. The group looked anxiously from the insulter to his target. Slowly a broad gold-toothed snarl of a smile formed on Zazou's face.

"It's hell, isn't it, boy, what love can do to you."

She slapped Roland on the back and gestured to the others at the table.

"Drink up, everyone. Go on, Berengère. Tell us more."

"Well," he continued, "morals had nothing to do with it. The Dowager Chateille was suffering from the green-eyed monster. She couldn't stand François taking so many vacations without her. She accused the poor hounded man of not attending to business. When he refused to discuss the matter, she set a private investigator on him. After reading the first report, she banished her son to his country consort."

Everyone smirked and chuckled at the gallery owner's fate. Inspired, Breton began to rhyme:

There once was a man named Chateille
Who was thought to be terribly shy
But ask his maman
And she'll tell you he can . . .

"But business comes first, so don't try," finished Bonfleur spontaneously.

Glasses were filled, clinked in companionable harmony, and downed. Roland blinked his eyes and looked hazily about. Had he missed something? Probably not, he concluded. It wasn't much fun tonight. He poured his glass full to the brim.

Morais glanced toward a commotion at the café's entrance. He poked an elbow at Roland.

"Look! Carteret has found Marguerite's replacement . . . or should I say, replacements."

Carteret strutted over to his friends' table with identical twins, one on each arm. Berengère rose and bowed. Bonfleur whipped out his sketch pad and Breton let out a war whoop.

"Back in action so soon, Camille?" purred La Maigre.

"You know what they say about me," Carteret said jovially. "Can't keep a big man down."

The twins tittered and blushed.

"Can't keep a good man down . . ." muttered an irritated Roland. Louder he gibed, "I see you're still in mourning, Carteret."

He pointed at the thin black armbands gracing the sleeves of the artist's red-and-white-checked jacket.

"This must be a new record. Marguerite's been dead a week," Roland jabbed, "and you still show evidence of remembering her. Or do you just like the effect of black against red and white?"

There was a long embarrassing silence.

Carteret whispered to Bonfleur, "No change yet?"

"No," answered André softly. "He's still at it."

"Well," boomed Carteret. "I brought just the right medicine, then."

He turned back to his miserable friend.

"Your wit is devastating as usual, Roland. I won't apologize. What can I say about poor Marguerite? She loved me; she bored me; she drowned herself. Such is the way for women like her."

Carteret sighed, then dipped his hands around both twins' shoulders so that his palms cupped a breast of each sister.

"It's life I seek, Roland. Life!" the outrageous artist shouted. "Look at these two ripe beauties, fresh from the country. Look at the life in them, *mon ami,* and take heart!"

He bussed both girls on their cheeks, sat down with

279

one twin on his lap, and patted the other twin's derrière in the comte's direction.

"Well, monsieur," came a butter-sweet voice. "May I join you?"

"If you wish," Roland answered noncommittally.

Across the table, Carteret's girl giggled, choked, and giggled again as he introduced her to the bitter green brew they all drank.

"May I have a drink too?"

Roland looked up at the young girl beside him. She couldn't have been more than fifteen. Probably she was even younger. Her flaxen hair fell in soft baby curls about a frank and open face. He stared at the familiar blend of urban naiveté, curiosity, and country wisdom all crowded together in her sky-blue eyes.

"You should be tending your mother's garden, not here in this godforsaken hellhole," he snarled.

"Pardon, monsieur?"

Her voice clouded with confusion. She looked over at her sister, who was preening about like a giddy hen in Carteret's funny jacket. She looked back at her gentleman, smiled bravely, and snaked one arm about his back.

"Don't touch me," he hissed.

Her hand jumped away as if singed by his rebuff. Shaking her head, she stood away from him. In a moment, she was off to her sister's side, planting herself on Carteret's free knee.

Sullenly, Roland watched her flit away. Like a moth to a flame, he thought, she doesn't know she's headed for inevitable ruin. He pulled a bottle closer to him. Feelings of isolation crept about him, building a wall against his friends.

Suddenly everyone was shouting for La Maigre to sing. Zazou pulled her out of her chair and escorted her to the small dark stage. Signaling to the concertina player, the lean angular woman with the catlike face began a ballad about an engaging flower seller who got engaged one time too many, finally marrying death.

Roland glanced about at the mesmerized faces of the café customers. They all believed the tripe La Maigre was dishing out. There's no wisdom in it, Roland wanted to shout. There's no great truth in the song. Hell, he mused, La Maigre was as false as the claptrap she sang about. She was an English girl parading as a street-wise Frenchwoman.

He was filled with abhorrence. He could feel it seethe and writhe within him. He looked about him. The foul drink, the bad jokes, his provoking friends, the noise and stench of the café—it was all too much. Slipping from his seat, he left, unnoticed.

Roland found himself wandering the streets of Montmartre but the usual quaint sight of oddly dressed, oddly paired couples left him cold. He only knew his pain, his torment over Tiane. He hardly noticed or cared where his feet led him.

Toward dawn, he recognized the tiny cemetery not far from his apartment. He recalled how Tiane spent hours, it seemed, staring out his windows at this very churchyard. He knew she was captivated by its silence and peace. He knew she felt the sharp contrast with the whirlwind of life he led . . . and had made her lead. He knew it all and had ignored it.

Entering the iron gate, he saw a tiny bent woman dressed all in black slowly walking toward a grave. In one hand she carried a posy of fresh violets. Roland knew her destination without being told and followed her to Tiane's favorite monument—the little angel with the cherubic smile.

The little old lady knelt down before the thin marble slab and closed her eyes in silent communication. When she was done, she picked a handkerchief from her pocket, polished the stone, and kissed it. She stood gazing upward at the angel.

"Until tomorrow, my bright and beautiful child," she murmured.

Removing the day-old bouquet from the stone hand's clutches, she put the new posy in its place.

"Until tomorrow," she repeated.

She caught sight of Roland as she backed away. Nodding to him as though she expected to see him there, she went on her way out the cemetery gates. Roland stared after the small black figure, her permanently tear-stained face etched in his memory.

Deeply touched by this vision of loyalty to a love wrenched away, he leaned against a low ivied wall and watched the dawn cast a pearly glow on the marbled monuments.

Before his eyes, a ghostly vision of Tiane dancing about in her *Echo et Narcisse* wisps rose up and gripped him. Elusive, ethereal, she was everything he yearned for. He was as tortured by her image now as he had been in St. Petersburg one moon-filled night. She lingered in his mind, in his heart, and he couldn't be rid of her. He didn't want to be rid of her.

As the morning light grew stronger, his vision faded. Tiane was gone. He realized that life without her was blacker than the worst moments with her. In rejecting her he had cursed himself with the living hell of her loss.

He searched out and recognized the windows of his apartment. For a moment he thought he saw a pink glow within. His heart thumped. Was Tiane standing there, waving for him to come home? He cursed hoarsely. It was only the first shafts of sunlight playing tricks on his eyes. Dejected, he looked away, down at the somber graves.

"What's the point of going home?" he muttered.

Slowly he strode away like an old man, weary of the world's burden. Maybe at the theatre I can forget, he thought with little hope.

He stood outside the locked theatre in the fresh morning air until Jacques arrived to open the building.

"Monsieur . . . Comte," the doorman mumbled apologetically, "if I had known . . . your own keys, where, sir? Pardon."

Roland wearily waved all excuses aside as the man fumbled with the door.

"At least I know you come to work on time."

He dragged a heavy hand over his face and through his hair.

"Coffee, Jacques. Get me the largest cup you can find. I've got one hell of a hangover."

"Right, boss," saluted the uniformed man. "I'll bring it to your office."

"No," Roland ordered. "I'll be in the theatre, tenth row or so."

Jacques started for the stage area.

"I'll turn the lights up for you . . ."

"No," barked the comte. "Just get the coffee."

Roland didn't enter the theatre until he saw the doorman turn the corner. Backstage, it was still dark as night and Roland left it that way. He groped his way forward, knocking over a couple of stools and an untended costume box, until his eyes adjusted to the gloom.

From the stage itself, he leaped down onto the floor of the auditorium. Rubbing his hands over the plush velvet backs of each row's aisle seat, he found his place and sank heavily into it. He was only aware of two things: his blinding headache and the empty stage before him. He sat staring, holding his head in both hands, oblivious to everything, even the coffee Jacques eventually left on the seat next to Roland.

As the theatre came to life that morning and the dancers and production workers trickled in to begin their day's tasks, Roland still sat in self-imposed isolation. Micheline Arnot sauntered down the aisle sporting a large emerald brooch. She spotted Roland and hurried over to him.

"I have you to thank for my beautiful expensive new pin, darling. The Duc d'Anville was so taken by my performance in *Echo*, he . . ."

The words died on her lips as Roland's glacial frown frosted over her. His eyes seemed to glitter a fiery greenish topaz through the hazy light filtering into the hall. The tight fabric of his coat stretched across his bunched shoulders in poised fury. The ballerina giggled nervously.

"A little tense today, darling?" she purred.

When he started to rise out of his chair, lurching upward with mute venom barely contained, Micheline gasped and backed off. Slowly he retreated back into the dark confines of his lair.

The other dancers, having been warned by the unlucky ballerina, steered a wide path around their brooding volcanic impresario. Léon finally arrived at noon. Before he could make his way to the stage, he had been cautioned five separate times about Comte de Valois's turbulent mood. The doorman, the lighting expert, the wig maker, a lowly corps dancer, even the company's leading male dancer all conveyed the same message.

In the wings, the dance master of the company's ballet classes stopped him.

"He's worse than ever," Émile hissed into Léon's ear. "I was only walking across the stage and he snapped at me."

"That's it," roared the old choreographer. "We've work to do, everyone. Get to your places, now!"

Léon heaved a weary sigh and strode out to face the incorrigible monster.

"This can't go on one more day," he muttered belligerently.

But when he saw the golden head rumpled and held low, he stopped and shook his own white mane.

"Only Dmitrova . . . she's the only woman who could've brought him to this," he murmured in sympathy.

Léon padded down a wood ramp erected by a company carpenter to bridge the orchestra pit by day. Gently he tapped Roland on the shoulder.

"My boy," he began.

A growl of nonhuman origin seemed to emanate from the crouched figure.

"Now, Roland," importuned Martinon, undaunted.

The miserable man gave Léon one swift glance which told all—the rumbling rage, the abject torment, the cage of conflicted emotions Roland was caught in.

"Drink your coffee," Léon said, and looked away.

Returning to the stage, he picked up his notes and examined them.

"Beg pardon, sir," Jacques said sheepishly, "but there's a young girl at the stage door, says she's got a letter of introduction for you."

Léon raised his bushy salt and pepper eyebrows.

"This is most irregular," he barked, and frowned. "Send the girl on her way, Jacques. I've no time for—"

"Excuse me, sir," the doorman interjected, "but she mentioned . . ."

He paused to glance out at the sulking figure in the audience and went on tiptoes to whisper in Léon's ear.

". . . she said Mademoiselle Tatiana told her to see no one but you."

Léon's eyebrows rose even higher.

"Tiane!"

The name loudly escaped his lips and his eyes flew to Roland. But the comte seemed not to have heard. He had finished drinking his coffee and now appeared to stare at the grounds left in his cup.

"Send her in," the choreographer hissed.

Jacques winked conspiratorially and left. Within minutes, he returned with a much too thin girl whose eyes told her life's story.

"Stand here," Léon commanded.

The girl stepped forward without hesitation and even ventured a shy smile.

"You're not afraid of me, are you?" he said, slowly circling the girl, eyeing her form.

"Everyone knows your reputation, sir," the girl said softly, "but Tatiana told me you were a pussycat."

The eyebrows stayed cocked.

"How do you know so much about me, about Mademoiselle Dmitrova?" he probed.

The girl laughed.

"We live practically next door to each other, monsieur, and we dance together every night!"

"Dance?" Léon exclaimed.

He looked around for a stool, retrieved one, and quickly sat down.

"Oh yes," replied the girl chattily. "Tatiana and I do the can-can at Chez Claude in Montmartre. She's very good."

"I expect she's the best," Léon said dryly.

He looked hard at this waif.

"What's your name, child?" he asked gently.

"Yvette, sir. Yvette Latour."

"Well, Mademoiselle Latour, may I see the note from . . . her?"

He glanced uneasily out into the cavernous hall. Roland hadn't moved. Léon turned back to Yvette who handed him Tatiana's letter. He read it quickly, stared again at the girl, and read the note a second time.

"Tiane says she taught you the opening section of *Giselle*. I want to see it now. Do you have shoes?"

From a threadbare purse, Yvette brought forth a pair of worn, secondhand point shoes. She smiled at Léon and showed him her prized possession.

"I see," he said in acknowledgment.

He went into the wings and yelled for a pianist.

"How the hell will she get up on toe in those things?" he muttered to himself.

The pianist appeared and descended into the orchestra pit. Léon bent down and gave her instructions. When he turned back to the girl, she had removed her shawl and put on a thin folksy vest laced with cheap ribbon. Léon nodded in appreciation.

"The tempo should be like this . . ."

He tapped his heel hard on the floor as the music began and Yvette took the first steps of her audition.

The gladsome sounds of Giselle's entry into her village square filled the air and disturbed Roland's gloom. He glared at the imposition of this merriment and went to snarl his displeasure. It was bad enough to hear the music Tiane had danced to, but to have to see the steps performed was almost unbearable.

"Lé—on," he growled, and then stopped short.

There, onstage, was a scraggly street urchin, a washed-out drab imitation of a female. Didn't she know, thought Roland angrily, Giselle was no streetwalker from Montmartre? She was gay with a young girl's strength and poignant with a heartbroken lover's fragility. Why was Léon sitting so calmly, beaming at this pathetic showing?

Roland stared hard, ready to snap at the first wrong move, the first inappropriate gesture, and he froze in his seat. In her opening set of pirouettes, this ragamuffin had set her foot forward, then cocked it ever so slightly. She proceeded to spin effortlessly and come down precisely in position, cocking her toe in place again. He had only seen one other dancer ensure her balance this way. Tiane had created this little correction for herself.

Now the girl posed, getting ready to jet forward across the stage. With a flutter of her wrist, she was off, soaring through the air. How often had Roland seen Tiane consciously flick her wrists before she leaped, as though testing the springiness of her wings. He couldn't believe his eyes.

When the girl landed, she dramatized Giselle's sudden sadness as only Tiane had immortalized it with a subtle slumping of her shoulders. Blood pounded through his veins. Who was this imposter mincing about, plying her wares, driving him mad with her counterfeit dancing? How dare she parrot his beloved Tiane, teasing him with his own memories?

He sprang from his seat like a lion uncaged. He ran down the center aisle, roaring his disapproval.

"No. No. Get off my stage," he shouted. "You can't dance . . . no one can dance like her."

Yvette shrank back, frightened by this bellowing, which seemed to come out of nowhere. She looked to Léon, who stalked forward with fire in his dark bright eyes.

"What are you doing, Valois?" the choreographer spat at the thundering impresario. "This is an audition, not a street brawl."

Roland pushed ahead, glaring at Martinon.

"Did you authorize this guttersnipe . . ."

He pointed at Yvette with unconcealed contempt.

". . . to enter my theatre, to audition for my ballet company?"

Léon boldly faced Roland.

"You're overstepping your bounds, Monsieur le Comte. You may find the talent but I judge it. This girl came highly recommended to me. *To me*," he emphasized, "and she's good."

He paused to smile at the quaking girl who clasped herself so tightly.

"I'm hiring her for the corps."

Yvette gasped and was compelled to come forward despite the comte's bullying remarks.

"Oh, Monsieur Martinon, *merci*. I'll work so hard for you . . . you won't regret . . ."

Roland turned a steely eye on her and smiled viciously.

"Whoever told you you could dance? You're nothing but a gold-bricking street rat. Go on," he prompted, nudging her with the flat of his arm, "crawl back to the alleys where you belong."

Yvette blanched and stammered, "Forgive . . . I only wanted . . . to . . . dance."

Léon put a firm protective arm about the girl.

"Listen to me, mademoiselle. You are hired, and tomorrow morning you will report to Monsieur Aubisson, the ballet class master. And perhaps you will be kind enough to accept the Comte de Valois's apology for his unfortunate behavior."

Yvette curtsied and dashed from the stage.

"How dare you . . ." Roland blustered.

"Shut up, man," Léon commanded curtly, and placed both hands on the taller man's shoulders. "You've got to get a hold of yourself. You're hurting everybody around you—that little girl, me . . . The company's falling apart. You're getting in the way of everything. Do you really want to ruin what you so painstakingly created?"

Roland sagged, the hot fight suddenly gone out of him. Léon caught and clasped the tortured man to his chest.

"What do you want me to do?" Roland asked morosely, clinging to his old friend for a brief moment. "I can't get her out of my mind."

Léon stood back with his wiry arms akimbo.

"Go see her. Resolve it once and for all, Roland."

Roland's eyes clouded over and the muscle of his jaw worked furiously. A rusty whisper emerged from his tight throat.

"Tiane . . ."

Chapter Seventeen

IT WAS MOONLESS, THAT NIGHT, AS ANDRÉ BONFLEUR escorted Roland to Chez Claude. It had been hard for the comte to apologize to André, but he had come to accept the innocent nature of Tiane's living arrangement with the artist. More importantly, Roland had realized there were greater issues at stake.

"You've kept your part of the bargain, oui, Bonfleur?" Roland demanded gruffly.

"Oui," replied the artist, "although I'm not happy about it. She doesn't know you're coming."

"Then I shall see . . . really see," the comte muttered to himself.

The two men walked past the more popular and notorious cafés.

"There," said André, pointing to a nondescript storefront.

Roland squinted in the darkness at windows black with soot. He walked closer. The doorway looked grim and uninviting. Over the entry a small placard declared "Chez Claude" in burnt letters.

"I don't know this place," Roland announced, unimpressed.

"It's not exactly your style," retorted the artist. "This is a workingman's tavern. Only Montmartre's own come to a place like this . . . or did until Tatiana arrived."

"Wait just a minute, André," protested Roland. "What're you telling me? That I don't work for a living? That I haven't taken Montmartre and its kind into my heart, into my life?"

André stood and faced his friend.

"Cruelty is not my forte, Roland, but look at yourself with open eyes."

Those green topaz eyes flickered and flared but the artist held his ground.

"You're an outsider, *mon ami*, a player, in love with the fast Parisian life. No bones about it, you're also a doer. You make life palatable for your friends. Without you, some of us would've already found a permanent home in the Seine. But you don't belong to Montmartre as we do. Hell, even Tatiana knows more about real life here than you."

Roland turned in a rage and said, "I don't have to listen to this."

He tramped away from the small café but André limped after him, grabbing on to the tail of his jacket.

"I think you do, Roland."

He held on steadfastly while Roland turned and glared at the artist.

"When you lost everything, we took you in and coddled you . . .".

"I landed on my own two feet," grumbled the irate comte.

"Yes," agreed André, still holding on to the jacket. "You remolded life to suit you . . . and it's almost been satisfactory. But look at what your overprotected, dreamy, emotional, hot-house dancing wonder of a child did. She lost everything too. But when she was ready, she took life as she found it, not as she wanted it to be, and mastered it."

He let go of Roland.

"You'll see," the artist said with pride in his voice, "she is the best of Montmartre."

Roland stepped back, straightened his jacket, and regarded Bonfleur with bitter scorn.

"No wonder you're an impressionist, André. You're blinded by the brilliant image of the surface of things. All color and light but when it comes to substance, pah!"

André looked back with pity in his sharp brown eyes.

"Need I look deeper when my friends wear their hearts on their sleeves?"

Roland snarled something unintelligible and pushed past André. He stormed into the café and took a table for himself at the rear. Bonfleur entered, unruffled, and was immediately greeted by Claude.

"Your usual table, monsieur, whenever you show up?" The dour, mustachioed proprietor grinned.

New to success, Claude was overwhelmingly jolly. He slapped André on the back with such force that the thinner man stumbled and almost fell. Claude grabbed for André and, with some care for the wispy artist, escorted him to a table close to the stage.

"A bottle of your finest for that man back there," André requested, indicating a sullen man with brown-gold hair.

"A friend of yours?" Claude inquired.

"Often," came the answer.

A bottle of Burgundy was duly delivered and a glass poured for Roland, but he pushed them both away. He had come for the show and nothing else.

He could hardly believe it . . . Tiane flaunting herself as a can-can dancer. The image clashed with everything he knew about her. She had been the most exquisite, unforgettable ballerina, stamping her artistry on the hearts and memories of all who saw her.

He had made her the toast of Paris. For what? he asked himself. To make a fool of herself in some dingy sideshow? How far she had fallen to use herself this way. It was a disgrace and a blow. He felt it as surely as she did.

His stomach knotted and a sour taste filled his mouth. He pulled his glass toward him and was raising it to his lips when the gay naughty melody of the can-can rang through the room. At once the garrulous crowd quieted and all eyes were fixed on the stage.

With a high-pitched squeal of raucous delight, a line of eight dancers sashayed onto the stage, flipping their white and black starched petticoats over purple or red sateened skirts to reveal similarly hued underdrawers. Roland put down his glass, intently studying the face of each chorus girl. Had Tiane changed so much he couldn't recognize her?

There was a sudden burst of applause and several shouts of *"l'étoile."* The rear curtain parted to reveal Tiane, the star of the can-can. Roland held his breath.

She was glorious, as radiant as he had ever seen her, and the constant ache within him galvanized and gripped him.

For an instant she stood there regally accepting her tribute. Her costume was the reverse of the others. Her petticoats were red and purple, peeking out from beneath a vertically striped black and white satin skirt. She wore a purple garter high on one thigh, and when she turned her back to the audience, she teased them with a brief display of black-and-white-striped pantaloons.

She joined the line and began to dance the can-can with panache and gaiety. Before his unbelieving eyes, Roland saw the usual tawdry exhibition illuminated into an art form. Tiane exuded a sexy charm which was only accentuated by her saucy attitudes, devilishly high kicks, and impossibly wide splits. She laughed while she danced, transforming the lowly café into a sunny carefree festival.

Roland stared, mystified, as a drumroll sounded. Tiane stepped forward. As though she had signaled to them, several men from the audience fought their way forward to crowd about the edge of the low stage. Roland found himself standing to see what the commotion was all about.

At another drumroll, the audience roared, "One!"

Tiane playfully chose an older well-dressed man sporting a high top hat. Aiming her toe, she deftly kicked his hat from his head. A tremendous cheer rose up.

The audience yelled out, "Two!"

Tiane caught sight of Bonfleur and expertly booted off his beret. The patrons continued to chant number after number as their queen acknowledged one after another of her adoring subjects with a swift turn of her toe.

Roland was thunderstruck. Tiane hadn't been brought down a single peg. In fact she raised the can-can a notch or two, imbuing the vulgar dance with life-appreciating spirit. While the café rang with explosive homage, Roland felt his heart tug at him all over again, drawn by her immense talent. He wanted to feed himself from the font of her strength and vitality, feeling their lack in him.

He grabbed for his wineglass and choked down the newly fermented liquid. It burned on the way down and he welcomed its cutting edge. He had to fight the temptation of her magic, knowing where it led, what it did to him. Her art hadn't changed; she was as superb a dancer as ever.

He sat down heavily and reached for the bottle to refill his glass. An overly efficient waiter materialized at his side and whisked away the bottle and glass before Roland could stop him.

Monsieur Claude crashed through the kitchen doors, his arms filled with cases of wine bottles.

"Champagne for all," he shouted, red-faced, "to toast our Tatiana's eighteenth birthday!"

Madame Claude, as rotund and florid as her husband, followed behind carrying a huge cake blazing with candles. The crowd broke into good-natured discordant salutations. Tatiana jumped down prettily from the stage and joined Bonfleur at his table. She gestured for Yvette to sit with them while she smiled and maneuvered the press of people who strove to touch her.

Eighteen, Roland pondered, was that all she was? It

seemed she had always been a part of his life. How could she only be half his age? What had he expected of this child, barely a woman when he had carted her off like some errant knight? He took the champagne pressed on him and felt its effervescence tickle and tease his upper lip.

Roland watched Tiane, surrounded by friends and admirers, and he was not among them. She was the center of attention and managing quite well, without him.

After Madame Claude cut the cake, the proprietor himself fed a thick slab to his dancing star. Tatiana laughed, wiping away the crumbs that stuck to her chin.

"Another slice for the belle of Chez Claude," he demanded of his wife.

"Whoa, Monsieur Claude," Tatiana called out, and grabbed his apron strings. "Can you imagine the expense of a costume six sizes larger than the one I wear now?"

"Remove the cake, Ernestine," he bellowed without a moment's hesitation. "We can't bribe her with food. How can we discourage her from accepting that offer from the Moulin Rouge?"

Loud howls emanated from Claude's patrons.

"She's ours."

"Keep her here at all cost."

"She's too good for the Moulin!"

Tatiana laughed gaily and waved her hand for attention. The crowd quieted.

"I won't go anywhere . . . yet . . ." she said coquettishly, tweaking Claude's long drooping mustaches, "if Monsieur le Propriétaire will give me my own dressing room."

She raised an eyebrow and glanced at her employer

with a devilish gleam of her shiny jet eyes. He formally presented himself before her in military style, clicking his heels and offering his mustaches to her.

"Tweak away, little moneymaker. The dressing room is yours. Just stay here long enough to make Chez Claude famous."

The customers trumpeted their approval and clinked their glasses to toast the fat businessman. Tatiana sat down to enjoy a moment with Bonfleur and Yvette.

Roland was astounded. Tiane had blossomed into the life of the party. She was as much in control of the social whirl as she was when she danced on stage. She'd grown up without him, in spite of him, and he'd forfeited his right to share her success.

Bonfleur was right about everything. Roland had turned his back on the one person who loved him for himself, not for what he could do for her. She had surrendered her whole being to him, trusting him with her feelings, her body, her talent, and her life. And what had he done? Abused them all. He'd killed their love with his blind pigheaded intolerance. Yet she'd survived and, he mused, from the look of things, done better than he, who'd only made a mess of everything he touched. He needed her more desperately now than ever and it was too late.

He slowly sipped at his champagne and stared at the startling, heart-rending, glorious, achingly desirable reality of a mature Tatiana. Seated next to her, Bonfleur caught Roland's eye and signaled him to come join them. Roland held his breath as he saw Tiane turn to the artist and, with a puzzled expression, follow his line of sight.

Their eyes met. Tiane put her hand to her heart as though it had stopped beating. Roland drank in her face until he could stand no more. Backing out of his seat, he saluted her and turned away, disappearing out the café door.

Tatiana turned abruptly to André, her eyes stinging with tears.

"Did you know he'd be here?" she demanded.

Bonfleur reached for her hand.

"Don't be angry. He asked me to bring him."

Wrenching her hand from the artist's gentle grasp, she held back her tears.

Defiant, she said, "Now he knows for himself. I didn't curl up and die without him."

She looked down at her costume, glanced at André and Yvette, gestured to the people she'd pleased.

"I'm glad he saw me like this."

Yvette smiled bravely and clapped her friend on the back.

"That's right. Take your fill."

She poured fresh champagne into Tiane's glass.

"Who knows when Claude will put on another show like this!"

Tatiana sat back, suddenly aware of the loud voices, the clumsy sloshing of champagne, the crush of people in the small café. Her feet ached and her head swam. She had danced and partied enough for one night. What she needed was fresh air and time to herself, to think about Roland . . . again.

Wearily she attempted a little smile for her two friends.

"I'm going home now," she announced.

She leaned over and kissed André on the corner of his mouth.

"Thank you," she said wholeheartedly.

He looked up at her with a worried expression.

"Did I ruin your birthday party?" he asked.

"No," replied the young woman emphatically. "You did the right thing."

Yvette jumped up.

"I guess I'll leave now too. No more late nights for me," she said with undisguised joy. "I've got ballet class tomorrow morning."

The two women withdrew to the dressing room and changed clothes in companionable silence. They walked home, linking arms. Yvette began to whistle a melody from *Giselle*.

"Please, Yvette, not that, not now," Tatiana begged.

Looking askance, Yvette said, "It can't be ballet music that's bothering you."

Tatiana gave a quick shake of her head.

"I know," the girl replied. "It's that awful Roland de Valois, isn't it?"

"He's not awful. Just unhappy, as I am," Tatiana said softly.

Yvette turned to her friend in surprise.

"I loved him very much, perhaps too much, Yvette, and I miss him," confessed Tatiana. "I would never have thought it possible, but when I saw him tonight . . . well, I believe he misses me too."

Yvette shook her head as if dismissing Tatiana's maudlin sentiment.

"Pah," she spat, as the two reached her door. "You're just eighteen. You've got your whole life ahead of you."

She turned the key in the lock and opened her door.

"As for men, there are a million of them out there. You'll find happiness again, I'm sure."

"No," Tatiana murmured, looking down. "I could

never find the kind of happiness I had with Roland and I won't accept anything less."

She looked up at Yvette and gently squeezed her arm.

"I've learned to handle my life and my unhappiness. I'm proud of what I've accomplished on my own," she said with a determined smile.

"You should be," responded the girl, hugging her good night.

Yvette watched her independent friend climb the stairs to her own little home.

Almost a week later, Tatiana wove her way back along the narrow passageway to her private dressing room after a late-night performance. Monsieur Claude had been true to his word and enclosed a little alcove off the kitchen for her use. An aromatic finger of hearty pot-au-feu beckoned to the young woman but she knew better than to disturb Madame Claude's culinary experiments.

Tatiana smoothed down her ruffled skirts as another bit of plaster was dislodged from the wall. Perhaps I should consider that offer from the Moulin Rouge, Tatiana mused. Chez Claude was so old and run down, and she found the stage too confining. The café was homey in an unconventional way but she knew the Moulin could offer more creature comforts, especially more space.

Lost in her thoughts, she pushed against the thin makeshift plank door of her dressing room automatically, weighing her future plans. The door was wedged against something in the room and wouldn't budge. She frowned and knocked loudly against the door. Comte Roland de Valois pulled the door open from within.

"Roland!" Tatiana exclaimed.

For a moment they didn't speak, only looked at one another. She glowed with womanly vibrancy, thought Roland, even in that ridiculous costume and stark stage makeup.

Tatiana took in his carefully manicured appearance— far neater than the last time she'd seen him—the enormous bouquet of spring flowers in one hand and his rich tawny eyes, soberly pleading his case. She took a deep breath and was certain he'd heard her inhale.

The dressing room seemed tinier than ever. There were only the two of them yet one couldn't move without touching the other. He was so close . . . Why?

She arched an eyebrow and deliberately went to her miniature makeup table, forcing Roland to step aside. She busied herself with her pots and jars, removing the kohl from her eyes and the rouge from her cheeks and lips.

Roland watched her precise movements, none wasted, all efficient. She seemed to know exactly what she was after, which seemed to him to be refusing to pay the slightest attention to him. Look at me, he wanted to shout. Listen to me . . .

He felt like throttling and kissing her, both at the same time. Roland grinned, aware of the exasperating, stimulating rush of love coursing through him, just like old times. No, he corrected himself hastily, this time it would be better.

He shuffled his feet back and forth, cleared his throat, and extended the bouquet toward his beloved. He had never felt so nervous.

"I would've been here sooner, Tiane," he began hoarsely, "but I had to clear up a few . . . loose ends."

Tiane. She thought she'd never hear the name spoken again. She maintained her calm facade and allowed herself one glance at him.

"Why did you come?" she asked in a low voice, ignoring the proffered blooms.

She'd never seen him so vulnerable, not since the first time they'd made love. She looked away quickly and busied herself with unknotting her hair.

"I have a confession to make, Tiane, and I hope you'll hear me out."

He paused and she nodded for him to continue. He leaned toward her and laid the flowers across her table.

"When my family died, I deliberately buried my emotions with them."

"I know this story, Roland," she interjected, brushing her long black hair over her shoulder.

She was so close, he thought. He reached out to caress the silky hair. His hand was trembling.

"When I lost you," he continued, "I tried to do the same thing. But I couldn't, Tiane. I couldn't bury you. You were everywhere—the stage, the apartment, the empty chair beside me, my bed . . ."

Tatiana looked up and stared intently at him, seeing the yearning in his eyes, the careworn lines in his face. His hand was open to her. She could have laid her cheek against it.

"I've suffered without you, my darling. When I saw you, so magnificent, last week, I knew I had to have you again. No matter what."

No matter what. She took the words in slowly and rolled them over in her mind. No, that was unacceptable now. She swiveled around on her stool and he knelt before her. She touched his face, brushing the lines at his eyes and his mouth with her fingertips.

"Dear, dear Roland," she murmured, withdrawing

303

her hand. "I would've died once to hear you say those words. All I thought I wanted was to have you 'no matter what.' I wanted one hundred percent of you, all the time, sharing you with no one."

She smiled sadly.

"I've changed, Roland, though I've never stopped loving you. That will never change."

She swiveled back, facing the mirror.

"But I need something different now. I need to be an equal with the man I love, not a mirror for his enthusiasms, not clay to be molded to his whims. I need a partner."

He rose and stood behind her, laying his hands on her shoulders. He looked into the mirror and spoke to her image.

"I took so much for granted, my darling. I was thoughtless, careless of our love. I assumed you would yield in all ways to me and I wouldn't have to give anything in return."

His grasp tightened and the words came fast.

"You're the only woman for me, Tiane, and I know I can't be happy without you. Let your pleasure be mine as I want mine to be yours."

He pulled her around to him and took her in his arms. He kissed her passionately, lingeringly, demonstrating his deep need for her. She accepted his kiss and savored it, tasting him, remembering him. He looked at her with demanding eyes, not letting go of her.

"Then you'll come back to me, darling?"

She gazed at this tawny lion of a man who seemed even stronger for his vulnerability. The light of his love warmed her once more, illuminating her with happiness. Smiling radiantly, she kissed away each downcurved line.

"We've both changed," she acknowledged. "Yes, yes, yes," she added between kisses, "I'll come back. However, I withhold my right to give up all my separate pleasures. I may take up painting next . . ."

He pushed her away in mock menace.

"Are you trying to rewrite your contract?"

She picked up his flowers with one hand and curled the other around his neck.

"Who needs a contract between friends?" she cried.

She threw the flowers up over their heads and joined both her arms about him. As they declared their love in kiss after kiss, the flowers danced and fell about them, forming a garden at their feet.

"Let's go home," he whispered urgently in her ear.

She leaned past him, extracted the key to her rooms from a drawer, and dangled it before Roland. His eyes lit up in delighted surprise.

"One moment, Roland."

She was out of her can-can costume and into a dress in a mere moment.

Scooping her up in his arms, he growled, "You might as well have left off the dress."

She threw back her head and laughed.

"I seem to remember having done that once or twice in this city."

Roland joined in her laughter and the two of them left Chez Claude, waving good-bye to the bemused proprietor, who quickly sized up the situation. I may not get to keep her, Claude mused ruefully, but the Moulin Rouge will never have her. There's some satisfaction in that. He nodded to himself and loudly smacked his lips.

It was only a short walk to Tiane's cozy room and then she was in Roland's arms. As if guided by one mind, they released each other and removed all their clothing, eyes locked in heated promise. They made love on her bed, rolling with abandon on the teasing fringes of a long Russian shawl.

As Tatiana's questing hands rediscovered the flat planes of Roland's golden chest, the sculpted hollows of his groin, the pulsing rounds of his buttocks, he cried out her name in joyous gasps. His fingers stroked her velvety skin, her rosy nipples pursed with longing, her quivering belly. Masterfully, gently, he caressed the moist center of her.

Mouth to lip, chest upon breast, thigh pressing against thigh, fingers intertwined, they sought the haven so long denied. Their love was reborn and flourished under the gentle torment of caresses and the welcoming storm of responses. Her hungry hand closed over him, rejoicing in his eager leap to her touch.

With one voice, they cried, "Now."

In perfect harmony, they thrust and arched, seeking love's sublime moment, reaching it together.

"I love you," they echoed to each other.

Later, resting side by side, Roland rained lazy kisses along Tiane's inner arm where the skin was especially soft and sensitive. When he finished, she draped her delicate limb over his chest, up and under his neck to fondle his golden curls. She gazed into his love-drunk eyes and extended her long neck, nuzzling under his chin as a bird might contentedly preen for her mate. Roland closed his eyes and grinned broadly.

"Still the swan," he murmured into the feathers of her hair.

"Perhaps," Tatiana cooed softly, "but certainly the happiest of women."

Epilogue

THE BANNERS OUTSIDE THE THÉÂTRE DE PARIS boldly heralded "A Night to Remember—A Season for All Time," and it seemed as though all of Paris had turned out to see history made by the Companie Valois. The rich mingled with the poor, top hats next to berets, furs and silks next to honest homespun. Inside, the first few rows were cordoned off for special guests. Their arrivals sent the inquisitive throng into gasps of both recognition and wonder.

The popular chanteuse La Maigre led the group from Montmartre to their seats of honor. She was escorted by Camille Carteret, dressed for the occasion in all polka dots, and a sheepishly grinning Georges Berengère. Roland had, at last, gotten the two men to work together. To their own surprise, they had designed and hand-painted the costumes for the evening's spectacle ballet in easy companionship.

André Bonfleur, the well-known artist, followed the trio. He was wearing an impeccably tailored new suit of English wool and sported an ebony cane, gleaming like polished marble, with a scrolled silver knob. Breton and Morais filed in next, each with an arm about the accommodating proportions of Zazou Picard.

Behind them came the Claudes, who, between them, filled the aisle. For the grand occasion Madame Claude had concocted an extravagant headpiece of dyed ostrich feathers and Monsieur Claude had waxed his mustaches into stiff artful curls.

Bringing up the rear was the distinguished choreographer Léon Martinon. With his shock of white hair and his keen eyes set in a tyrannical blaze, he marched to his seat with dramatic fanfare. At his side was a striking woman swathed in sable and diamonds. Her lustrous dark hair, flashing eyes, and electric smile set off a spontaneous buzz in the auditorium.

"This way, Madame Dmitrova," Léon barked in a deliberately loud voice, and glared at the curious multitude, ending all speculation about the exotic woman's identity.

Lydia Petrovna settled decorously in her seat, spreading her luxurious fur coat about her. She accepted a program from André, squinted prettily at it, and dug her long fingers into her beaded bag. Extracting a mother-of-pearl lorgnette, she read with interest the notes about *Sol et la Lune,*" the evening's premiere ballet.

"Why, Monsieur Martinon," she said with a provocative ring. "A costume ballet? No one has staged one of those in decades . . . centuries!"

"Precisely, madame," Léon said crisply. "Can you think of a better, more original idea than to update the past to current tastes?"

Lydia read on, searching for her daughter's name and credits. At the title page, her eye was caught by an unusual line.

"Léon Martinon, master choreographer," it read, "dedicates this ballet to the reunion of the Companie Valois's impresario and its greatest star."

Lydia raised her thin eyebrows in surprise. *Sol et la Lune?* Roland de Valois and Tatiana? The sun and the moon? She glanced at the artist seated next to her.

"Do you know what this means?" she inquired of Bonfleur.

"Hush," hissed Léon. "My ballet is starting."

The curtain rose to reveal an old-fashioned allegorical tableau straight out of Louis XIV's court, modernized to suit the fin-de-siècle ambience. Among heavenly clouds of hazy rose dawn, the nine immortal Muses floated in bevies of three. In short divertissements, each trio danced a paean to those areas of learning or art over which they presided.

Apollo appeared, bringing the light of day with him. He called the demigoddesses to his side. In eloquent mime, the sun god directed the Muses to find him the perfect partner, a goddess worthy of as much inspiration and reverence as he. The Muses flocked together, then scattered about the heavens in search of the divine creature Apollo described. Slowly, grandly, he paraded across the stage, and when he exited, the light dimmed.

The scene changed to the deep shade of an ancient forest where a shimmering pool rippled and swelled. From its mysterious depths, Tatiana emerged in silver frost and glided from the water onto the soft bed of primeval foliage. An ivory cap covered her hair, set off by a glittering crescent that blazed with its own light.

As if waking from a long spell of enchantment, the moon maiden stretched in languorous fluid movements. She seemed boneless, each part of her slim body undulating in sensuous coiling arabesques. Then she came alert to the trumpeting call of distant horns. Unaccustomed to her surroundings, she dashed about in wild abandon, but from every corner of the forest a Muse appeared to prevent her escape. They converged on their quarry and bound her in silken bands, leading her captive from the glade.

Back among the fleecy kingdom of clouds, Apollo waited for the arrival of his bride. The Muses came forward one by one, each dancing the praises of the lady moon. At last she appeared, head unbowed. Ice seemed to drip from her. Apollo leaped to her side, immediately in love with this creature so much his opposite. He unleashed her hands and attempted to kiss and caress away the humiliation of bondage. She ran from his grasp, alarmed at the unfamiliar heat he stirred in her. But the sun god was quick and his desire aroused. He lunged for her, and in a dazzling *pas de deux* of lightning-fast runs, extraordinarily high leaps, breathtaking dives, and a searing tight clinch, the moon was wooed and won.

In the final scene, the sun and moon appeared in their wedding raiment, flanked by the immortal pantheon. Apollo wore a tunic of gold brocade and was crowned with a thin circlet of the precious metal. Tatiana, the moon queen, attended by the nine Muses, was cloaked in a diaphanous robe of shot silver gossamer. Her lustrous crescent tiara gleamed with milky pearls. They stood with hands joined together atop a tall staircase emblazoned and canopied with stars. In stately pomp the divine couple descended to take their places among the gods and goddesses and the curtain rang down.

The audience leaped to its feet in a tumultuous ovation. Whistles and cheers sang out from the balconies and those closer to the stage threw flowers. The group from Montmartre furiously hugged one another and the Claudes even kissed.

"Dmitrova!" came the uniformly exultant scream from the audience. "Dmitrova!"

The theatre lights blinked and blazed, shedding a bright sheen across the lush curtain. Roland de Valois in resplendent evening dress stepped out before the audience. Recognizing him, the audience shifted gears and shouted its admiration for the great de Valois.

"Many, many thanks, ladies and gentlemen, for attending our gala season opening," he declared. "I must beg your indulgence and announce a last-minute change in the Companie Valois. It may distress a few but it pleases me more than I can say."

He paused dramatically, knowing the ballet patrons were poised on the edge of their seats.

"The great and beautiful ballerina, Tatiana Ivanovna Dmitrova, will not dance again on this stage or any other stage in the world!"

His announcement was met with shocked gasps, groans of despair, and much booing. He held up his hands to quell the clamor.

"Her place will be taken by my new wife, the incomparable Tiane de Valois!"

Turning toward the wings, he signaled to the ballerina to join him onstage. Tiane came out in her moon bridal costume, stood serene at her husband's side, and accepted the audience's adulation. Deafening applause surged through the theatre, rippled with shouts of approval and relief.

Lydia Petrovna leaned over confidentially to André.

"I knew he would marry her," she boasted, "from the first moment I saw them together."

The couple smiled triumphantly at the crowd. Roland took Tiane's hand in his and raised it high over their heads. Then, with an adoring glance, eyes only for each other, they strolled offstage.

The curtain parted to let the other dancers accept their acclaim. The nine Muses curtsied and Apollo bent his head reverentially.

"They don't want us; they want Tiane," he hissed to the Muse representing Dance. "Where is she?"

Yvette cocked her head toward the wings where Tatiana was locked in Roland's worshipful embrace.

"There's only one voice she hears."

And Roland was showering his ballerina with words of love and devotion, transporting her to their private heaven on earth.

Tapestry

HISTORICAL ROMANCES

POCKET BOOKS

886